Deadly Catch
By
Crispin Nathaniel Haskins

This book is dedicated to:
Monica Halsey
&
Penny L. Samms
I would not be a writer without either of them.

1

Charles' face exploded through the water to find the hot July sun waiting for him. It did not take long for the coolness of the ocean to drip away and the warmth of the mid-summer rays to heat his skin. He couldn't have asked for a more beautiful day. July on Martha's Vineyard was full of flawless days. One hundred and twenty five thousand annual tourists could attest to that. Charles looked back over his shoulder at the now familiar Fuller Street Beach. There were quite a few families on it today. In the past, Charles had swum in the early morning and the beach had been quiet but today he was swimming at peak time and he had a lot of company. Swimming parallel to the beach, he did the breaststroke for a while before breaking into a full front crawl.

*   *   *

The man thrashed desperately to stay afloat, just to keep his head above water. Without hands and feet, his severed limbs flailed but made little difference. The more he splashed, the more he bled. The water around him was deepening from pink to dark crimson. His arms stretched out but ended in bloody, severed stumps. He could gain no advantage over the water. He was sinking. He couldn't even flip onto his back. On his back, he might be able to calm down- float and breathe. He swallowed water. His blood made the taste metallic.

*   *   *

Charles floated leisurely on the ocean. The salt of the Atlantic carried him around like a king. How had he gone a whole year away from this place? It was so good to be back. Toronto was a fantastic city and definitely his home but there was something special here. Something rejuvenating. As soon as he stepped off the ferry that morning, he had felt it. It had been good to see Laurie again. Police Chief Laurie Knickles. They had kept in very close contact all year. There had even been some brief talk about her coming up from Edgartown to spend Christmas with Charles and his family but it hadn't panned out. No matter. He was here now and it was great to see her. She had tried to insist that he stay with her but he was emphatic about staying at The Edgartown Inn on North Water Street. They almost had quite a fight about it, now that he gave it some thought. He was such a private person. He really liked his space.

Charles straightened up from floating and started swimming back toward his towel. He swam in the direction of the Edgartown Lighthouse. Chappaquiddick crested the horizon behind it.

*   *   *

The man went under. His lungs burned with a desperate plea for oxygen. A kick with a footless leg got him up quickly but briefly. He inhaled. There were black spots floating in his eyes. He hoped that he would bleed out before he drowned. He went under again. He was blind under water. There was too much blood. His limbs were numb. They slowed. His lungs gave up what little air they had and he gagged. Wretched. He could feel himself sinking. Blackness. No sound. It was so quiet. His blood swathed and warmed him like a sleeping bag as the life left his body.

*   *   *

Charles swam back to shore. Making his way onto the beach, his body glistened in the warm, yellow sun. He was in no hurry as he walked toward his knapsack and his towel. Families flew big red kites around the lighthouse and young couples lay reading on the sand. He couldn't stop smiling. He loved seeing happy people. Charles was so glad to be back on Martha's Vineyard.

2

Charles walked down North Water Street toward the Edgartown Inn. The summer was in full swing and the street was jammed with tourists and SUV's. Charles didn't drive and he certainly couldn't imagine driving in Edgartown in the summer. He had never had a license so he didn't miss it. When he was younger, it had been a plus because he never had to be the designated driver. Now, it was probably one of the things that kept him healthy. Charles walked a lot. He loved walking. As a teen, Charles had found himself between jobs a lot. More often than not, it came down to a dollar for the bus or a dollar for a bottomless cup of coffee at Denny's with his friends. It was a half an hour walk to Denny's but he always chose the latter. Armed with his Sony Walkman, and then subsequently Discman, and then iPod, Charles got into the habit of walking anywhere that time would allow. Now, living in downtown Toronto there was really no need for a car. In fact, there had been studies done proving that it was actually cheaper to take cabs everywhere than it was to own your own vehicle. Between gas prices, insurance premiums, and parking prices, it wasn't hard to believe. Charles thought that walking and biking were the way to go. His relatives all lived to be nonagenarians and centenarians and Charles attributed that to the amount of cardio exercise that they all did. They were all big walkers. Good genes to have.

North Water Street was flawless. If you were a walker, thought Charles, this was the place to be. The captain's houses were exactly where he had left them a year ago. They were exactly where they had been left four hundred years ago. They stood like great oaks: stoic, strong, and comforting in their uniformity. Their white pillars and black shutters stood at attention for Charles to admire as he walked by. The blue and pink hydrangeas, as much an island tradition as the houses they trimmed, were in full bloom. There was a spring in Charles' step that he was sure was absent in Toronto. He really wasn't sure why. The last time he had been on the Vineyard was exciting but certainly not relaxing. It had been more stressful than anything else. JAWSfest had been fun but he had been chased through Manuel F. Corellus Park by a murderous thug. He had been smashed on the head with a revolver, he'd been in a car accident, and he'd watched a friend of his get shot in the face! The more he thought about it, the more it seemed like he should never have wanted to come back at all but he did. He really did. He remembered it as the best trip of his life. All of the good memories were there too: the island, his friends, the Edgartown Inn, *breakfasts* at the Edgartown Inn, and Laurie. Laurie had been the best part without question.

Laurie Knickles, his childhood friend, who had shown up as the Edgartown Police Chief. Charles had certainly not seen that coming. How could he have? How could anyone? They had spent a lot of time together and it had been wonderful. Charles had long thought of himself to be a confirmed bachelor but there was something in Laurie that had made him think differently. He didn't know what it was. All he knew was that she made him smile when he thought about her and that was all he needed to know... for now. Their kiss had been warm and nice. He could still feel it and smell it and taste it. Yes, Laurie Knickles had made quite an impact last summer.

Charles passed the red brick Edgartown Library on his right and looked across the street to the Court House on his left. The Kelly House, of which The Court House was a part, was a beautiful hotel. A lot of the tragedy of last summer had taken place there but it was all long forgotten. It was back to its full majesty and filled with guests who either hadn't heard anything about it or just didn't give a damn. The Court House was a grey cedar shingled house with white trim as were many of the buildings on the island. The window boxes were stuffed with red geraniums and the wrap around deck was neatly appointed with wicker chairs. A few steps further and Charles was home. The Edgartown Inn.

Charles bound up the stairs greeting his fellow guests on the porch with a smile and a "hello". It was such a comfortable place to waste an afternoon. The white wicker chairs and over-stuffed pillows had drawn Charles in every morning last summer. He couldn't wait to get sucked in to them again tomorrow morning. Edie would have his coffee ready and waiting in his usual American flag coffee mug unless he missed his guess.

"How was your swim?" As if on cue, Edie walked into the foyer from the kitchen as Charles opened the screen door. Edie was still as pretty, warm, and welcoming as always. She tottered around the inn all day on high-heeled mules. Her blonde curls bounced when she walked.

"Fantastic! Thank you!" Charles pulled his room key out of his knapsack and opened his guestroom door. By request, he had been given the same room as last year. The door swung open and he was greeted by the cool air and fresh scent that had drawn him back from the year before. The blue cornflowers and the red poppies still peppered the wallpaper and the immaculate white bedspread still covered the queen-size bed. Charles dropped his bag on the green leather wing back chair in the corner and went into the bathroom. He looked at his watch; it was 1:30pm. He had time to take a shower and then put on some fresh clothes before heading into Edgartown for some lunch. He was starving. The afternoon was his but then he was meeting Laurie after her shift for supper.

*   *   *

Charles walked down Daggett Street to get to the Harbour. He was heading for the restaurants. This was the long way around but he liked taking this route because it was a JAWS route. This was the road that Mayor Vaughn had driven down with Deputy Hendricks, Meadows from the Amity Gazette, and Doctor Beller to meet Chief Brody on the Amity On Time ferry. Charles wondered if he would ever get that movie out of his system- probably not. Why should he? It gave him an enormous amount of pleasure and didn't bother anyone. Actually, sometimes it probably bothered a great many people. Charles could go on about it. He thought about his friend, Mike Burroughs and winced. Mike had been the biggest and best of the JAWS fans and it got him killed. Charles had seen him get shot. One shot from a forty Glock and his head had exploded all over that pristine beige and black living room. He had never hurt anyone. On the Vineyard last summer, Mike got caught up in the greedy scheming of Tim Oakes and Rebecca Thompson. Neither of them was around anymore and Charles had to admit he was pretty happy about that. Well, Rebecca was still alive, rotting away in a prison somewhere, but Tim Oakes was good and dead. What a waste of space that guy had been. Charles still had nightmares about being chased through the woods by that guy in the middle of that brutal storm. Enough, thought Charles. He was not back on the island to dwell on the ghosts of vacations past. Oakes was gone and he wasn't coming back. Mike was gone and would want Charles to be enjoying his time on the island. If there had been

12

anyone who loved Martha's Vineyard as much as Charles did, it had been Mike Burroughs. He would want Charles to enjoy himself.

When he reached the On Time ferry, Charles turned right and headed toward the tourist restaurants and shops of Edgartown. Weather beaten shingles, green lawns, and meticulously clean streets all being milled over by tourists. On his left, sailboats cruised on the blue waters of the harbour; overhead, the ever-present gulls cheered them on.

Charles stood in line and waited for a slice of Edgartown Pizza. Everywhere Charles looked there were signs and pamphlets for the Monster Shark Fishing Tournament. Apparently, it was happening that weekend. He had no idea that he would be on the Vineyard at the same time. He was surprised that Laurie hadn't mentioned it. Shark fishing was not Charles' favourite thing. It always amazed him how people would never entertain slaughtering a cat or a dog or club a baby seal but if an animal doesn't have fur? Who cares? Granted, sharks were getting a bit more protection these days. At least, they were in the Western Hemisphere. There had been a mass execution of sharks in the seventies and eighties. Sadly, it all started after JAWS, thought Charles. "A good shark is a dead shark!" They used to say but people had changed. A lot of them had come around in their thinking. Shark Week on Discovery Channel had seen to that. Younger people really liked sharks now. Shark Week was the highest rated week of the year for that channel. That was cool- education was a wonderful thing. Ironically, none of that would have happened if there hadn't been JAWS. JAWS had been responsible for their slaughter in the seventies but it was responsible for their redemption in the nineties and the new millennium too. Charles ordered two slices of cheese pizza. He shook a generous helping of Parmesan onto them both and went to sit at a small, wrought iron table and chairs. There was a brochure for the Shark Tournament at the table. He picked it up and perused it while he ate his pizza. Charles decided to learn more about this shark hunt. When he was finished, he would head over to the Edgartown Library and see what they had on the subject.

3

Charles briskly stepped up the front stairs at 72 Peases Point Way and walked in the double front door of the Edgartown Police Station. He thought it was an odd looking building every time he saw it. Not unattractive- just odd. The finish was in the traditional Vineyard grey shingle and white trim but the design of the building itself was more modern. Charles appreciated what the designer was trying to accomplish- new meets old and all of that. He just wasn't sure that he had made a success of it.

"Hi Mr Williams! She's back there." The desk sergeant motioned over his shoulder as soon as he looked up and saw Charles.

"Thanks, sergeant." Charles felt a little awkward at being referred to as 'Mr Williams'. It was his name but the sergeant was a cop after all. If anything, Charles should be deferring to him. Besides, every time Charles heard 'Mr Williams' he looked for his dad.

Charles walked down the hall to the office of Chief Laurie Knickles. The chief was at her desk and on the phone. When Charles got in the doorframe, he hesitated before entering but Laurie motioned for him to sit down. He stepped into the office and sat down in one of the leather chairs facing the chief's desk. She was off the phone almost immediately.

"Hey you!" Laurie smiled at Charles and for a brief moment, the real Laurie Knickles shone through. The Laurie Knickles that was fresh and feminine and exuberant. Someone knocked on the door and she was gone, replaced by Chief Knickles.

"You wanted to see me, chief?" The young sergeant, who had been at the front desk when Charles came in, poked his head in the office.

"I did. If you're still looking to make some extra cash, Chief Jefferies is looking for some warm bodies in Oak Bluffs this weekend. You're not on my schedule so I thought you might want it." Chief Knickles looked at the sergeant with an almost expressionless face.

"I would! Absolutely! Marcie won't be that happy about it but her mother's on the Vineyard this weekend, she'll keep her occupied. She hates when I work weekends but she loves spending the paycheques! She always goes down-"

"Sergeant Burrell..." The chief's expression had become weary.

"Yes chief?"

The chief motioned to Charles.

"Oh! Sorry! Thanks again chief." Sergeant Burrell left quickly.

"My pleasure." The chief looked back at Charles who was grinning ear to ear.

"Who was that?" Charles laughed.

"My new, very new, sergeant. He's a really good kid, he's just nervous. He never shuts up!" She laughed. "I like him though."

"How did you warrant a new sergeant? I mean how many do you need?"

"Jeff's gone." Laurie raised an eyebrow at Charles.

"Aw man! Really? I liked Jeff! He was a dude!"

"Calm down. He still is a dude- that is, assuming he was one to begin with." She shook her head. Laurie settled back in her chair so that her news would have full effect. "Jeff is now Police Chief Peter Jefferies of Oak Bluffs."

"No way!!" Charles was genuinely thrilled and made no attempt to hide it.

"Way. I told you he'd make a good chief."

"That's fantastic! When did that happen?"

"About a month ago. He's doing an awesome job too. I still hear from him quite a bit- questions here and there. He's got his work cut out for him this weekend, I tell you, with that Monster Shark Fishing Tournament going on. I'm glad that I'm down here in cosy Edgartown."

"I can't believe that you didn't tell me about that! I probably would have come at another time if I'd known that was going on."

Laurie looked stricken, "I never thought. Oh Charles, I'm so sorry. I didn't even think about the Shark Fishing Tournament being here! It didn't even occur to me! I'm such an asshole. It's like I invited Martin Luther King to a KKK rally!"

"Well, I wouldn't go that far but they're certainly not my crowd- that's for sure." Charles laughed. "Women are always comparing me to black men. Must be my-"

"-Moves on the dance floor?" Smirked Laurie; cutting him off.

Charles stood tall and tried to look boastful. "Well, actually, I was going to say my-"

"It's your moves on the dance floor." Laurie was shaking in her seat as she tried to contain her laughter. She stared at Charles; her blue eyes sparkled mischievously.

"Well, whatever the reason," Charles did his best to sound irritated. "I'm sure it's a *big one*!"

Laurie laughed out loud. "Get out of my office or I'll never get this crap done."

"Give me your house keys. I'll go to your place and make us supper. What do you say?"

"Are you kidding? That's the best offer I've had this week." Laurie reached into her desk drawer and tossed him a set of keys. "Those are my spares. You can hold onto them while you're here. How are you going to get there?"

Charles shrugged. "Bus, I guess."

"*Jack!!!*" Laurie yelled so loud for her sergeant that Charles jumped. Sergeant Burrell came running back to the office with a look that told Charles that he was afraid he was going to be fired on the spot.

"Yes chief?" The sergeant was wide-eyed.

"Will you drive Mr Williams to the Stop & Shop and then take him to my place please? You're heading up that way anyway."

"Oh, sure thing, chief. Anything else?"

"Nope. That's it. Oh, Jack, don't talk his bloody ear off the whole way, would you?" The chief snickered half-teasingly.

Sergeant Burrell blushed and looked sheepishly at Charles by means of a premature apology. "Aw chief! I won't. You ready to go Mr Williams?"

"Only if we straighten out one thing first."

"Sure thing, Mr Williams."

"You're going to have to call me Charles."

*   *   *

Sergeant Burrell pulled up in front of the chief's grey shingle house on East Chop. The sun was low in the sky and the light that it cast across the ocean was pure gold. Charles looked out across the bay before getting out of the parked squad car. "It sure is beautiful here," he said. He said it more to himself than to anyone else.

"It really is! When I first moved here with Marcie, that's my wife- Marcie Cunningham, we couldn't get over just how beautiful it was! We were out every minute of the day, I'll bet you! Well, not every minute but a lot! Good thing that we have cell phones or no one would ever get a hold of us!" Sergeant Jack, as Charles had decided to call him, barely took a breath. He was a really nice guy; Charles liked him a lot.

"Sergeant Jack?"

"Yeah Mr Williams? Sorry, Charles. I'll get it don't you worry! It might slip out once or twice but you won't have to tell me more than once-"

"Sergeant Jack!" Charles exclaimed. The sergeant looked at him again with a slightly embarrassed smile. "You've got to relax dude! Take a breath for Christ's sake." Charles smiled at him.

"You're right. Sorry. It's just that you're the chief's buddy and all and I haven't been on the job that long." Sergeant Jack slouched in his seat like a dog that knew that he shouldn't have ripped apart a pillow but just couldn't help himself.

"I know. Chief Knickles told me."

"She did? Oh that can't be good. I'm out of here for sure!" He threw up his hands in exasperation.

"What? Why would you think that? If you're going to continue as a police officer, you're going to need better instincts than that! Chief Knickles told me how much she liked you and that you were new. That's all she said." Charles shook his head in disbelief at the young officer. God, thought Charles, was I ever that young?

"She did? She likes me?" Sergeant Jack was wide-eyed and started to sound a little too much like Rudolph The Red-Nosed Reindeer for Charles. "She likes me!"

"I'm outta here. Have a good night sergeant. Thanks for the lift." Charles got out of the black and white cruiser and closed the door. "Oh and hey," he leaned in the open window with a closing thought. "Say hi and congratulations to Chief Jefferies for me. Would ya?"

"Sure thing, Mr- Charles!"

"Getting better..." Charles stepped back and the car drove off of East Chop and down toward Oak Bluffs and the brewing Monster Shark Fishing Tournament.

With grocery bags in each hand, Charles walked up to the front door and fiddled with Laurie's keys. The sea air freshly skirted his nose as he tried to manage balancing the bags in his hands and fitting the key in the lock. Accepting defeat, he put the bags down and opened the door.

Laurie's house was warm and inviting. Mismatched wood furniture and multi-coloured woven rag rugs drew Charles in just as they had last summer. There was a lot of light. Several of the original walls had been taken down in favour of the more modern 'open concept' look. The many windows let in enough natural light that only in the evening or during a storm would you need to turn to electricity.

Charles kicked off his shoes in the foyer. He picked up the groceries, carried them into the house, and set them down on the kitchen island. He went over to the sink to wash his hands but stopped short before turning on the tap. Centred on the windowsill just above the sink was a framed photograph of two young teens. They beamed at the camera arm in arm. It was a photograph of Charles and Laurie. Charles was in a Blondie T-shirt and shorts; Laurie was in a halter-top and shorts. Charles didn't remember the picture being taken but he guessed by their age and dress that it must have been the early eighties. He picked it up and stared at its faded colours. Charles could tell that they had been running around for hours prior to the picture being taken. Their hair was messy and it stuck to their foreheads. They were both so tan. Long summers spent entirely outdoors will do that to you, thought Charles. They didn't have videogames. Videogames were around in their most rudimentary form but neither of their parents was throwing money around on things like that. Charles wasn't even allowed to have a T.V. in his room. In hindsight, Charles thought that had been the right thing for his parents to do. This photograph might not have existed otherwise. Charles wondered where Laurie had unearthed this. Of course, he had several pictures just like it buried deep in a Toronto closet. Briefly, he felt badly for not digging one up himself. It just hadn't occurred to him. He had thought about Laurie constantly. Men just didn't think to do things like this. Charles loved that she had framed this and put it out in such a prominent spot. He set it back down. He turned on the tap and squirted a dollop of lavender Dr Bronner's Magic Soap into the palm of his hand. It lathered quickly. Charles looked out over Vineyard Sound as the natural lavender scent filled the kitchen.

Drying his hands, Charles thought about his research in the Edgartown library that afternoon. The Monster Shark Fishing Tournament was due to start on the 18th. That was tomorrow. The more Charles had read the more he was curious to check things out for himself. He didn't see the point to killing sharks but that was because he loved sharks. If he gave himself an honest answer, if it was the Monster Tuna Fishing Tournament, he wouldn't be giving it a second thought. He'd probably be down there in the hopes of scoring some free tuna- he loved tuna! What if it had been salmon or swordfish? What was the difference? Charles' research had been quite surprising. He had been shocked to discover that the tournament was 97% catch and release. Why didn't they broadcast that? They also didn't tell people that the fishermen were restricted in what they were allowed to catch. It wasn't just a free-for-all. You couldn't go out and haul back an enormous Great White Shark for example. Great Whites are protected. The fishermen in this tournament are only allowed to fish for three types of sharks and none of them were on the endangered list. Makos, Threshers, and Porbeagles were on the menu and each boat could only bring in one shark per day. The sharks were all caught a good distance from the shore too. That way, catching them had little effect, if any, on the eco-system. Charles paused and gazed out at the ocean. The contest itself was its own worst enemy. Calling it 'The Monster Shark Fishing Tournament' was awful. It was almost a misnomer. They should at least take the word 'monster' out of there. It gave the whole thing a slaughter and circus feel.

Charles reached into two of the bags of groceries and pulled out the hamburger, pasta, cheeses, canned tomatoes, tomato paste, and onion. He was going to make lasagne. The other bag had the fixings for wicked Caesar salad and garlic bread. If that wasn't comfort food, he didn't know what was. Charles looked through Laurie's cupboards until he found a pot the right size. He put it on the stove and tossed in the ground beef. Before he went any further, he walked across the kitchen. He took a bottle of cabernet sauvignon off the rack at the end of the counter, pulled out the cork, and poured a liberal glass. Charles sipped it and smiled. You can't cook Italian food without wine, he thought.

*   *   *

"It smells amazing in here!" Laurie came home and the smells of fresh home cooking hit her before she even opened the front door. "I can smell this from the driveway! What are you trying to do? We're going to have all the god-damned neighbours in here!"

"Welcome home." Charles got up from his spot on the sun porch and walked into the kitchen. "Would you like a glass of wine?"

"Absolutely. Can you pour me one while I run upstairs and get changed? I won't be a sec." Laurie hiked up the stairs in her uniform. A couple of minutes later she came down with her hair in a ponytail, her face freshly scrubbed and pink, wearing a baby blue set of yoga pants and hoodie. She looked pretty. "Where's my wine...and what's for supper?"

"Lasagne, Caesar salad, and garlic bread." Charles held out a glass of wine and she took it.

"Holy crap! That's like my favourite thing! Did you remember that?"

"I did actually. I remember my dad making it and you weaselling invites out of them if you found out!"

"Your dad made the best lasagne ever." Laurie sipped her wine.

"Well, this is his recipe. I hope I did it justice."

24

"I'm sure it will be great." Laurie topped up her glass and then topped up his.

"Speaking of justice, how was your day?"

"Swell." She took another healthy mouthful of wine. "The shark tournament starts tomorrow and no one seems to be able to get a hold of the organiser. He's also the emcee so everyone's in a panic. I'm not too worried about it though. He's a good guy. Somebody has his or her wires crossed. He'll show up tomorrow for sure. He's put a lot of time and money into this." Laurie walked over into the sun porch and Charles followed her lead. "How soon until supper?"

"We can eat anytime. The oven is turned down and just keeping the lasagne and the bread warm. The salad is in the fridge; I'll put the dressing on just before we sit down to eat. So, whenever really." They both sat down on the overstuffed burlap and oak couch that faced the beach and the sea.

"God, that sounds so good. Let's just relax for a bit then, okay?"

"Absolutely. I'll open another bottle of wine."

Laurie jumped up. "I'll do it! You've done enough. You sit down." She walked across the floor with a happy bounce. "Oh! Jeff says, "Hi!" I was talking to him today." She opened another cabernet.

"Hi Jeff."

"He invited us out to supper tomorrow in Oak Bluffs. I said yes. I hope that's all right." She came back with the wine. "We can cancel if you want to do something else."

"No. That's totally cool. I'd love to see Jeff. I was thinking of spending some time in Oak Bluffs tomorrow anyway."

"Why?" Laurie looked at him with disbelief.

"I want to check out this competition." He saw her face change to a snicker. "No, I'm serious. I did a lot of research on it today."

"Of course you did." She rolled her eyes.

"Of course I did and I want to check it out. As it turns out, I was under a lot of misconceptions about it and I'd like to see it for myself."

"All right. I have the day off so I'll go with you. I've never seen it either."

"It will be interesting. We don't have to stay all day or anything."

"No worries. I'm just glad you're here." She reached out for his hand and found it.

"Me too babe."

4

Charles and Laurie drove up Beach Road toward East Chop. They had just finished a delicious albeit early breakfast at The Artcliff Diner in Vineyard Haven. Charles had noticed Larry David from Curb Your Enthusiasm in one corner of the restaurant. When he pointed him out to Laurie, she had said that she didn't know who he was. Charles wasn't sure if he believed her or not. She had pointed out one of the guys from 60 Minutes. Charles had never heard of him. There was almost an entirely different cast on that show than when Charles had watched it. In fact, sitting in the car crossing the Lagoon Pond Drawbridge from Vineyard Haven to Oak Bluffs, he couldn't even remember the anchorman's name. Charles wasn't sure that Laurie believed that he didn't know who the guy was. People are funny, he thought. Charles leaned forward and motioned to his left, across the street, to a park and beach. "What beach is that?"

Laurie looked out of reflex even though she had driven this route several times. "Eastville Point Beach."

"I haven't been on that beach. Is it nice? I mean, it's a beach on Martha's Vineyard so I doubt that it's too shabby but by Vineyard standards, is it nice?"

"It's a nice beach for sunsets but there are much better swimming beaches on the island. It's a really calm beach so a lot of parents go there with toddlers and picnics. No big swimmers like State beach, The Inkwell, or Lucy Vincent." Laurie steered the patrol car smoothly up along East Chop Drive. The ocean sparkled a magnificent blue reflection of the perfect summer sky. The houses along this street were immaculate. Greyed cedar shingle with white or black trim marked the tradition of the island. A warm breeze marked by the swaying of the sea grass wound its way around the houses and through the meticulous island gardens.

It wasn't long before they rounded the chop, passed the lighthouse, and drove into Laurie's driveway. "I'll just be a second." Laurie hopped out of the cruiser and ran into the house. She was off-duty and wearing a white Star Trek T-shirt tucked into a pair of tight blue jeans. Her make-up was minimal. She didn't need it.

Charles turned his gaze to the sea. It was hypnotizing. It didn't matter how old you were, as soon as you saw the ocean, you were a kid again, he thought. He wasn't sure whether it was because it reminded you of how small or insignificant you were in the grand scheme of things. Maybe it was because it was just beautiful. Whatever it was, Charles couldn't help but be affected by it every time he saw it and he certainly wasn't the only one. People came to the ocean in droves. What was it? It wasn't just sun and swimming. People would have lost their use for the ocean and its beaches when they invented pools if that was the case. There was something about the sea. Studies must have been done. Charles made a mental note to look that up later. Lakes were wonderful. There was a rejuvenating feeling about being on a lake. Charles loved being down by Lake Ontario on Toronto's harbour front and for all intents and purposes, it was big enough that it looked like the ocean but it was different. The smell wasn't there; the tide wasn't there. This was the ocean…and it was magnificent.

"Man, you're like those senior citizens in old folks homes! The attendants park them there in front of those fish tanks and leave them there all day!" Laurie laughed as she jumped back in to the car. She had changed in to a pair of navy Gap Capri pants and a white and navy horizontal stripe T-shirt. She looked very nautical and very pretty.

"What are you talking about?" Charles blushed.

"I saw you. I know you. I could diaper you up and leave you to stare at the sea forever." She backed out of her drive.

"It's sad but it's true." Charles didn't see any point in arguing.

"Nothing sad about it. Quite the contrary, I think it would be sad if someone didn't see the majesty in it. The view is spectacular." She looked quickly out at the ocean herself before focussing back on East Chop Drive and putting the car in drive.

"Then why are you giving me such a hard time?"

"Honestly?" Laurie grinned. "It tickles me. Oh, and by the way, of course I know who Larry David is."

He shook his head. "I don't know why I came back here." He deadpanned.

Laurie drove up East Chop.

*   *   *

East Chop Drive became more congested the closer they got to the harbour. Cars were parked on both sides of the street and people were everywhere. Charles figured that if he and Laurie weren't in a police cruiser, they wouldn't make it through at all. Pedestrians always had a way of making you feel like you were in the wrong if you were in a car. It didn't matter whether or not you had actually done anything wrong, pedestrians glared at you like you were the skinniest person at a Weight Watchers meeting. They all had a look that said, "What the hell are you doing here?" Charles smiled politely at them but it didn't help.

"I'm going to pull over and park. We can walk from here." Laurie said. Laurie squeezed them into a tight spot along Washington Park and they got out of the car.

Even from their position on East Chop Drive, Charles could tell that he had never seen anything like this before on the Vineyard. Throngs of people were yelling and jeering. It reminded him of the group of yokels in JAWS who were all out to avenge the death of Alex Kintner... and receive the three thousand dollar

30

reward of course. "Say, I hope you're not going out with those nuts, are ya?" He could hear Ben Gardner saying it in the film now. Ben could very well be talking about the scene in front of Charles at this very moment. Boat motors hummed and buzzed under the din but far above it, there was the sound of one man with a microphone. Charles couldn't understand what he was saying over the din but his tone was irritating.

"Jeff sure has his work cut out for him. I'm glad I sent Jack to give him a hand. I wonder if I have any other officers who could help out." Laurie grimaced at the scene unfolding in front of them.

They crossed the street and made their way in closer to the emcee and centre stage.

"You want to protest? BRING IT ON!! Who the hell do you think you are anyway? I'm the one who works for the safety of the fish, year in and year out! You don't have a clue what you're talking about!" The man with the microphone spoke in a condescending and disgusted tone to the crowd. "You come out here from your cushy little jobs in accounting firms and grocery stores and take your pious stance *'Oh Save Our Sharks!'* then go back to your lives and forget all about this. You think that these protests vindicate you somehow from all of your sins. Probably makes you feel superior at dinner parties; you can refuse to eat tuna and pontificate at length as to why everyone in the room is so horrible for doing so. *Well, I have news for you!* I fight for sharks all year in *Washington and on state boards.* I make sure the fisheries are protected. Without them, I'd be out of a job!"

Charles turned to Laurie. "Who is that guy?" He couldn't believe what he was hearing.

Laurie did not look pleased. Her brow was furrowed and her lips tight as she watched the man with the microphone belittle the protestors. The negative energy was palpable. "His name is Bill Cunningham."

"He really knows how to charm a crowd, doesn't he?"

"I don't know why he's emceeing this event at all. He's done it in the past and I was sure that I had heard that the committee had voted against electing him again this year. He's belligerent and mean-spirited. He's right in what he says but his delivery is less than pleasant. I was under the impression that they had gone with Steve Christie this year. Not quite as qualified as Bill but a helluva lot more pleasant. Steve has a great way with people." Laurie watched as Bill continued to throw nasty insults out at the crowd.

"This guy's awful." Charles cringed. He hated negative energy. He had always thought that you could say anything you wanted to anyone and they'd thank you for it. You just had to find the right way to say it.

A voice came from behind them, "Yes, he is."

They turned around to find a tall thin man in uniform. It was Chief Jefferies.

"Jeff!" Charles yelled. "How are you? Congratulations on the promotion, man! Do they call you 'Chief Jeff' now?"

"Charles! Welcome back!" The two men shook hands vigorously. "It's really good to see you! No, now that I'm the chief in these parts, it's a little more

32

professional. I'm Chief Jefferies now, which is even more confusing with my dad still being Fire Chief Jefferies but at least he's in Edgartown and I'm over here. Did Laurie tell you that we're going for supper tonight?"

"Wouldn't miss it."

"Laurie, why did you send me Jack Burrell of all people?" Chief Jefferies looked seriously dismayed.

"Why? I thought you would need bodies."

"I do, chief but I've got Bill Cunningham down here and you know how he gets."

"Sadly, I do but what I don't understand is why Cunningham's here at all. I was under the impression that Steve Christie was supposed to emcee this circus. The committee hates Bill!" Laurie stared across the crowd in bewilderment.

"I know they do but Christie didn't show up." Chief Jefferies threw his hands up.

"Didn't show up? That's not like Steve."

"Don't I know it." Chief Jefferies lifted his cap and rubbed it along his head before returning it to its original position. "There's no answer at his house and his car is gone. His boat is here though. It's in its slip right over there in the marina."

"Weird." Laurie and Charles spoke in unison.

"Well, I wouldn't have sent Jack if I knew that Bill would be here. Sorry about that."

"What's the problem?" Charles turned and looked at Laurie.

"That asshole up there with the microphone, Bill Cunningham? That's Sergeant Jack Burrell's wife's father."

"Of course! Marcie Cunningham! Jack told me her name in the car."

"Of course he did." Laurie shook her head and both chiefs chuckled.

"Five minutes in a car will get you that boy's life story." Grinned Chief Jefferies. "Anyway, I'd better get back to work. I'm keeping Jack as far away from Bill as I can. I've got him directing traffic. I am glad that he's here, really. Thanks for sending him. I will see you guys tonight!" Chief Jefferies walked into the crowd and was gone in a matter of minutes.

"So now what?" Laurie turned to Charles. Before he could answer, Bill Cunningham started up again on his microphone.

"It's hard to believe folks, it's so early, but it seems that we have our first weigh-in of the contest!" He bellowed.

Charles started in to get as good a look as he could. "I want to see this!"

Laurie lunged through the crowd in his wake. "Why?" She knew the answer before she asked the question. Charles wanted to see it because he had never seen it before. It's just the way he was.

Charles was tall and could see clearly from his vantage point in the second row. He watched as the fishermen tied a rope around the base of the tail and the winch squeaked as it hauled up a large mako shark.

"Now, ladies and gentlemen, let's remember in order to qualify for the contest, a mako shark has to weigh in at a minimum of two hundred pounds to make a point for the team. If it's less than two hundred

34

pounds, the team gets docked one hundred points! Let's see how the vessel 'Hot Wave' has made out!"

The fish twisted and its weight strained the pulleys until it was no longer touching the wet wood docks. It was a good-sized fish. Charles found it hard to watch. If this were a tuna-fishing contest or a salmon-fishing contest, Charles would probably be feeling hunger pangs and drooling at the prospect of sampling Team Hot Wave's wares. It was strictly an emotional response that had him feeling this way. It was completely irrational; however, they were his feelings and he didn't like this contest. Everything that he had read in the Edgartown Library yesterday told him that this was an ecologically safe contest and in fact, a lot of scientific information was gathered at these events that benefitted sharks in the long run. Somehow, he needed to wrap his head around that fact.

"Two hundred and thirty-two pounds ladies and gentlemen! Let's give Team Hot Wave a round of applause!!"

On one side, the shark hung silver and dark blue, glistening and wet, smooth and flawless in the mid-day sun. When it spun around, Charles winced. A mess of alabaster white belly marred by a thick dark stream of blood that ran the entire length of the fish. The mixture of blood and seawater ran down half of the underside of the mako shark until it dripped from its bottom jaw in a cold puddle onto the harbour. Its mouth was open displaying rows of very sharp, long, triangular teeth. Mako shark's teeth were some of the most distinct shark teeth, thought Charles. They looked the most vicious. The fisherman, who had captured the shark, grabbed the fish by the snout and pulled its mouth open wide and aimed its maw at the eager onlookers. The crowd yelled and jeered as if to demonstrate their own power over this vicious beast. Charles looked closely at the shark and noticed that the shark's gills were still flipping, just a little- tiny lingering pleas for water. He wondered if anyone else noticed or cared that the shark was still alive. Hung in front of all of those people, being poked and prodded, and alive for the privilege. Charles was sickened by his fellow man sometimes. This was one of those times. He certainly wasn't alone either.

A large portion of the crowd was carrying signs of protest. The police stood at a makeshift, metal barricade that had been erected for the event. The contest was being held on private property; therefore, they had the right to keep protesters out- a smart political move by those in charge of the tournament. Charles surveyed the sea of signs bobbing up and down together like buoys. "Save Our Sharks", "Killing Sharks Is Killing Our Oceans", "Catch And Release Only", "The Only JAWS Here Is The One Eating Money". The last one made Charles smile. It was his favourite sign. A pretty, redheaded woman with big sunglasses held that one. She was very vocal. She screamed "Catch and Release!" so often that Charles was sure that she would wake up hoarse the next day. Her thick red hair was back in a ponytail and she was wearing a 'Save Our Sharks' T-shirt with khaki shorts. "Killing our oceans means that there will be no environment left for our kids!" She screamed out as loud as she could. Charles was somewhat glad that she didn't have a microphone of her own. As it was, the police were having a tough enough time keeping her behind the barricade. An officer gently pushed her back and Charles watched as she stopped to take a bit of a breather. She set her sign down and pulled a slice of pizza out of a Jurassic Park knap-sac. Taking a big bite, she looked intensely into the crowd. Charles followed her eyes. He was sure she was looking for someone.

"Officer! We have another one over here!!" Bill Cunningham yelled for an officer and was pointing into the crowd right in front of him. A policeman that Charles had never seen before weaved his way into the mêlée. A couple of minutes later, he re-emerged pulling with him a large bearded man carrying a sign and a camera. Once out of the crowd, the man shrugged off the policeman and walked toward the woman with the red hair. How he managed to slip past the police in the first place was anybody's guess. He was over six feet tall and covered with tattoos. He reminded Charles of the Ray Bradbury story, *The Illustrated Man*. It was a book about a man who was covered in tattoos and when you looked at one, you were drawn into it and the story that it told. Good book, thought Charles. The redhead and the tattooed man spoke under their breath to each other. They did not look happy. The redhead reached into her dino-bag and handed the illustrated man a slice of pizza. There was no way that Charles could hear them even if they spoke aloud with all of the ambient noise.

Charles tapped Laurie on the shoulder and motioned toward them. "Do you recognise those two?"

Laurie turned her gaze in the direction he was pointing. She shook her head. "No, I would remember them. Especially him. Why?"

"Just wondering. They seem particularly intense about their protesting. Nothing really, I suppose."

"Oh." Laurie looked back at Bill Cunningham and his microphone. She looked just as unimpressed as the protesters.

Charles decided that he'd seen enough for now. He looked down at Laurie, "I think I'm good. Let's go." He turned slowly through the crowd and headed back toward the corner of East Chop Drive and Lake Avenue. Once he was there, away from the maddening crowd, he took a deep breath and looked back. "That was gross!"

Laurie looked up at him with concern. "Are you all right?"

"Oh yes." He smiled faintly. "I'm fine."

"That was your idea. I don't know why you wanted to go there in the first place."

"I'm an idiot sometimes. My own worst enemy." Charles managed a small grin.

"Your own worst enemy, I believe. An idiot? Never." Laurie looked around before returning her eyes to Charles. "Come on. Let's lighten this party up!" She took him by the arm and started leading him down Lake Avenue toward downtown Oak Bluffs.

"Where are we going?" He pretended to resist but he followed her every step.

"We're going to get something to eat and then ride the carousel!" She was grinning like a six year old.

"We just had breakfast!"

"Yes but I want to go to Mocha Mott's for an apple fritter!!"

"Of course, you do."

5

Lake Avenue was busy at that time of day, especially with the Monster Shark Fishing Tournament taking place. There was a wooden boardwalk on the north side of the street along the Oak Bluffs harbour. On the south side of the street was Sunset Lake nestled in a ring of grass and set back from the road by a split rail fence. Charles and Laurie walked the boardwalk quietly for a while past the long line of mid-sized but still very expensive white boats that were moored in every slot along their path. Each boat gleamed clean and bright in the sunshine. They all showed pride of ownership. There was a lot of the "best in show" mentality in owning a boat. Charles sized them up one by one. He had never really taken in a fishing tournament before and was curious about the vessels that would be appropriate. There were a lot of centre console boats, which made sense as it left a large wrap-around deck for fishing. There were sportier boats with closed bows. It seemed to Charles that they would be better for water sports but they probably worked for salt water fishing as well. Almost all of the boats seemed to be inboard cruisers and the larger boats all had a sedan bridge. That made perfect sense for fishing as it gave the fishermen a much better visual. Charles absorbed the particulars of each one as they walked along the largest harbour on Martha's Vineyard. Some boats were empty and some were filled with people drinking and barbequing steak and seafood. It smelled delicious. Charles wondered if any of the seafood was shark. He would never have wondered that before today. Occasionally, a boater would wave a pair of barbeque tongs at them. Sometimes it was just a friendly greeting but most of the time a "Hey chief" accompanied it. Laurie smiled and waved back. A couple of times she warned them that they had better not be going back out if they were drinking. At that point a designated driver invariably stood up and assured her that he or she was sober. It seemed to be responsible fun for the most part.

"You can always tell when someone's up to something," said Laurie. "When I walk by, they get very quiet. They try to be invisible. Ironically, that's what makes them stand out." She laughed. They took a few more steps. "Speaking of standing out, have you ever noticed that almost all boats are white? You'd think that someone would want to mix it up. Someone would want to be different. Cars are all different colours, why not boats?"

Charles looked across the sea of white cruisers. "They're all made of plastic. I imagine that anything but white would absorb the heat and heat up the cabins quite quickly. It would be impossible to control. Toward that end, sitting on a dark coloured deck in the hot sun, wearing a bikini or shorts would not be comfortable either."

"Of course," said Laurie. "I should have thought of that."

Charles shrugged. People always said that to him.

They passed Siloam Avenue as it branched from Lake Avenue to the south beside the lake. The Wesley Hotel kept a watchful eye over the entire harbour. It was all five stories of shingles and white painted balconies. With a widow's walk in the centre, it looked very prestigious indeed. After The Wesley Hotel, followed large multicoloured gingerbread houses for which Oak Bluffs was famous. Houses of purple, green, yellow, blue, crimson red, and baby blue- all of them heavily latticed. They were getting closer and closer to downtown Oak Bluffs.

"Funny about that guy- what was his name? Steve?" Mused Charles.

"Steve Christie." Laurie confirmed.

"Yes, that's it. Funny about him not showing up for the contest." Charles looked pensive.

"I've been thinking the same thing. It really isn't like him. I like Steve; he's a good guy." Laurie was deep in thought too. Charles could tell with a quick look that her wheels were turning.

"What does he do?" Asked Charles.

"He owns a restaurant in Edgartown. The only Chinese restaurant on the island, actually."

42

"Is it any good?"

"Very good. Well, actually, I've never eaten there but it has an excellent reputation and you know what these people are like. An excellent reputation isn't that easy to come by." Laurie smiled at her own cynical observation.

"I wonder if anyone has asked any questions in there. Have you?"

"Of course I haven't. I didn't even know he was missing. Technically, he's not missing yet. No one's filed a formal complaint either. He's not married so I'm not even sure who would. He might be seeing someone on the island." Laurie kicked a stone off of the boardwalk and into the harbour. It hit the water with a pleasing plop.

"Maybe we should take a trip down there... just sayin'..." Charles tried to sound nonchalant but failed.

"Well, what I was thinking was that we would hang out up here for a bit and then we could check out Christie's house when I dropped you off at The Edgartown Inn before supper."

"That sounds good. I think that you and I should see it for ourselves." A missing person peaked Charles' interest, he could not tell a lie.

"Yes but in a very unofficial capacity. I don't want to step on anyone else's toes. I need to find out who rang his doorbell before we do. Find out whose toes we would be stepping on, so to speak. I know Steve so there is no harm in us going down to call on a friend." Laurie's official face had returned. It looked very out of place without her uniform.

"What about the restaurant?" Asked Charles.

"I don't think that we'll have time to do both."

"Couldn't we go there for supper?" Charles grinned at his friend.

Laurie smiled broadly, "yes, yes, we could." She took his arm and pulled him across the street toward Circuit Avenue and Mocha Mott's. "I'll call Jeff."

*　　*　　*

Laurie drove the police cruiser smoothly down Beach Road as they headed toward Edgartown. This was one of Charles' favourite strips of highway on the island. At least technically it was a highway. The definition of a highway was "a main road especially one connecting major towns or cities"; however, to Charles, a highway had six or eight lanes and a speed limit of 100 kilometres an hour or 60 miles an hour. Beach Road consisted of only two lanes with Sengekontacket Pond snuggled in on the west side and the Atlantic Ocean sprawled out to the east. The speed limit was only forty-five miles an hour. It just didn't seem like the same thing at all.

The windows were rolled down and the warm summer air blew in at a rapid pace. Charles had plugged his iPod into the car stereo and they were listening to a genius mix based on The Rolling Stones' song, Sympathy For The Devil. Right now it was The Doors' Love Me Two Times- a great song, thought Charles. Charles remembered reading that Ray Manzarek had just died recently. Too bad, he was a talented man, thought Charles. He wondered if Robby Krieger and John Densmore were still alive. They were the only two members of The Doors left if they were. He would have to look that up later.

Charles watched as Joseph and Sylvia State Beach began to unfold in front of them on the driver's side. It was a beautiful and popular family beach. The sand was light and smooth and the water was relatively calm. People waded waist deep in the ocean, seeking relief from the hot summer sun. Others lay on multi-coloured striped beach towels, reading summer mysteries no doubt, thought Charles. One young man stood up and shook the sand off his towel. Charles couldn't help but smile when he made out the thick, red lettering and the all too familiar blue and white picture. He had a JAWS towel. Awesome, thought Charles. All too appropriate, he thought. Charles looked forward as the cruiser took the JAWS Bridge. Kids and adults alike were jumping off the bridge, swimming to the side, climbing onto the long, distinct, rocky jetty and getting out to repeat the whole process- summer on the Vineyard.

With the beach behind them, the road closed in again with tall, thick trees as they headed into Edgartown proper. Cars were few and far between. That surprised Charles. In fact, there were more cyclists on the bike path beside Charles than there were cars on the road. It was good to see. They drove past a sign for cow crossing. That was good to see too, thought Charles. It was just a big outline of a black cow followed by an X.

"I love that sign," said Laurie without taking her eyes off the road. "I'd love to have it in my house somewhere."

"It would be awesome in the kitchen." Charles grinned.

"Exactly!" Laurie laughed.

Sunshine sprayed the car in flecks through the thick woods. They drove past Trapps Pond Road and the trees briefly made a complete canopy of greenery before opening up again. Charles winced at the sudden catch of sunlight. It was bright and yellow. Peaked red roofs and grey-shingled homes began to peer out of the trees on the passenger side of the cruiser. These homes were built like the subdivisions of townhouses back in Toronto, Charles thought. It always took him aback when he saw a design style of the modern world creep its way onto the Vineyard. It seemed to be so out of place to him. These would have been perfectly lovely homes anywhere else but here they seemed awkward and uncomfortable. They looked like they wanted to go home. That's how Charles saw it anyway.

After Beach Road merged with Edgartown-Vineyard Haven Road, the tone changed dramatically. The two streets became Upper Main Street and they were in town at that point, no question. Trimmed shrub fences lined yards and white picket gates blocked driveways. One trimmed shrubbery after another picket gate led them further and further into town. They drove past the Stop & Shop where Charles had picked up their groceries the day before and past the Mobil Gas Station that was advertising a seven dollar and ninety-nine cent cheese pizza. Charles wondered if that was where the red headed protester had bought the pizza in her bag. After Cannonball Park, Laurie turned the cruiser onto Edgartown West

Tisbury Road and then took an almost immediate left into a beautifully manicured driveway.

There was a fair sized front lawn in front of the Christie house. The traditional Vineyard hydrangeas in brilliant blues and blushing pinks surrounded the perfectly green lawn. The ell shaped house was a white two-storey with black shutters framing each window. The long side of the ell was parallel to the road and fronted by a welcoming porch. On the second storey, there were three peaks and a shuttered window sat comfortably in each. It was a lovely home, thought Charles.

Laurie parked and turned to Charles. "Remember, this is completely informal. Just looking for a friend out of concern."

"Got it." Charles agreed. He didn't really see what the difference was but if it made Laurie feel better, so be it.

They both stepped out of the car and closed their doors behind them. The sun was high and made the home look all the more inviting. Charles remembered that on the island, if a police cruiser pulled up, the people inside were likely to come to the door to greet them. No one came out of the Christie house. Laurie walked up to the front door and rang the doorbell. They both waited in silence for signs of life from within. There was nothing. She opened the screen door and knocked a little harder than usual. "Steve?" There was nothing.

"In North Bay, people are just as likely to come calling to the back kitchen door as they are to come to the front. You know, for a casual visit. What do you think? Would that be out of the ordinary here?"

Laurie looked at him intensely. She had her cop face on. "Not at all. I'll lead the way though." She stepped around him and headed down the porch to the end of the house. When she got there, she jumped down and walked around to the back.

At the end of the drive was the inevitable second building. Almost every property had two buildings. Every islander wanted to capitalise on the summer D.I.N.K.s and everyone had a cottage to rent. This was a garage on the first floor and a small cottage on the second. A wooden staircase ran up the side of the building to a door on the side. The whole building had been appointed to match the main house in white with black trim. Laurie and Charles walked past it and around to the kitchen door. Again, Laurie opened the screen door and knocked heavily. "Steve? You in there? It's Chief Knickles!"

"So much for unofficial." Charles gave Laurie a mischievous half-grin.

She looked at him and shrugged. "Habit." she whispered.

There was still nothing coming from inside.

Charles leaned over the flowerbed at his feet and looked in the kitchen window. There were utensils on the cutting board and eggs on the counter. He turned to Laurie, "Is the door locked? It looks like someone's in the middle of something."

Laurie tried the doorknob; it opened easily. She poked her head in and called him again. "Hey Steve! It's Laurie Knickles. Are you all right?" Still nothing.

48

She pulled her head back out of the house and turned to Charles. "You stay here. I'm going to go up to the second floor and make sure that he's not in bed with meningitis or out cold after hitting his head in the shower or something. I'll be two minutes."

"You got it chief."

Charles watched her disappear into the house and then turned toward the backyard. There was enough manicured lawn to have a cocktail party but with a beautiful pool in the centre. Hedges ran all the way around the yard giving a good amount of privacy. Steve Christie must do all right for himself, thought Charles. His family had probably been on the island for a few generations, he surmised. He stepped away from the door and looked up to see if he could see Laurie; he couldn't. There was a stone path to the steps on the second building. Charles decided to follow it. It seemed doubtful that Steve Christie would be up there and not have heard the cruiser drive up, let alone not heard them knocking and calling but it gave Charles something to do. The stones were large and well spaced; Charles easily took one per step. At the foot of the staircase, he grabbed the railing and walked up the thirteen steps. There was a screen door at the top. Charles opened it and knocked much as Laurie had at the main house. "Mr Christie?" He tried the doorknob; it was locked. He really hadn't expected anything to come of this. Charles turned around and looked out at the yard. From this vantage point, he could see the whole thing. He froze. His heart beat wildly as he absorbed the scene in front of him. His skin felt like it was on too tight. Finally, he pulled his iPhone out of his pocket and called Laurie. "Get out here now," he said. Almost immediately, Laurie came out of the kitchen door. She looked up at him in bewilderment. He pointed. She followed his finger. "The pool!"

Laurie walked quickly across the lawn and Charles made his way down the stairs. He jumped the last two and met Laurie at the edge of what was marked as the shallow end. The cover was pulled over from one end to the other but it was easy to tell that there was something wrong. The translucent pool cover did not shimmer bright blue but rather a murky brown. Spits of water spurted out from under the lip of the plastic sheeting in the same colour of rot. It was only now, standing at the edge that they could smell it. It smelled of decay. That sick sweet smell of cold earthy pits and rotten wildlife that came with death. This was slightly different. The mix with chlorine gave it a tang that stuck to the back of Charles' throat. Charles looked out over the pool and he could see that there was something underneath, something more than water.

He pointed toward the largest mound. "Look."

Laurie walked around the pool to the deep end. Charles followed. The pool cover came to a spool there with a large wheel to roll it back. She took a hold of the handle and started cranking. As the cover slid back, the smell filled the backyard. Instinctively, Charles covered his mouth and nose. It didn't help. It was a bright blue day. The pool should have looked bright, blue, and inviting. Instead it was feculent, brown, and repulsive. Charles could see there were pieces in the pool. The pieces were more than likely Steve Christie.

The corpse was mostly in one piece but it was missing its hands and feet. They looked like they had been severed cleanly just above the wrists and ankles. Charles was able to make out one foot bobbing along the side of the pool. His stomach turned and he shuddered involuntarily. He didn't know what to make of this. He looked at Laurie. She stood up when she had finished rolling back the cover.

Laurie looked at him. "Jesus H. Christ," was all she said.

6

"Any guesses?" Laurie asked Charles as she typed her password into her office computer.

"Exsanguination." Charles sat in one of the leather chairs that faced Laurie's desk.

"That's what I figure too. We won't know for sure until we get the autopsy report back and find out if he had any water in his lungs." Laurie began to type. "Look, I'm going to have a lot of paperwork here. Can you walk back to The Edgartown Inn?"

"Absolutely. Are we still on for dinner?" Charles stood up again.

"I think so. My team should be finished at the Christie house. Detective Meadows will take a team through the house and report back to me. I'll take his report and go through the house myself when they're done. I can take an hour or two for dinner. I'll call Jeff because I really do want to go to Steve's restaurant now."

"No kidding." Charles turned to leave.

"I know that I don't have to say this but keep it to yourself, all right?"

"Of course." He said. She was right; she didn't have to say it.

Charles stepped out into the late afternoon sun. Steve Christie murdered in his own pool. There was no formal paperwork but Charles was pretty sure that Steve hadn't had his hands and feet hacked off in a cooking accident. It was so gruesome. Somebody was really trying to drive a point home. Who would do that? What point was so important that they would go to such extremes? Martha's Vineyard was not turning out to be the tranquil vacation spot that was in all of the brochures! Twice Charles had come to the island as an adult and both times someone had been murdered. If this happened in a book, people wouldn't believe it, thought Charles.

He turned and headed down Main Street. He loved this part of Edgartown. In fact, it was his favourite part of the island that was "in town". The Old Whaling Church built in 1843, the Dr Daniel Fisher House built three years prior in 1840. He loved the Greek revival architecture. Trees that had to be as old as the houses and magnificent gardens made it easy to forget the brutality that Charles had witnessed that morning. He had no reference point for people on the island, no ideas as to who could have perpetrated such a crime. The chief would have a better idea there. All he had to go on was the crime itself. Everyone did everything for a reason. When he got back to The Edgartown Inn, Charles was going to do some research on crime with similar modus operandi. There must be at least one on the Internet somewhere.

The lower that Charles got on Main Street, the busier the sidewalks became. Young professional couples, known locally as "summer D.I.N.K.s" (dual income-no kids), bobbed and weaved in and out of the tiny boutiques and shops that had taken over Main Street a long time ago. If you were bobbing and weaving as well, you would have no problem but if you were walking down the street with a purpose- good luck. Charles fought his way through, making his way toward North Water Street. Once there, he stopped briefly to smile. The corner of Main Street and Water Street was JAWS central and Charles doubted that he would ever get over it. Once his imagination was sated, Charles turned up North Water Street and walked on.

North Water was equally beautiful and had the perk of not being made up entirely of shops. There were some but they were interspersed between hotels, restaurants, and art galleries. Charles walked up past The Fallon of Edgartown and Murdick's Fudge. On past The Gardner Colby Gallery and The Eisenhauer Gallery with their fresh white trim and wide welcoming windows. Charles stopped briefly to look in each one. There was real artistic talent on this island, he thought. Because of the tourist market, most Vineyard paintings were of the Vineyard itself but each with its own interpretation, each with something to say.

A man and woman stopped to look the paintings beside Charles. "Aren't they lovely Frank?" she asked.

"How many times can you paint a beach?" Frank snorted.

Charles looked him straight in the eye, "About as many times as you can sing a song about a beautiful woman." He looked at Frank's wife, "Have a nice day." The woman smiled at Charles before he turned and walked away. He did not look back. Mostly because he was pretty sure that if he did, he'd get punched in the nose. What an asshole, thought Charles.

The sun began to cloud over and the breeze felt cool without it. Charles passed the Kelley House and crossed the street to his home away from home, The Edgartown Inn. He climbed the stairs to find Edie cleaning on the front porch. Her curls bounced as she wiped at cup rings on the glass-topped coffee tables.

"Hi hun! How was your day? Missed you at breakfast this morning." Edie smiled her smile that had been warm and welcoming since he had first seen it last year.

"It was good, a good morning. Breakfast was nice- not as good as yours, you understand but you have to go out occasionally to make sure that you really appreciate yours for what it is!" Charles grinned.

"That was pretty slick! Okay, you're forgiven." She laughed. "What else did you do?"

"We stopped to watch some of that Monster Shark Fishing Tournament. I wasn't impressed." Charles grimaced at the memory.

"Why on earth would you stop and watch that? You of all people!" Edie stopped what she was doing and put her hands on her hips for effect. She looked like she was scolding a child.

"I don't know." Charles slumped down into his favourite chaise and watched the tourists walk by on red brick sidewalk. "I'd never seen one before this morning Edie. It was horrible, like a three ringed circus for slaughtering sharks." He shook his head.

Edie sat down on the armchair across from him. Leaning forward and crossing her arms on her knees, her face was one of concern. "Then what made you go?"

"I went to the Edgartown Library here," he motioned over his shoulder. "I read everything that I could find on the tournament. On paper, it actually doesn't sound that bad. It turns out that ninety-seven percent of the sharks caught are released. There are always marine biologists from Woods Hole on the scene to take samples and study the sharks caught- we learn a lot from them, a lot of things that we wouldn't have the opportunity to learn without contests like that one. Don't get me wrong; we might still learn these things but certainly not as easily or as inexpensively. That leaves funds for other things which is good- it all sounds so good!" Charles was exasperated. He hadn't intended on getting so emotional about this.

"But..." Edie pushed him on.

"...But in reality, it's horrible. It's barbaric. It's negative energy and ignorance frothing at the mouth. It's helpless animals that have just been slaughtered being strung up for the world to see, poked and jeered as monsters. In Africa when people are after elephants, rhinos, lions, or gorillas, we call them poachers and they get arrested! They're tried and put in prison! We all take such a superior stance and point our fingers at the governments of those countries. In North America, as soon as the animal isn't cute, if you can't make its

56

likeness into a cute stuffed animal, it's game on! It's human beings at their worst. Well, I suppose human beings at their worst would have to be when they do that to each other *and they do in some places*." Charles briefly saw Steve Christie floating in his pool. "This is of the same mindset though. It's such a sour and hateful energy." Charles sat back in his chair. He felt a little worn. The morning at the tournament and then the afternoon at the Christie house had been a lot to take.

Edie was quiet for a while. "Sit here, I'll be right back." She stood up and went back into the inn. It wasn't quite time to come back and dress for dinner yet so the inn was quiet. Charles wasn't sure if there was anyone else there besides him and Edie or not. Edie would know, Charles knew that for sure. She returned carrying a tray with two mugs and a pot. She poured them each a cup of tea and then settled back down onto her chair. "You're Canadian, right?"

Charles looked at her quizzically. "Yes." He was leery; he didn't know where she was going with this.

"You ever eat rabbit? Pheasant? Moose? Bear? Deer? Caribou?" She looked at him with a very direct look.

Charles nodded his head. He should have seen that. "Yes- all of the above."

"You're a smart man and you're the shark guy."

"Am I?" Charles grinned in spite of himself.

"According to Chief Knickles you are and she is nobody's fool. That one is as smart as a whip. So tell me, the sharks they are catching, are they endangered?" Edie was determined to make her point.

She sipped her tea and Charles could see that she found satisfaction in its warmth and subtle flavour.

"No, they're not." Charles brought his mug to his face and deciding it was still too hot, blew on it gently.

"I didn't think so. If you don't like the tournament then don't go to it. It's as simple as that. There will always be fishermen and there will always be sharks caught and killed for food in the ocean. You should be thankful for that fact because it means that sharks are still bountiful enough to be caught."

Charles stared at her. "That's a good way to look at it." He smiled.

"Of course it is. Me? I love bunnies so don't ask me to shoot one or eat one." She smiled. "Have you seen the bunnies that we have living in the backyard?"

"No." Charles shook his head and then sipped his tea. It was delicious.

"Next time you are up and around at night poke your head out the back door, you'll see them. They come out at night. They're the sweetest things." Her expression was back to warm and friendly. "How's your tea?"

"Delicious, thank you. I needed it."

"A good cup of tea will cure anything. So will a good glass of wine for that matter." She took another sip and stood up. "All right, you sit here, drink your tea, and relax. I have books to tend to before I go home."

"Thanks a lot Edie." Charles smiled as she squeezed his shoulder on her way back into the inn. The screen door closed behind her with a whine and a clack that only seemed to be heard in summer. It left

Charles in almost perfect quiet. A car drove by occasionally and of course there were the ever-present gulls but for the most part, it was quiet. It was still. Charles drank his tea and it did seem to calm him. Everything around him was wrapped in the island's greenery. He stared out at the sun-streaked street, trimmed with trees and the beautiful Kelley House, surrounded by shrubs, flowers, and trees. Downtown Edgartown was still one giant green space. Charles thought that was so important to easing a person's state of mind. Nature had a profound affect. If he turned his head the right way, he could see past The Kelley House and catch a glimpse of the ocean, Edgartown Harbour. No matter what was going on, you could always turn your head just the right way on Martha's Vineyard and there would be a view reminding you that everything would be okay, thought Charles.

On the other hand, the Christie murder was still clear in his head, at least the aftermath was. Charles could see it like a photograph. He could pin it like a bulletin on a board. The only other bulletin was the tournament. Charles would have to find out what else was going on right now on the island. Could Steve Christie's death be related to the Monster Shark Fishing Tournament? Charles couldn't see how. Steve was supposed to work the tournament but there was no obvious link between the tournament and the crime. Charles hoped that it would stay that way. The tournament would make investigations that much more difficult. There were a lot of tourists on the island.

Charles finished his tea. He looked at his iPhone and got up. He wanted to have a short nap and a shower before going out with Laurie and Jeff. He got up and headed in. Edie was hard at work in her office, so Charles walked to the back of the inn and put his mug in the kitchen. Then, he walked to his room and pulling his key out of his back pocket, he opened the door.

The fresh, cool air rushed at him and drew him in. He put his key down on the night table and took off his shoes and socks. A thirty-minute nap was all he needed. Just thirty minutes and he would feel grand. His head felt heavier than it really was as it sank into the clean, white pillow. He went over the details of the crime scene in his mind. Charles felt that there was something that he wasn't seeing. He also hoped that Laurie had sorted out their dinner plans with Jeff. He really wanted to go to that Chinese restaurant and talk to Steve Christie's partner. He also wanted to hear more about the tournament from Jeff. There was something there but Charles had no idea what it was.

7

The Golden Dragon was on Winter Street just off of North Water Street in Edgartown. It was small and unassuming. In fact, if you didn't know it was there, it was easy to miss. Charles always thought that it was very impressive when a restaurant survived purely on reputation. Most restaurants would find it extremely difficult to survive without a strong street presence. In Toronto, all of the Chinese restaurants were red and gold. Large dragon sculptures guarded the doors, paintings of traditionally drawn Chinese people by flowing streams filled the outdoor murals but not on Martha's Vineyard. The restaurant was grey-shingled, white-trimmed and half-shaded by a large maple tree just like everything else. That made Charles chuckle. The wooden sign hung on a wrought iron bracket. The font was vaguely Oriental but not overly so; however, it was painted in red- a lucky colour in Chinese culture.

Charles had decided to walk to the restaurant. When Laurie had called to say that she was on her way to collect him, he had asked where it was. It was so close to the Edgartown Inn that it seemed ridiculous for her to come and get him. He could walk to the restaurant in the time that it would take her to turn the car around on Water Street! Well, not quite but close. Charles opened the door by the brass door handle. It was a small restaurant with more traditional décor on the inside than out. The lighting inside was all Chinese lanterns. He saw Laurie immediately and walked over to her.

"Hi!" He sat down opposite her, at a table for four, in the chair against the wall.

"Hey. How was your walk?" She smirked.

"Brief." Charles looked around and took in the smells and the atmosphere. He liked it quite a bit. "Kind of a cool place, eh?"

"It is actually. I don't know why I haven't been here before now." She looked around too but less enthusiastically than Charles. "It makes for a nice break from the traditional island fare."

"That traditional island fare is pretty damned good!" Charles smiled. "It would be tough for me to take a break from that."

Laurie smiled, "Yeah, I guess that's it."

"Have you seen Christie's partner yet?" Charles scanned the employees for possibilities.

"No. He's not here but they're expecting him. I don't think that anyone here knows anything. They would have said something to me. Certainly asked some questions or been a little bit upset."

62

"Who's here?" Charles picked up his menu and perused it carefully. Every time that he went to a Chinese restaurant, he scanned the menu for shark fin soup. If they did offer it on the menu, he wouldn't eat there. It was legal in the state of Massachusetts but, thankfully, the Golden Dragon did not sell it. Shark-finning itself was illegal but serving the soup wasn't. That kind of thing drove Charles crazy.

"Two cooks in the back and two waitresses are all I've seen so far." Laurie, who had only been giving her menu half of her attention looked up when the door opened. "The rest of our party is here!"

Charles looked up as two gentlemen made their way in to the restaurant. The light from outside was behind them but the room was lit well enough that he could make out their faces. The first one was Chief Jefferies but he didn't think he knew the second one; however, he looked vaguely familiar.

Laurie stood up and greeted them both warmly. "Hey guys! How are you doing?"

Charles couldn't help but feel a mild pang of jealousy when Laurie leaned in to hug the second man. He was very well built and very handsome. The fact that he was a stranger to Charles didn't help either.

"Good! We're good!" Jeff pulled out the chair beside Charles and sat down. "Hey man!"

"Hey!" Charles shook his hand and looked quizzically at Jeff's friend.

"Charles, this is Chris Johns-"

"The hockey player!" Charles exclaimed in realisation. "I knew you looked familiar! It's really good to meet you!" He extended his hand and shook it energetically. "You were with the Chicago Blackhawks, right? Defenseman?"

Chris laughed, "I'm flattered. I've heard a lot about you from Jeff here. He speaks very highly of you. You made quite an impression last summer."

"Well, I don't know that I did anything all that special but it was great getting to know Jeff." Charles turned to Laurie. "You didn't tell me that you knew Chris Johns!"

"Oh." She glanced at Jeff. "Well, I wasn't sure if I was supposed to make it public knowledge or not. I figured you'd meet him eventually." Laurie looked a little sheepish.

Charles watched her face and thought her reaction was a little odd. He turned to look at Chris and Jeff and realised that there was a lot that was not being said. He focused on Jeff and raised an eyebrow in an unspoken question.

There was a brief pause and then Jeff said in a very matter-of-fact tone, "Charles, Chris is my husband."

Charles looked up dramatically and exclaimed, "Oh, thank god!"

Chris grinned, "We haven't had that response before."

"Is that all? Jesus, you scared me! I thought someone had cancer or something!" Charles took a deep breath. "Well, congratulations! How long?"

"Six months almost to the day." Jeff grinned across the table at his husband, Chris.

"Well, that's great. Good for you. I had no idea." Charles looked at Laurie.

"I was dying to tell you but I didn't think that it was my place to tell you...or anyone for that matter. I'm not that big on 'outing' people."

"I'm surprised that I didn't read about it in the papers with your NHL background Chris."

"We've kept it pretty quiet for just that reason. I don't feel like I have anything to hide but we lead a quiet life and that's the way I'd like to keep it if I can. Having the ceremony here on the island helped. Everyone stays away from America over here."

"Well done." Said Charles. He loved that islanders called the mainland, 'America'. It showed how much they felt like the island was their own world. That was the appeal of Martha's Vineyard. Since 1642, when the island was founded, the islanders had created their own world and they had done a miraculous job of keeping it that way.

"We're still a little tentative when it comes to telling people but we figured that you'd be cool with it." Jeff said.

"I live in downtown Toronto. Straight white males are the minority! I couldn't care less. Actually, that's a terrible way to put it." Charles rethought what he had said, "That sounded uncaring and dismissive which was not my intention. What I should have said was, I think it's great."

"Thanks." They said in unison. There was an awkward pause.

Charles laughed, "Ok, so now what?" they all laughed then.

"We hear you guys had a bit of excitement this afternoon." Chris started.

"That's putting it mildly." Laurie rolled her eyes. "It was a shit show. I have never seen anything like it on the island. I rarely saw anything like it in the city. Wait until that hits the papers. I bet it goes national."

Charles watched as Jeff and Laurie both put on their business faces. Even without their uniforms, they became chiefs again. He looked at Chris and smiled.

"Here we go." Chris said.

"You're damned right, 'here we go'." Jeff looked around to be sure that nobody else was listening. "You found Steve Christie floating in a pool with his hands and feet removed?"

"We did." Laurie nodded.

"What the hell is that about?"

"I have no idea. Everyone does everything for a reason. I'm going to have to figure out what that reason is. It means something."

"Who do you have going over the crime scene?" asked Jeff.

"Jack Burrell is the lead and he has a couple of other guys. Jack will come here and tell me when he's done. I'll go over it myself then. I'm curious to see what they come up with. Maybe they'll find something to explain the hack job."

"It's biblical," said Charles.

"What do you mean? What's biblical?" asked Laurie.

"In the book of Samuel, David has Rechan and Baanah killed, their hands and feet cut off and their bodies hanged by the pool at Hebron." Charles searched the faces of his three tablemates for some sort of recognition but they all just stared at him in disbelief. "What?" They still just stared.

"What the hell are you talking about?" Laurie asked. Her face was squinted in disbelief.

"I was an alter boy and I don't even know what he's talking about!" Said Chris.

"In the bible! Rechan and Baanah killed Ish-Bosheth, the son and successor of Saul, and presented his head to King David. They thought that this would put them in David's good books but David did not see the son of Saul as an enemy but rather as an honourable man. So, he killed Rechan and Baanah by cutting off their hands and feet and hanging them by the pool at Hebron. Hebron is a Palestinian city twenty miles south of Jerusalem."

"*How do you know that?*" Exclaimed Chris.

"See what I mean." Jeff shook his head in disbelief.

"When did you get so religious?" Laurie asked him incredulously.

"I didn't. I'm an atheist; however, whether I think it's true or not, I can't argue the fact that the bible is by far the most influential book in history. I had to read it."

Laurie sighed and grinned at her friend. "Of course you did."

"Well, that's quite a coincidence, don't you think?" said Jeff.

"I do." Conceded Laurie.

"I still don't believe in coincidences," said Charles.

"I can't believe that you just knew that!" exclaimed Chris.

"I know, right?" Jeff smiled at Charles and nudged him with his elbow. "Well done buddy."

Laurie tried her best not to smile. "It gets kind of obnoxious." She couldn't help herself though and she kicked him playfully under the table. "Can we order? I'm starving."

"Absolutely!" Said Charles.

"Tomorrow, maybe we'd better start this investigation at the church." Laurie said to Charles. "If you'd like to come with me in an unofficial capacity."

"That would be great." Charles tried not to sound too overly excited but the truth was he loved being a part of this sort of thing. "Shall we all share some starters?"

"Perfect. What do you suggest? This is a little out of my league. I know sweet and sour chicken balls and then I'm out." Jeff laughed at himself.

"I say we get satay chicken skewers, spring rolls, sesame prawn toast, and vegetable samosas. Then, we can just divide them all up." Chris suggested.

"I'm all over that! Laurie is that all right with you?" Charles asked.

"Absolutely. Let's get our waitress over here."

"The only word I knew in there was 'chicken'." Jeff grinned.

"You'll love it," said Charles.

They placed their order and the waitress came back with a pitcher of beer and four glasses. Chris poured one for each of them and they talked about the wedding and Chris's hockey career. The food came quickly and they ate almost ferociously. It made Charles laugh. All four of them had been really hungry, much hungrier than they had been letting on. Charles sat back when he had eaten enough appetizers and quietly watched the others eat and chat. They were lovely people, he thought. He really liked all three of them. He was in a good place. He was happy except for one thing. There was still something gnawing at him. There was something telling him that he was overlooking something... something obvious... something important.

8

The fish swam smoothly and silently through the open water. Food had been scarce and she was hungry. She was a lot leaner than she could be. Her black back and white belly were narrower than she would like them to be. Instinctively, she swam west. She knew there would be meat there. There would be food closer to shore. Seals. She was larger than most of her kind, larger than any she had ever come across, and therefore needed a lot more food. Still, her tail swept smoothly, silently. She was not in a hurry. She could not give any sign of distress, no sign of weakness. That could be life threatening out here. Most of the wildlife in the ocean gave her a wide berth but fear could be smelled miles away. Once it was in the water, predators would come looking for it, for her. They'd take her down if they knew she was weak. Her torpedo snout bore scars of previous battles. Battles that she had fought and won. She was undefeated. Gouges in her back told similar stories. Those were from battles with men, men in boats. She hadn't won those but rather escaped them. That was winning of a sort. The gouges interrupted her otherwise sleek skin. She was designed for power and speed. Each tiny scale on her back formed to push water over her as fast as it could go. When she had decided that something was prey, it rarely had a chance. The fish moved along with her mouth cracked in a Cheshire grin. Her eyes were black and seemingly bottomless. It was an evil combination. The expression was that of a clown doll that a child couldn't bear to have in his or her room at night, the doll that had to have a blanket thrown over it in protection against nightmares. There was no throwing a blanket over this nightmare. Three tonnes of muscle swam at an even pace pushing seawater over its serrated teeth and out of its rippling gills.

In an instant she was alert. There was something in the water. The senses in her snout came alive and at once her whole body was wired. Her pace quickened. Her jaw was electric, primed with almost four thousand pounds of pressure. She knew where it was, where she had to go. The water was getting shallow. The shark was headed toward land.

9

Chief Laurie Knickles' police cruiser pulled up into the drive of the Christie house for the second time that day. Charles looked up at the house and it seemed to look back with familiarity and menace. The sun had almost completely set leaving the large white house entirely backlit. The lights were on inside. The chief and Charles already knew that the other officers were inside. Sergeant Jack Burrell had called them just as they had finished their dinner at The Golden Dragon. They had said their good-byes to Jeff and Chris and come straight over. When they arrived, yellow police tape was stretched across the entire property. Neighbours' prying eyes were peeking out of every house. Some people were out on their front porch. Charles looked up at the once inviting Vineyard home. The windows looked empty and soulless. Charles had thought this house to be beautiful when they had driven up for the first time but now, after seeing the corpse chopped and floating in the pool this

72

afternoon, it looked eerie and cold. It even looked threatening. It filled Charles with a sense of foreboding. That was just foolish. Charles always had a vivid imagination. The combination of high intelligence and high emotion was what did it, he figured. He was smart enough to think up all of the possibilities and emotional enough to feel them.

Seemingly unaffected, Chief Knickles got out of the car and walked up to the house. Charles hesitated slightly but in the end, followed her up the stone path. They stopped at the front door. "Here, put these on." The chief passed him a pair of latex gloves. She put on her own pair and reached for the doorknob. "I want you to stay in the background for the most part. Try not to touch or disturb anything. By all means look around and tell me what you see. It certainly couldn't hurt to have your brain and your eyes in here with me."

"I'll do my best." He tried to sound as humble as he could but he was still quite chuffed when someone mentioned his intelligence.

"I should probably just deputize you." She stared at him for a moment, thinking.

"Is that a very involved process?"

"Hmm, I don't know. I hate paperwork."

Charles made a mental note to look that up later.

The chief opened the door to find three police officers working diligently on the main floor. One of them was Sergeant Burrell. The sergeant scurried over when the chief entered. "Hi chief! Mr- Charles."

"Jack, what are you doing? You told me you were finished." The chief's voice was deeper and more serious than it had been all evening.

"Oh! We are! I just thought that it wouldn't hurt to triple check everything while we waited for you to get here. We double-checked before I called you. I think it's good. I hope it's good. I was really good at crime scene forensics in school. It was one of my best things. That and marksmanship were my best-" The chief held up her hand, silencing Jack Burrell.

Charles had to turn away so that the sergeant couldn't see him grinning. Jack was a really good guy but boy, did the chief make him nervous. Charles inhaled deeply and turned back toward the police officers.

"Walk me through it, sergeant." The chief said.

"Yes chief."

"I'm going to stay back and think for a minute if that's all right. I'll be along in a minute." Charles said.

The chief nodded her approval while following Sergeant Burrell into the kitchen.

Standing at the front door, Charles looked around the room. Two soft lights with cream coloured shades lit the room with a warm yellow hue. The furniture was navy blue and the woods were dark. The room hinted at a nautical theme that showed up fairly regularly on the island. The artwork was also very typical. There was a painting of the Edgartown lighthouse over the large sofa and a collection of beach photographs over the matching chair. The room was very pleasant if lacking in imagination, thought Charles. He walked over to the dark wood desk and

74

looked at the papers piled on top. They had been carefully organised. What he had seen of the rest of the property was also meticulously kept. The hedges and lawn were extremely tidy; coffee table books were lined up neatly. Charles assumed that Steve Christie had left the room and his desk this way. There was a cord feeding into a wall jack but no phone. Someone so tidy would have removed the cord with the phone, thought Charles. There was a pad of yellow lined paper but nothing had been written on it. Charles reached into his shorts and pulled the receipt from their dinner out of his pocket. He placed it on the top left hand corner of the pad where someone would be most likely to write. With a pencil from the cup on the desk, he softly coloured in the receipt until the indentations from the yellow paper below the receipt left a pattern. The pattern was a list. A list of oriental names- Pink Pagoda, China Pearl, Chang Lee's, House of the Orient, and Hong Kong Cuisine had been written on five lines on a piece of paper that had since been discarded Charles checked but there was nothing but a Coke can in the trash. Perhaps the police had collected it. He doubted it but it was possible.

Still using the pencil, Charles lifted various pages to read the papers underneath. There wasn't much of interest. There was what you'd expect, bills, bank statements, flyers, and restaurant pamphlets. Charles would have dismissed them but the first one caught his eye, Pink Pagoda. He lifted that one and looked at the next one. It read, China Pearl. He read the third, Chang Lee's; the fourth was House of the

Orient; the last one was Hong Kong Cuisine. That was too much for Charles.

"Hey Chief! Can you come in here for a minute?"

There was no response. Charles turned around and walked toward the back of the house. When he got to the kitchen, he could see the chief and the sergeant through the plate glass window that faced the backyard. The sun was gone. They were just silhouettes but he could see them by the pool, illuminated by the light on the side of the garage.

Charles walked through the kitchen and out the backdoor. The air was cooler and Charles could smell the freshness of the evening dew when he inhaled. The sweet changed to sour, as he got closer to the pool. It was still being drained. Even though the body parts had been removed, the water that was being pumped out was brown, bloody, and rancid. The metallic smell of blood mixed with heavy chlorine. Charles was careful to stay on the patio stones as he walked back to meet Chief Knickles and her sergeant.

Laurie turned to greet him as he came closer. "Hey, how are you making out?"

"Um, okay. I might have found something interesting. Should I wait until you are done here?"

Laurie shook her head. "By all means what have you found? Jack will come with us."

Charles looked down into the darkness of the emptying pool. "Did someone check the temperature of the pool before they drained it? At least checked the thermometer?" Asked Charles.

"Seventy-two degrees, Charles," said Sergeant Burrell promptly.

76

"Why do you want to know?" Asked Laurie.

"When we found Mr Christie, he was floating. A body doesn't float right away- it sinks. It will rise after gases build up and make it buoyant. The temperature of the water in a heated pool will speed up that process."

"Cool!" Said Sergeant Burrell. He regained his composure and said, "I mean, that's very interesting."

The chief smiled. "It's all right Jack, I thought it was cool too." She turned back toward Charles. "So, what brought you out here to me? It wasn't to check the pool temperature."

"Oh right! Jack did you go over the contents of the desk in the front room?" Charles asked. He turned to walk back toward the house but tripped when his toe caught on a patio stone. Jack jumped forward to catch him. Charles straightened and they continued. "Sorry about that."

"No problem. We did go over the contents of the desk. We have an itemized list of the contents of the drawers and of the items on top of the desk as well. There wasn't much there. Nothing that stood out at this time anyway- might be important later."

"May I see that list sergeant?" Chief Knickles held her hand out and waited for the list.

"Did you take anything out of the garbage can?" Charles continued.

"No. It had a Coke can in it. That's all," said Jack, passing the list to Chief Knickles.

Chief Knickles read the list carefully as they stepped into the house and walked back into the living room. "Jack's right, Charles. I don't see anything here that really jumps out at me. Are you setting us up?"

Charles walked over to the desk and motioned to the yellow note pad. "I took an etching of the note pad using the receipt from our dinner and there was an itemized list of Chinese restaurants on the missing page."

"So?" Laurie stared at Charles with a furrowed brow.

"The same names match the pamphlets for the Chinese restaurant in this pile on the desk. They should be on your list from the sergeant." Charles looked at Jack for confirmation.

"They're there! Absolutely!" Sergeant Jack nodded.

"Also, the phone is missing." Stated Charles.

"What phone?" Asked Sergeant Jack.

"Exactly." Charles reached behind the desk and pulled up the phone cord that was missing an owner. He looked at the two of them and shrugged.

Jack went as red as a tomato and looked at Chief Knickles. "I didn't catch that. Sorry Chief."

"Good catch, Charles. Sergeant, find me that phone."

"I'm on it." Sergeant Jack made his escape as fast as he could, eager to redeem himself.

"Nice observation with the phone." The chief pulled the pamphlets out of the stack of papers and flipped through them. "Do you really think that there is something to the Chinese restaurants?"

"Well, it's curious. Don't you think? Why would he have these pamphlets at all and why would he be

78

writing them down on a pad of paper? It was a list that was either important enough for him to take with him or for someone else to take. No one threw it out or it would still be there with the Coke can." Charles looked over the chief's shoulder at the pamphlets as she scanned them. "They're all in Boston. That's curious too. They're too far away to be competition for his restaurant here. Do they all have the same owners? They all look to be traditional Chinese food not take-away crap."

"True." The chief put the pamphlets back down on the desk.

"May I?" Charles motioned to the pamphlets.

"Oh, I'm sorry. By all means..."

Charles picked up the pamphlets and started reading each one carefully from cover to cover. "Did you guys find anything interesting out back?"

"Not really." Laurie looked at the lists that Sergeant Jack had given her. Each one was an itemized list by room or section of yard. "I'm anxious to see if there is anything else at the bottom of the pool; it's still draining. It was too murky to see to the bottom as it was...and it's too dark now anyway."

Charles grimaced. "Ugh."

"I know- pretty gross."

Charles placed the pamphlets back on the desk grimacing like he'd just found rotten fish in the refrigerator. "Let's go home. I could use a glass of wine."

"You're on."

10

Oak Bluffs had first been settled with the rest of the island in 1642. In the beginning, it had been a part of Edgartown but had incorporated as a town of its own in 1880. It was the only town on Martha's Vineyard designed specifically with tourism in mind and it still stood out as the biggest tourist location on the island. Like the rest of the island, there was an amazing history and beautiful beaches; however, there were also more shops selling cheap mementoes, T-shirts, and other souvenirs than any other township. There were more bars and pubs too. Souvenirs could be purchased all over the island. If you wanted an original oil painting, Edgartown was your town but if you wanted a JAWS T-shirt and a pen in the shape of a lighthouse, you looked in Oak Bluffs. Three thousand, seven hundred people lived in Oak Bluffs year round and in the summer, the tourists were uncountable. Right now, almost all of them were still asleep.

At dawn, Oak Bluffs was quiet. There was no one on the street and Seaview Park was empty except for dog walkers. There was nowhere to get coffee yet. At six o'clock a few hardcore coffee goers and photographers would be up and out but for now, it was still quiet. The sun hadn't technically risen although there were signs that it was imminent. The sky had been a deep midnight black not moments ago. In a very short period of time, it had become a vibrant cobalt blue, still speckled with stars. The cobalt plunged toward the skyline in every direction but changed dramatically to lemon yellow and then exploded in a flash of orange before reaching the horizon.

The ocean waves rumbled softly, beating the shores all the way around the Bluffs. The Inkwell Beach was devoid of people but the waves crept in and out anyway like a midway ride awaiting its first fare of the day. It was quiet enough inland that the waves could be heard anywhere- soft and comforting. The ocean was just waking up. It was a Martha's Vineyard morning.

The downtown streets wound through long morning shadows. Lake Avenue lay quiet and sheltered behind the hundreds of boats that rocked quietly in their slips. Fibreglass hulls groaned against wooden docks. Bells rang in the gentle rocking. The morning sun continued to rise, hitting the masts one by one turning them golden in the early glow. Each mast reached desperately for the promise of the warm sun that would eventually heat up their decks. Whether the boats were occupied or not was impossible to tell. If they were occupied, their occupants were sleeping and quiet.

Lake Avenue directed the occasional vehicle up toward downtown or away across the chop. Each driver passed the stage where the second day of the Monster Shark Fishing Tournament would take place. The posters all hung as they had the day before. Their messages now flickered with the dawning sun. Garbage cans had been emptied in preparation for the overflow of a new day. All signs of yesterday's catches had been rinsed away to make ready for future fish to be caught.

Bill Cunningham hung like a prize shark. His feet were hoisted high above his head and tied with a thick rope. A large fishhook pulled his head back. His mouth was misshapen where the hook disappeared and punctured his palette. His nose was torn where it reappeared through his right nostril. Bill's eyes were dry and staring lifelessly upward. His face was one of permanent fear and horror. Blowflies were already arriving to lay eggs in the nooks and crannies of his wounds. The blood had drained from his hoisted legs leaving them pale and grey. His torso was swollen and his arms hung low like pectoral fins. His fingertips swelled around his fingernails. They were livid and black, the skin tight and engorged. His body swayed slightly when the breeze picked up and when the sun caught his bare flesh... he was grey and shiny.

11

Charles got up very early, showered, and headed out. It was still dark when he left the inn and started walking through Edgartown. North Water Street was quiet. The Kelley House was still and the businesses were closed. Even the omnipresent gulls were still sleeping. Main Street was just as quiet. Two of the corners of Water and Main were banks and it was certainly nowhere near banking hours. Charles continued down South Water Street. The white homes were still and dozy behind their rolling green lawns. Everything lay contently bedded under the heavy blanket of trees. He turned left at Katama Road and kept walking. Katama was a very busy street during the day, especially now during peak season; however, there was no one on the street at this hour. The stillness of town and Water Street became the stillness and quiet of nature as he passed the heavy woods on Katama. It was beautiful. There were still houses but not as frequent as back in town. Most of them were newer and built on their own cul-de-sacs. The older houses were on their own drives hidden deeply behind the woods to Charles' left. Behind the split rail fences and past the thick mix of deciduous and coniferous trees, they would all be on their own private beaches on Edgartown Harbour. Charles would love to have a house in there. Eventually, the houses disappeared behind him and the long grass of Katama Farm swept the edge of the road. Inhaling deeply, he could smell the rich combination of trees, grass, and the sea. He knew he was getting close to his destination. Charles had passed this field the year prior. It had been during the day and he had seen cows grazing. Now, it was too dark. If the cows were out, they must be on the other side of the vast pasture and out of Charles' line of vision. Everything was so quiet. Katama took a sharp turn west, wrapping around the southern end of the farm and then turned south, leaving the farm behind completely. Charles could hear waves in the distance. They were the soft waves of morning, not the heavy waves of mid-day. In the distance, Charles could see the dunes, black silhouettes in the barely lit sky. He had reached his destination, South Beach.

Charles walked through the gap in the dunes that led to the beach. He sat down on the side of a dune and reached out to untie his shoelaces. He removed his left shoe and then his left sock, careful not to get sand in either one. Then, pressing his bare left foot into the cool sand, he repeated the production with his right foot. Both feet bare and pressed into the sand, he stood up and walked toward the surf. The beach was empty. That didn't surprise Charles for that time of day. He did think that he might bump into one or two people walking their dogs or a few photographers here and there. On the Internet, there were always beautiful pictures of early island mornings but there was no one out taking such shots today. At least, not that Charles could see. He walked far enough down the beach that when the waves came in, the water hit his feet. He didn't flinch at the water's temperature; it wasn't that much cooler than the beach itself. He walked along low enough that the water would cover his feet, maybe rush up his calves but not wet his shorts. Rhythmically, the water rolled in, frothed, and rolled out. The next wave was lapping at the beach before the last had completely washed away. Charles closed his eyes for a moment and listened. The ocean hissed like bacon frying as it pulled away from the sand. Charles loved this beach. The opening scene from JAWS was filmed on this beach. Spielberg had made it look like the first victim, Chrissie, was attacked here but in actuality that was filmed on the other side of the island; however, the bonfire was filmed here and Chrissie and Cassidy ran along the dunes here. The rest was spliced in- magic. That was it. Anyway, movie magic aside, it was still pretty cool. Charles remembered swimming here as a boy with his parents. He remembered being on this beach, body surfing, with his Dad when a guy caught a shark with his line not far down the beach from where they were swimming. He thought it was cool at the time. He wasn't sure how cool he would think it was now. He looked out into the now pale yellow light of morning. The long seemingly unending golden swath of sand wound down the island until there was nothing more to see. South Beach was always on the list of the world's best beaches. Charles liked that. Another wave rushed at him. It swirled around his legs; it felt smooth and inviting. He looked out over the dark Atlantic. It was so beautiful. There was still no one on the beach. "If there was ever a chance to go for a skinny dip on South Beach, it was now", thought Charles. Before he could give it anymore thought, his phone went off. It was Laurie. He could tell by the ringtone, "Hail To the Chief".

"Hello?" He said once the phone was at his ear.

"It's me. Where are you? I'm coming to pick you up." Laurie's tone was abrupt. Charles knew that something was going on.

"I'm on South Beach."

"*South Beach!* What the hell are you doing on South Beach at this time of the morning? You're not swimming are you?"

"Not yet. I was thinking about it." He looked out at the open ocean.

"Well don't. Where are you *exactly*? South Beach is three miles long."

"Where they filmed the opening scene in JAWS."

"Of course you are. I should have known; this is a JAWS thing." The chief was almost barking at him. "*Where the hell is that?*"

"What's the matter with you?" Charles asked calmly. "If you are going to be like this then maybe I'd rather you didn't pick me up."

There was a long pause on the other end of the line. Charles let it go on until Laurie was ready to speak again. "I'm sorry." She said quietly. "There has been another murder. I would like to come and collect you. I find you helpful and calming." She chuckled sheepishly. "As you can tell, I could use some calming."

"Another murder! Who?" This time it was Charles who was alarmed.

"Bill Cunningham."

"The asshole from the tournament?" Charles' mind was reeling.

"The one and only."

"I'm at the bottom of Katama Road." He said.

"Oh good. That's easy. I'll see you in ten." She hung up the phone without saying good-bye.

Charles gave his feet one last swish in the water and headed back toward the break in the dunes. Back on the road, he sat on the brown wood bench at the bus stop and began meticulously brushing the sand off of his feet. There were few things worse than sand in your socks, thought Charles.

Bill Cunningham, dead. That wasn't going to be an easy thing to sort out. All Charles had ever heard about the man was that nobody liked him. Certainly, that was going to make it that much harder to find a suspect. This also made Charles think differently about the murder of Steve Christie. There hadn't been any real reason to imagine that the Christie case and the tournament were connected but now, this morning, this was a whole other kettle of fish. Steve Christie was supposed to emcee the tournament but he was murdered. Bill Cunningham steps into his shoes and he is murdered after one day at the job. There was no way that anyone could convince Charles that the two murders weren't connected now. He was sure that Laurie would feel the same.

With nothing but the flat Katama Farm field between him and Katama Road, Charles could see the headlights of Laurie's cruiser a long way off. He stood up and inhaled the salty sea air once more. It was cool and it was wonderful. The cruiser turned onto the last stretch of road and Charles walked toward it.

Chief Laurie Knickles pulled up in front of the beach. Sand ground between her tires and the pavement. "Good morning!"

"Hi! Good morning to you!" Charles said as he slipped into the car. Laurie had been driving with the windows down and the cruiser had that fresh feeling. It was nice.

Laurie looked ahead into the beams of her headlights. They shone directly on the entrance between the dunes. "So, that's where they filmed the opening to JAWS, eh?"

"Yep." Charles nodded.

She nodded in mild appreciation. Still looking straight ahead, she spoke. "Sorry I kinda yelled at you."

"That's okay." Charles smiled. "Let's go. I could really use some coffee."

"My treat." She said. The chief pulled the cruiser back while pulling the steering wheel to the right. She then, pulled it to the left and drove forward up Katama Road.

88

*   *   *

The parking area surrounding the market and the Oak Bluffs Harbour that had been packed full of spectators and fishermen not twenty-four hours before was now sectioned off with yellow police tape. As Chief Knickles pulled her cruiser up to the guard, Charles could see that most of the fuss was around the stage where Bill Cunningham had been poised with his microphone. Charles could see the gallows where first the shark and now Bill had been hung. Charles felt queasy again. He also felt mildly guilty that he did not feel queasy for Bill. Once past the police guard at the yellow perimeter, they drove smoothly up to the other squad cars and parked.

The chief turned to Charles and pulled out a badge. "I'm deputizing you."

"*You're what?*" Charles nearly spit out his mouthful of Mocha Mott's cappuccino and apple fritter. He choked on his mouthful of food.

"Sorry. You want to swallow that?" Chief Knickles smiled at him.

Charles nodded while processing what he had just heard.

"You ready?"

Charles nodded again.

"I'm deputizing you." Laurie handed him the badge. "Don't lose it. Keep it on you at all times. You're not a deputy forever but for the number of days that it takes for us to apprehend the person or persons behind these crimes, you're a deputy. Is that all right with you?"

Charles nodded again.

"Is that it? You don't have anything to say on the matter?"

Charles shook his head. "I think it's kinda cool!"

"Technically, I'm not sure I can deputize a Canadian citizen but being Canadian, I know you're not going to shoot anyone." She winked at him and grinned.

"That's true. We just use harsh language."

"That's fine." The chief opened her door. "Let's go."

"There is a precedent for deputizing Canadians. The Department of Homeland Security implemented agreements under the Intergovernmental Personnel Act allowing non-federal employees to be temporarily assigned to federal agencies to meet the need. At the 2006 Super Bowl, Canadians were deputized so they could make arrests."

"Really?"

"Yep."

"Well, who am I to argue with the Super Bowl? Let's go."

They both stepped out of the car and closed their doors softly. Charles followed the chief's lead toward the crime scene and he took in everything that he could. Several officers were standing under the shark gallows. One of them was Chief Jefferies. They headed in that direction.

"Jeff?" Chief Knickles called out to him.

At the mention of his name, the chief turned. He looked worn. "Oh, hi guys. Thanks for coming chief. It's good to see you Charles but I'm not sure if you should be here."

"I deputized him." Laurie said.

"Oh! Can you do that?"

"The Super Bowl says I can. Besides, by the time anyone checks- if anyone checks, we'll have this thing wrapped up and it won't matter any more. What exactly happened Jeff?"

"Someone is not happy. This was no simple crime. Bill was hoisted up like a prize shark. Feet in the air, hook through his face. I have no idea what the cause of death was yet. We're still waiting for the hospital to collect him. He's over here."

Jeff walked them over to a lump of garbage bags. He lifted one to reveal Bill's disfigured face. Rigor had set in and the hook was still in his mouth. His mouth was gaping and twisted in a permanent silent scream. His neck and cheeks were livid and bloated with blood. Jeff began to reset the bag over him but Laurie stopped him.

"Take the bags off of him, Jeff."

Jeff looked at her questioningly, "Why?"

"You've been watching too much CSI." Her remark was flippant but her face was serious. "I know you want to keep anyone from seeing the body but you're contaminating the crime scene. Who knows what elements you're introducing. If it ever comes up in court, a defence attorney will have a field day with that. They'll say you introduced trace evidence. We called them 'funglets' in Boston- fungus blankets.

"I didn't think about that." Jeff looked embarrassed.

"Don't sweat it. Everyone does it the first time. I did. I got in royal shit for it too."

Jeff removed the garbage bags carefully and they returned their attentions to Bill.

"It's not good," said Charles.

"No, it most certainly isn't." Laurie shook her head and led the three of them away from the corpse. "I'd leave you to it Jeff but I have a sneaky feeling that your corpse and my corpse are related. There's no way that they couldn't be."

"I agree."

"How do you feel about working together on this?"

"I'd love it. I want this done and over with. The more heads the better. I have no idea what I'm going to do about the Fishing Tournament. It just started! There are a lot of people on this island. If I cancel, we'll have a mob on our hands for sure. Not to mention the business that people will lose. I can't do that to them but I have a crime scene to consider."

"Can't you move it?" interjected Charles.

"What do you mean?" asked Jeff.

"Well, as long as the crime scene is protected, there is no reason for the tournament not to continue is there? Can't you just have them move it further down the harbour? It will also keep a lot of the tourists out of your hair, keep them occupied."

"I like it. Nice work deputy! I'll talk to the harbour master." Chief Jefferies called over one of his sergeants and asked him to organise a makeshift tournament headquarters further up the harbour. By the look on his face, Charles didn't think that the sergeant had any clue how he was going to accomplish that task but he said that he would. Chief Jefferies turned back toward Chief Knickles. "How's Sergeant Burrell?" he asked.

"I don't know. I called him and told him about Bill this morning. He's at home with his wife. He said to tell you that he would come in and identify the body when Marcie's ready to be left alone." She turned to Charles. "We should probably be heading over there actually."

"Sure thing." said Charles soberly.

"Jeff, if you come up with anything, let me know would you? We'll go back to Edgartown and see if we can finally talk to Steve Christie's business partner; he never did show up at the restaurant."

"Sounds good."

Laurie and Charles walked back toward the car. The doors weren't locked and they both slipped into their seats. Charles automatically opened his window all the way.

"What do you think will happen to the tournament?"

The chief shook her head. "Nothing."

"No?"

"It's a circus...and the show must go on."

"Where are we headed first?" Charles asked. He watched Sengekontacket Pond go by outside his window.

"Well, I think that it's a bit too early to go and talk to Christie's partner or Jack Burrell. I thought that we could grab some breakfast." Laurie didn't take her eyes off the road.

"Excellent idea. I'm starving. I want more coffee too. Where do you want to go?"

"How do you feel about going back to the Edgartown Inn? I love Edie's breakfasts and I haven't had one in ages. Also, it's close to The Golden Dragon and Burrell's house. We could walk from there."

"You are on top of things this morning, Chief Knickles aren't you?" Charles grinned at her affectionately.

"I'm trying." She smiled briefly at him before returning her eyes to the road. "This isn't exactly the trip I had planned for you."

Charles laughed. "I hope not! …But I'm enjoying it nonetheless. You know, in a creepy, fascinating kind of way."

"I didn't want our time together to be creepy and fascinating," said Laurie. There was sadness in her voice.

Charles hadn't realised how upset she was about this. He reached out for her hand. She hesitated but took it. "No one could have known that this would happen again but it did. We still get to spend all of our time together. In fact, because of this case, I'll bet that we're spending more of our time together than we otherwise would have."

Laurie stared intensely at the road. Charles could tell that if she looked at him, her emotions would take over. She was fighting it all the way. "How do you figure?"

"If everything was business as usual, you'd be in and out of the office with little things every day. You'd tell me to wait at home or to meet you here and there- you'd be distracted. Unintentionally, of course, but distracted nonetheless. It wouldn't bother me. I'm just saying that maybe this case has focused our time together. It's given us a common cause so to speak." Charles smiled reassuringly.

"Maybe." Laurie didn't sound convinced. She rubbed her hand over her blonde ponytail. "I just would have preferred if our common goal was just being us."

"It is babe." He reached out and squeezed her neck affectionately. "We are being us."

Laurie smiled and a tear ran down her cheek. She wiped it away as quickly as she could. Laurie had never been good at showing emotions. She perceived them as signs of weakness. "I'm starving. That apple fritter didn't cut it."

Charles took a deep breath but tried to keep it as inaudible as possible. He didn't like to see her upset. "Me too. I can taste Edie's homemade bread already." He turned to look at Laurie again. "Let's have supper together tonight. Just the two of us."

Laurie visibly brightened. "Good idea! Let's eat in. A bit of a hideaway at home is probably exactly what I need. Are you cooking? I'd say that I would but you will probably have more time and frankly, you're a better cook than I am."

"No problem. I'll figure something out. How about this: I'll prepare the meal, you bring the wine and the conversation."

"Deal!" Laurie smiled her first full smile since they had been back in the car. That made Charles happy.

Edgartown was busy. The driving was much slower than it had been when Laurie had collected him from South Beach. Early rising vacationers were headed out for breakfast. Some were just out for coffee and the morning paper. Sailing camps were in full swing and the young sailors were headed toward the harbour. Upper Main Street led them closer and closer to the centre of town. They drove past the Mobile gas station. At this point, Main Street was still largely residential. They passed shingled homes and stone homes, manicured lawns, manicured hedges, and white picket fences. If you were going to raise kids, this was the place to do it, strong community and beautiful green neighbourhoods. It was idyllic for families; however, Charles knew that quite a bit of it was seasonal living. High priced seasonal living at that. He would love to come and see the island off-season. He always said that but it still hadn't happened. As they came up on Point Peases Way, Charles watched as Laurie looked in the direction of the police station. He could tell by the way that she was biting her lower lip that she was tempted to make a quick stop. She turned to look at him. They spoke without speaking. He could see her debating.

Laurie could tell that he knew what she was thinking. She thought better of it, and made a left hand turn in the direction of the inn.

Charles smiled to himself.

North of Main Street, Point Peases Way wound through the middle of Edgartown. It was busier than some of the streets because it wasn't a one-way. Prime Edgartown real estate, the houses were impressive and elegant. The hedges got higher to afford the residences more privacy. Large trees swept over the street and over the heads of the pedestrians who walked on the elegant red brick sidewalk.

"It's pretty here." Laurie seemed to be reading his mind.

"It is." Charles looked across the street and back. "This would be a great place to live really. The houses are stunning; the trees are big and beautiful. It's a nice street. I like it."

"Living in a beach house wouldn't be good enough for you? You have to be an Edgartown snob?" Laurie smiled at him but she was only half-joking.

"I do love Edgartown it's true but there is no place I would turn down on this island. A beach house on East Chop would suit me just fine." Charles smiled.

"Well, if I see any for sale, I'll let you know." Laurie said mischievously.

Laurie turned right onto the narrow Simpson Lane. There was a small parking lot on the right hand side. Laurie turned in and smoothly slipped into an unmarked slot. She turned off the engine and pulled her keys out of the ignition. "Let's eat!" She said.

The two of them walked up the lane in quiet and came up on the back of The Edgartown Inn. "I love that sign." Said Charles. He pointed at the red, white, and blue inn sign with the black wood whale. "I'd like that on a T-shirt."

"That would be cool." Laurie nodded her agreement. "You should tell Edie that. She could sell them here."

"Absolutely!" Charles mind started spinning.

Laurie watched his face. She laughed. "I'd be willing to bet a pay cheque that you're wearing one of those T-shirts by next season!"

"Maybe not just me!" Charles stepped back chivalrously and let Laurie climb the front steps ahead of him. On the front porch, he reached ahead and opened the screen door for her.

"Thank you." Laurie said as she walked through.

The homely, inviting sounds of clinking silverware and conversation led them back through the foyer and into the dining room of The Edgartown Inn. The dining room was nautical American camp and Anne of Green Gables chic all rolled into one. The lower half of the walls were dark stained wood and the top was warmly striped wallpaper. The entire kitchen was trimmed with immaculate white wainscoting and baseboards. The shutters and back door matched with coral paint and the woodwork on the windows was the same. All of the art and wall ornaments were nautical in theme. Whale carvings and clipper ship drawings were elegantly placed between blue and white ceramic plates and tea sets. There were tables against the windows and tables in the centre of the room. It wasn't a large dining room by any means but the space it had was well used without feeling cramped. Charles thought it was very homey. Senior citizens occupied three of the dining room tables. It didn't matter what the weather was like, seniors always seemed to prefer to eat indoors. Charles wasn't sure why but he figured, with any luck, he'd find out eventually.

"You'd rather sit outside, wouldn't you?" Laurie looked back at him.

"Oh absolutely." He nodded. They headed toward the back door.

"Well, it's about time you made it in here for breakfast! I'd given up on you this morning too!" Edie came in tottering on wedge mules with an ease most people reserve for running shoes. "Chief, you're due for a good breakfast yourself! When was the last time you were here?"

"It was just after you'd opened this season, I think." Laurie thought about it. "You had that truck illegally parked in front of your place."

"Oh, that's right! What a bugger that guy was. Honestly, I don't know where people's manners are sometimes." Edie shook her head. "Why don't you two take that table at the back by the wall. That was your regular table last year Charles."

"That's right! Good memory Edie!"

"Only when it comes to my guests. As soon as I leave this place, my entire brain flat-lines." Edie used her left hand to demonstrate. In her right hand was the seemingly permanent coffee pot.

Charles and Laurie sat down at the table and without asking, Edie filled their mugs with coffee. "You both want coffee cake right?"

"Yes, ma'am!" They answered in unison.

"Comin' up!" Edie teetered away in the direction of the kitchen and the two of them were left alone with their coffees.

They sat in quiet for a few minutes admiring Edie's garden. The flowers were in full bloom and the back garden was a true oasis. Nestled between the Inn and the vine-covered cottage. The garden was comfortably laid out with tables for two and tables for four, all covered in blue and white chequered tablecloths. A couple of tables were still free but most were occupied with guests and islanders alike. The Edgartown Inn was known to have the best breakfast on the island and it wasn't only inn patrons who ate there on a regular basis. It didn't take long before Laurie's face took a more serious tone.

"Bill's murder was discovered too late to hit the morning papers. That bought us a bit of time. Martha's Vineyard Patch will be putting out a 'Breaking News' email though, you mark my words."

"Consider them marked." Charles took his iPhone out of his pocket and set it on the table with the JAWS case facing up.

Laurie looked at it and chuckled.

"I call it my 'iJAWS'." Said Charles.

"Of course you do." Laurie sipped her coffee and their waitress brought them their coffee cake.

"I subscribe to Martha's Vineyard Patch on my phone. I'll let you know when they release something."

"Shall I get you some more coffee?" The waitress smiled. She was young, blonde, petite, and pretty.

"Yes please." Charles answered. The waitress left to retrieve the coffee pot.

"I say we go to Jack Burrell's house first. I'd like to get that over with. Then we can head over to the Golden Dragon and back here for the car. It's sort of a loop."

"Sounds good." Charles leaned back to let the waitress refill his cup. "I'm kind of dreading going to the Burrell house. That won't be pleasant."

"You don't really have to come." Laurie said.

"I don't think that I should back out now. I should either be in this thing or out."

"Fair enough."

The waitress had been standing politely waiting for a break in the conversation. "Are you both having the full breakfast or the continental?"

"Full, please. We'll both have our eggs over-easy and bacon please. What's the toast today?" Charles ordered for them both.

"We have the white and the cinnamon raisin today." The waitress smiled genuinely.

"Could we both have one of each?" Charles smiled as charmingly as he could. It was genuine.

Her smile broadened. "Sure. Keep it under your hat." She collected their menus and left to place their order.

Laurie shook her head.

"What?" Charles grinned.

"You could sell an Eskimo snow. That's what."

"I was just being nice. That's all." Charles chuckled.

"Sure you were and what if that's not what I wanted? You didn't even ask me!"

"Was it what you wanted?"

"That's not the point." Laurie was trying not to smile but she couldn't help it. She liked that he had ordered for her.

"It's entirely the point." Charles settled in his chair with the grin of the Cheshire cat on his face. "I know you well enough by now. You never eat sausage. You think it's gross. As for the bread, I've never seen you turn away a slice of homemade bread in your life."

Laurie laughed heartily. "I do love Edie's bread. You think she'd give us another slice if you asked?"

13

The Burrell house was small. Charles and Laurie had finished their breakfast, said their goodbyes to Edie, and had headed back up Simpson Lane. At Point Peases Way, they had turned right and headed north. A few houses in, just at Sherriff's Lane, was the home of Jack and Marcie Burrell. It was a grey shingle bungalow with white trim and black shutters. The front door was centred and Jack had painted it black to match the shutters. There was a big picture window on either side of the door and an evergreen shrub between the door and each window. The lawn was small but tidy and enclosed in a pristine white picket fence. There was a driveway on either side of the house. Typical of the island, the second one was for a rental cottage in the back.

Laurie led Charles past the break in the picket fence and up a short walkway to the front door. There was a second door with a small porch on the side of the house. Laurie opened the screen door and knocked gently. It wasn't long before Sergeant Jack answered.

"Oh, hi chief. Hi Mr Williams. Come in." Jack looked tired. His usual bounce and enthusiasm was gone. His short, thickly muscled body seemed small and limp. "It sure was nice of you to come over." Jack stepped back and they stepped into the small kitchen. "Would you like some coffee? I was just about to make some."

"No, that's fine Jack. We just had quite a bit at Edie's place. Do you want anymore coffee Charles?" Laurie looked at him quizzically.

"No, I'm fine. Thanks."

"I like that Edie over at the Inn...she's a nice person." Jack seemed distant and confused. He didn't look at either of his guests when he spoke. There was a lot going on in Jack's head and it was taking up all of his energy.

A small kitchen table with four chairs filled out the corner of the room. Charles and Laurie pulled out two of the chairs and sat down. The set was wood and each chair had a yellow seat cushion that was tied to its back. Four yellow knitted placemats each marked a place setting. Charles thought they looked homemade. There was a fake yellow rose in a slim vase in the middle of the table.

"How's Marcie holding up, Jack?" asked Laurie. She was using her comforting tone. Charles had heard it before when she talked to people in times of stress. He thought that she was very good at this sort of thing.

"Um...she's okay. She's sleeping a lot. That's probably good."

"Probably. It's a defence mechanism." Laurie ran her hands over the placemat in front of her. "Jack, I know that Bill wasn't exactly the most popular man on the island but can you think of anyone in particular who would want to harm him in any way? Had there been any altercations with anyone lately?"

"I don't think so. I tried to ask Marcie that but she wasn't really in the headspace to answer any questions." Having police questions to focus on seemed to help Jack regroup. "The guy was kind of an ass but they had a good relationship. He was a good dad. I'm a bit worried about her. He did have a bit of a fight with the board about the tournament. You know, when they said that he couldn't host this year. When they asked Steve Christie to do it. But that seemed to blow over when they came back to him when Christie disappeared. Well, was killed. We didn't know that at the time though. He was just missing, well not legally a missing person. We just couldn't find him. Right?"

Laurie smiled in spite of the sombre situation. It was nice to see a glimmer of the real Jack shine through.

"Jack it does seem that the two murders must be connected as they were both doing the same job when they were killed. How well did they know each other?"

Jack thought before answering. "Fairly well, I guess. They were both islanders. I don't think they were friends though. I think they travelled in different social circles." Jack poured himself a cup of freshly brewed coffee and then sat at the table with Charles and Laurie. "Steve was more the science guy. He came to the sharks from the school side. Bill came to it from the fishermen's side. More blue collar, ya know?" Jack was quiet for a minute and then spoke again. "He knew your buddy, chief."

"Who?" Laurie looked surprised.

"The fisherman, Keith Hurtubise and his wife Catherine. They went to church with Bill and Virginia before the divorce. With Ginny gone, Bill stopped going."

"Really?" Laurie was clearly intrigued by this bit of information. "Thanks Jack. We'll check that out." She paused for a minute. "Jack we're going to need you to identify the body."

"I already did. I went down this morning when Ginny was here with Marcie."

"Where's Ginny now?"

"Grocery shopping." Jack sipped his coffee. "I could have gone but I think she wanted to get out for a bit."

Laurie stood up and Charles followed suit. "Take care of yourself Jack. I'll call you tomorrow and see when you think you might come back to work. Take what you need but come back as soon as you can. We need you." Laurie put her hand on his shoulder. "You're a good cop, Jack. Give my love to Marcie." Laurie motioned to Charles and they made their way toward the door. Jack stayed at the table uncharacteristically quiet. "We'll let ourselves out."

That seemed to wake him up. "Oh! I'm sorry chief. I guess I'm a little out of it. I should lie down maybe."

"I think that's a good idea buddy." Charles reached out and shook Jack's shoulder gently. "Call us if you need anything at all. All right?"

"I'll do that. Thank you Mr Williams."

Charles chuckled slightly at being called 'Mr Williams' but he didn't say anything.

Charles and Laurie stepped out into the sunlight of mid-morning closing the kitchen door behind them. They looked at each other and exhaled deeply. Neither of them spoke until they were back on Point Peases Way and a fair distance from the Burrell house.

"That sucked," said Laurie.

"Yes, yes it did." Charles shook his head. "He'll bounce back."

"Oh, I know. It's not seeing Marcie that concerns me. The only reason that Jack is so shaken up is because of her. That really worries me. I can't imagine the state that she must be in to do that to him." Laurie thought for a minute. "I wonder if she's seen a doctor? We should have asked."

"Everybody deals with grief differently. Wait a day or two. Maybe she'll be all right. If not, you can suggest it. Do you know a good one?" Charles looked at her. The road was quiet.

"Several. The island is lousy with them this time of year."

"Yes, I suppose it is."

"Charles, I was thinking..."

"Yes?"

"About dinner tonight, would you mind if we went to Keith and Cathy's? They've been asking me to come over because it's been a while and now with this connection to Bill Cunningham, maybe it would be a good idea."

"Sure. That's fine with me. Are you sure they won't mind me coming along? I didn't really get the impression that Captain Keith liked me all that much. He kept calling me 'smarty-pants'."

Laurie laughed out loud. "He still calls you that."

"What do you mean he still calls me that? Why would he have reason to mention me at all?"

"When I go over for Sunday suppers, he always asks about you." Laurie puffed out her chest and spoke in a deep, terrible French-Canadian accent. *"How's smarty-pants doing? Are you still talking to him?"*

"Oh yes. It sounds like he's my biggest fan!" Charles rolled his eyes.

"Don't be an idiot. If he didn't like you he wouldn't ask about you and he wouldn't bother to tease you. He wouldn't waste any energy on you at all. Doesn't that sound familiar?" She nudged him with her elbow.

"What's that supposed to mean?"

"Oh give it up! You're exactly the same! I can always tell when you don't like someone. You ignore them completely. You think they're just not worth your energy."

He shrugged. "That's true." Charles grinned. "Anyway, I wouldn't mind going to the Hurtubise's for supper. Call them and see if they're up for it. I'd like to meet the missus."

"Awesome. I'll call them when we're done at the restaurant."

*   *   *

The Golden Dragon was not yet open for business but the lights were on. Laurie reached for the handle and pulled the door open with ease. "Somebody's home." She said and they walked in. The tables were all empty but there were noises coming from the kitchen. Laurie called out. "Hello?"

A well-built man walked out of the kitchen. "I'm sorry, we're not open for another hour or so." He had short salt and pepper hair and a tan. His eyes were a piercing blue.

"I'm Police Chief Laurie Knickles. This is my deputy Charles Williams. I'm looking for Richard Brooker."

"You've found him, Chief... I've been expecting you." Richard walked over to them and held out his hand. "I'm glad you're here."

Laurie shook his hand. "I'm sorry that I wasn't here sooner but it has been a busy twenty-four hours."

"I imagine it has. First Steve and then this morning poor Bill, Its awful."

Laurie and Charles looked at each other. "How did you know about Bill Cunningham?"

"On this island? I don't even know why they waste the ink on a newspaper. Everyone knows everything before it hits print."

"Fair enough. We'd like to ask you a couple of questions if that's all right. It won't take too long." Laurie was speaking in her official voice.

"Certainly. Would either of you like a coffee?" Richard motioned for them to sit down at the same table where Laurie and Charles had eaten supper the night before.

"No, I think we're fine. Thank you." The three of them all took seats. "Mr Brooker, how long have you and Steve been in business here?"

"We've had this restaurant for three years now. Not that long really. It's going well."

"How did you come to know Steve?"

"We owned a restaurant in Boston together but moved out here. It was intended to be seasonal but we both liked it here so much that we kept it open year round. We sold the Boston restaurant."

"You live on the island then?"

"Yes, ma'am. I have a house with my family in Vineyard Haven. We've been there two and a half years." Richard checked his Blackberry compulsively.

"When did you first notice Steve was missing?"

"I didn't actually. I was told he was missing when the shark tournament started calling for him. They noticed he was missing, not me. He was supposed to be off from the restaurant to emcee the tournament. I assumed he was there."

"That makes sense." Laurie paused to collect her thoughts. "Can you think of anyone who would want to harm Steve, especially so violently? I mean whoever it was didn't just kill him; they took out some serious anger."

"I'm sorry, I'm afraid that I don't know the details." Richard looked back and forth from the chief to Charles and back again. "What happened?"

110

"I guess the town criers and the newspapers don't get everything after all." Laurie said. "Steve's hands and feet were cut off and he was left to die in his pool."

"Jesus. Who would do something like that?" Richard Brooker brought his hand up to his mouth. His expression was one of revulsion.

"That's what we're trying to find out." Said Laurie.

"So he drowned then?"

"We're still waiting for the coroner's report." Laurie pulled out her note pad and scribbled something down. She flipped back a couple of pages and read her notes. "Mr Brooker, do you know if Steve was a religious man at all?"

"I would say that he was but then again, I'm not at all. He certainly wasn't a fanatic but he did go to church occasionally. He always went on the holidays but it was more than that, maybe once a month?"

"Do you know which one?" Laurie asked.

"Sure. Our Lady Star of the Sea in Oak Bluffs." Richard answered. "He was Catholic."

"Ok. Thank you very much Mr Brooker. That's all for now." Laurie and Charles stood up.

"My pleasure Chief Knickles, Deputy Williams. If there's anything else..."

"Oh, maybe one thing... Where were you two nights ago? The night before we found Steve?"

"I was at home."

"Can anyone vouch for you?"

"I don't think so. My family is on the Cape." Richard reached out and shook their hands. "I guess that's not so good."

"Not necessarily. Have a good day Mr Brooker." The two of them made their way toward the door but before the chief reached it, a large blonde man pulled it open. With the sun behind him, his features were hidden in shadow.

"Goodbye Chief Knickles." Called out Richard.

The two of them let the man pass and they slipped out in his wake. Before the door clicked in the latch, Charles heard Richard Brooker speak one last time. "Come on in Frank; lock the door behind you." He said.

14

Charles sat up on his white bed at the Edgartown Inn and looked around. The room was bright with the afternoon sun. With the extra light, the red poppies and blue cornflowers seemed to jump from the wallpaper. The warmth was comforting. Charles decided that a nap was in order. He never napped at home but seemed to do so regularly on the Vineyard. He chalked it up to the sea air, the extra excitement, and the fact that his room at the inn seemed designed for doing so. He got up and walked to the bathroom to wash his face. Standing in front of the spotless mirror and sink, Charles turned on the faucet, adjusted the temperature, and leaned over. Cupping and filling his hands with warm water, he splashed his face. He stood up straight, reached for one of the pristine white hand towels that had been placed in his room, and patted his face. The water felt so good that Charles decided to have a shower and start the day again. He had some time to fill before Laurie collected him to go to the Hurtubise's for supper. He was looking forward to the home-cooked meal and it would be nice to go bright and fresh. He reached past the shower curtain and turned on the water. The spray of the hot water was inviting. Charles stripped down and stepped into the big, square tub. The water beat down on his head and ran off in every direction it could find. It felt good. Charles felt that a layer of grime, a film had been covering him and he desperately needed to rinse it away, a film of death and ugliness. The foul slick of discovering Steve Christie the day before still lingered and the residue of the sight of Bill Cunningham's mangled corpse was fresh. Now, in the hot shower, Charles felt them wash away. Out of his head, off of his torso, and down his legs, they all washed away in little rivers toward the drain and he was happy to have them gone. Rinsed clean, Charles felt better equipped to think. There was a lot to sort out.

Steve and Bill had known each other; this much was certain. They travelled in different circles so the likelihood of them being introduced socially was minimal. So if not social, it had to have been professional. What else does a grown man have? The connection was a straight line, thought Charles. It was the tournament. It was fishing. Sergeant Jack Burrell had said that Bill knew Keith Hurtubise. Over supper, he and Laurie would have to find out if Keith knew Steve Christie as well. If fishing was how they knew each other, it stood to reason that fishing got them killed. The two big hitters on the murder hit parade are always love and money. Charles was willing to bet that

114

greed was the real reason the two men were murdered. That brought Charles back to how they were killed. They were both killed gruesomely. Both murders made a statement. On the surface, they were killed very differently. One was murdered on land and hung while the other was dismembered and thrown in a pool. Not the same thing at all but when you put the two murders twenty-four hours apart, they seem to have a lot more in common.

Charles dried off after his shower and put on his island uniform of a navy blue golf shirt and khaki shorts.

Still, he thought. There was something more that he hadn't put his finger on. The biblical reference that Charles had made at supper the night prior no longer pertained as far as he was concerned. No matter how hard he tried, Charles could not think of any biblical figure being hanged by his feet. It was kind of surprising actually. You'd think that the Bible would have had someone knocked off in such a simple and gruesome way. There were those who believed that the apostle Peter requested to be crucified upside down. The story was that he did not believe that he was worthy of the same crucifixion as Christ but there was no proof of that in the bible. That left them back on the island and out of the church as far as Charles was concerned. He hadn't relished the idea of going into that Catholic Church and questioning the priest anyway. One headache avoided.

Still having plenty of time, Charles headed out to the front veranda to watch the people go by and do a little more thinking.

"Charles!" He hadn't had time to lock his room door when he heard Edie calling him.

"Hey Edie. What's up?" Charles smiled broadly at her as she sashayed her way out of the kitchen. She was wearing a black dress and a pink cardigan.

"What can you tell me about this?" Edie held up the island newspaper.

Charles took the paper and unfolded it to get the full effect of the front page. There were two photos side by side of the victims. Not dead but rather how they had been in life. Thank god for small mercies, thought Charles. There was also a photograph of a fisherman talking to a reporter beside a boat. The photo of the fisherman caught Charles' eye in particular. It was taken at the tournament. Not quite at the scene of the Bill Cunningham murder but further up. It was definitely at the Oak Bluffs Harbour. The fisherman must have been a contestant because attached to his boat was a dead shark. It hung off the stern of the boat probably post weigh-in. They had started to fillet it. The fins were sliced off. Then it hit Charles like a tonne of bricks. It was what he had been overlooking all that time. It was what had been nagging at him constantly but he couldn't get it out. Edie must have seen it in his face.

"Charles? What's the matter, hun?" She started to look worried. "You did know about this, didn't you? I mean you must have!"

"Oh yes, Edie. I'm sorry. Yes. I knew about this. I couldn't tell you about it. I wanted to but I couldn't."

"What do you see in this photograph? You were white as a sheet a minute ago."

116

"Oh, I'm fine Edie. Say, Edie, can I have another cup of tea on the porch? I'm going to sit out there while I wait for Chief Knickles." Charles didn't take his eyes off the paper. "May I keep this?"

"Oh sure, hun. I have a couple for the Inn. I'll get you that tea. You go sit and I'll bring it right out."

"Thanks Edie; you're the best." Charles headed out to the porch and sat in his usual green and white chaise. He was sure that he was right. Charles sat on the chaise and unconsciously rubbed his stomach. He had butterflies. Charles had what he figured cops called a "gut-feeling" and it was absolute. Steve Christie had been finned like a shark and thrown back in the water. It also fit the Cunningham murder as well. Bill had been strung up like a prize shark. Turns out that the murders had a lot more in common than they had originally thought. They were both more than just a little fishy, thought Charles. He didn't even smile at his own bad pun. Instead, he stared across the street, past The Kelley House and beyond to the small blue glimmer of ocean. It always seemed to come back to sharks for him on this island.

*   *   *

"Holy crap!" Laurie exclaimed. "You're a god damned genius! Well, we already knew that but...holy crap!" Laurie hit her steering wheel with the palm of her hand. She was doing her best to focus on the road but she couldn't help but take quick glances at Charles. She was grinning ear to ear. "It's the only thing that makes any sense. I figured that it had something to do with the tournament. Well, we knew that from the fact that they were both emcees but this is excellent news. Well done, babe." Laurie stared at Morse Street in front of her and turned left onto Point Peases Way. Beautiful heritage homes and trees that had seen homeowners come and go surrounded them but neither Charles nor the chief saw any of it. They were focused on their case and the tiny steps of progress they were making. "Thank God we don't have to go to the church. I was dreading that."

"Me too." Charles agreed.

"We'd better make sure we ask Keith whether or not he knew Steve Christie. I want to know how many ways we can tie these two men together. If we can only tie them with the tournament, we will need to look at it closer."

"Terrific." Charles rolled his eyes only half-jokingly.

"Sorry about that. I'm sure that I'll be able to cover most of the hands-on tournament work. We'll try to keep you away from it if we can."

"No. I'm here for the full Monty. I can't pick and choose what I see and do. Nobody else can; I shouldn't either."

"All right." Laurie nodded. "If you're sure."

"I'm sure." Charles turned his attention back to the island flashing past his window. They drove Point Peases Way until they hit Main Street and they turned right. They followed Main under the flickering shade of a green, leafy umbrella. They passed the Hob Knob Inn and the Mobil gas station until they hit Edgartown West Tisbury Road. As they turned left, they both

118

looked out the driver side window at the Christie House. Still surrounded with yellow tape but quiet inside. All the lights were out. Neither of them said anything. They followed the Edgartown West Tisbury Road clear across the island. As they left the centre of Edgartown, the houses became fewer and farther between. The trees became denser. They drove through the Sweetened Water Preserve and Ben Tom's Preserve. Charles thought that the island's interior had a beauty that rivalled the beaches that framed it. The island was known worldwide for its beaches, idyllic townships, and quaint fishing villages but very little was ever mentioned of its wildlife preserves. Charles thought that was too bad.

The road took a darkly familiar turn. Charles' chest tightened. Laurie looked at him quickly but didn't say anything. They were driving through Manuel F. Corellus State Forest. Charles still remembered all too clearly the last time he was through here with Laurie in the police cruiser. That psychopath Tim Oakes had crashed into them deliberately. Laurie had lost consciousness and Charles was forced to run through the forest for his life. He had nearly lost too.

"Still with me?" Laurie reached out and grabbed his hand. He gave it a squeeze.

"I'm fine."

"We were through here after that incident with Oakes you know."

Charles liked the fact that she knew exactly what was going through his mind. "We were?"

"Sure. On your last day on the island, I took you to The Black Dog for your last meals. It was a very nice morning. You kissed me after breakfast. Focus on that instead."

Charles had forgotten that they had driven this road that day. He hadn't forgotten anything else. He smiled. At the mere mention of that day, Charles could feel Laurie on his lips. He could still smell her hair. That helped.

Laurie felt the tension leave him. "Forced yourself on me really." She said matter-of-factly. "Didn't ask or anything... No warning..." She shook her head.

Charles laughed. "You wish!"

"Practically assault!" Laurie tried to stay straight-faced.

"As if! More like practically begging!!"

"I did not!" Laurie punched him in the shoulder.

Charles grabbed her leg just above the knee and gave it a Charlie-horse squeeze.

She hit his arm hard. "Don't do that!! I hate that!!" She laughed.

"Well then..." That was exactly what Charles had needed. By the time they had finished their laughing, they were past the airport and through the forest. All of the bad memories left behind them.

The Edgartown West Tisbury ended at State Road. The options were marked with two signs. The first pointed south for Chilmark and Aquinnah; the second pointed north for Vineyard Haven and Oak Bluffs. Without pause, Laurie chose the former. Other than the occasional rock wall and split rail fence, State road was nothing but woods. It was beautiful. Green spaces were good for a person's state of mind. There had been several studies done that proved just that. Charles had read papers on the subject and was always trying to get his clients in Toronto's financial district to get out of the office at least once a day and enjoy a tree or parkette. There were green spaces all over Toronto. Science had proven that sitting in a green space for fifteen minutes a day had a significant affect on stress levels. Charles deeply inhaled the fresh air coming in his open window. It was rich in natural scents. They passed another stonewall. "I love those." He exclaimed.

"Me too. They must have taken forever to build. They've been there for centuries." Laurie stated.

"Amazing." Charles watched as they passed more fields and more stonewalls. Soon they passed the Chilmark Cemetery. "I love cemeteries. They're so peaceful."

"I don't. They're sad." Said Laurie. "What's the difference between a cemetery and a graveyard anyway?"

Charles shook his head. "Nothing... at least not now. There used to be. Graveyards were always attached to churches while cemeteries stood alone. The word 'graveyard' comes from the old Scottish word 'kirkyard' meaning 'churchyard'. Now, because of property values and people not always being affiliated with religion, more often than not, graveyards aren't attached to churches. So the two are more or less synonymous."

"Interesting. If graveyard comes from kirkyard, where's the word cemetery come from?"

"The French, 'cimetière'." Charles said matter-of-factly.

Laurie nodded her head as she took in this information.

The Hurtubise house was on Larsen Lane almost right down at Menemsha Harbour. The lot was well wooded so there was no view of the harbour even though it was within walking distance. Charles didn't figure that an ocean view was too much of a priority for a seaman. It would be like being able to see the office from your kitchen window. He could be wrong. The house was a sprawling wood bungalow with a dark brown stain. The door was off to the right side and standard sized windows broke up the siding. Mrs Hurtubise must be something of a gardener, thought Charles. There were flowers of all kinds with a long line of Maximilian sunflowers running along the entire front of the house. Not the usual hydrangeas for which the island was famous. Charles liked that. They walked up to the front door and Laurie walked in without knocking.

"Hi! We're here!" She called out.

Charles stepped in to the doorframe and a familiar voice, "Well, if it isn't smarty-pants!"

Charles laughed in spite of himself.

15

"Keith! Be polite for crying out loud!" A very attractive woman with long brown hair came out of the kitchen. "You must be Charles; I've heard a lot about you. I'm Cathy."

"It's nice to meet you ma'am. I've heard a lot about you too." He reached out and shook her hand. She had a warm smile and smelled of patchouli.

"You can stow that 'ma'am' crap right now. I'm not the queen of England." She laughed at her own joke. "Let's get you some wine or would you prefer beer?"

Keith jumped in. "Don't let her kid you, young man. She thinks she is the queen of England, true enough!"

"Oh shut up." Cathy rolled her eyes. "Honest to god!"

Charles couldn't help but laugh at the two of them. Something about them made him feel right at home. "I'll have a white wine, Cathy. Thank you."

"Coming up." Cathy went back in to the kitchen.

"Let's move into the living room." Keith leaned in to get a kiss and a hug from Laurie. "How are you mon petit chou?"

"I'm good, old man. How about you?"

"Just great. Just great. Catherine is tickled pink to have you here. Wait until you see what's for supper!" Keith ushered his guests into the living room with an enthusiasm that made Charles think that it was really Keith who was tickled pink to have the company.

The living room was pine floored with a vaulted pine ceiling. In the centre of the ceiling was a large fan and placed high on one of the walls was a brass arrangement of maple leaves, a symbol of their Canadian roots. The furniture was dark brown and overstuffed. It looked a little dated but very comfortable. Keith motioned for them to sit down and they did. It was a nice room, thought Charles. There was a large picture window and Charles sat so that he was facing it. It looked not toward the street but rather into the large and wooded backyard. Charles thought that was a brilliant idea. Most people would think the house was backward.

"You're wondering why we built the house like this, aren't you? Figure it out smarty-pants?" Keith grinned warmly.

"I think I've got it and I think it's brilliant."

"Well, tell me then."

124

"Why would you want to waste a view on cars going by? Who wants a view of the street? You have a huge, peaceful backyard; why not look at it all day? It's quieter too. At night, I wouldn't imagine that you get a lot of traffic out here. Do you get any traffic out here?"

Keith shook his head. "Not even in high season."

"Well then, why not?" Charles looked down through the picture window. "You have a huge deck. It looks like we're over a walkout basement too? This is a great set up. It's like being at the cottage. If you have kids over, you can see them playing in the back rather than by the road. All houses should be built like this. Besides, I always liked a kitchen at the back of the house anyway."

"You're all right with me, Charles!" Keith grabbed him by the shoulder and laughed.

"What did I tell you?" Laurie motioned at Charles. "I told you that you guys would get along you grumpy old man."

"When did I say that we wouldn't?" Keith asked innocently.

"Ha! Ha! That's a joke!" Cathy walked into the room with a bottle of wine to refresh their glasses. "You warned Laurie about Charles' intentions left, right, and centre."

Keith squirmed in his seat and looked a little sheepish. "I was just looking out for our girl! D'accord??"

"All right." Cathy gave him a squeeze and sat on the arm of the couch beside him. "He always goes French when he gets emotional."

"That's all right. I speak French." Charles said.

"You do?" Keith, Cathy, and Laurie all answered in unison shock.

He looked at Laurie. "Why are you so surprised?"

He looked at Keith. "J'ai étudié le français à l'école pendant huit ans. J'essaie de l'utiliser si je ne l'oublie pas."

Keith's eyes lit up. "C'était excellent, mon ami!"

Cathy looked sideways at Laurie and rolled her eyes. "Uh-oh, they're bonding. Now he's 'mon ami'!" She chuckled. "That's enough you two."

Charles looked at Cathy apologetically. "I'm sorry Cathy."

"For what? Never apologise for knowledge. Especially for knowing a language! That's wonderful! Now come on, everyone at the table for supper. It's ready!"

The living and dining were in the same room. They got up from the couches and headed over to the dining room table. It was oak with a medium finish. It had the feel of elegance and antiquity. Cathy left the room and came back immediately with a large tray. "Christmas in July! I thought a turkey dinner with all the fixings was just what the occasion called for."

Charles' face betrayed his exuberance. "Holy crap! That's amazing! What are you trying to do to us? We may never leave!"

Keith got up in his spot and began to carve the turkey while Catherine brought in the side dishes.

"Do you need some help bringing things in?" Charles asked.

"You stay where you are, mister. This is your first time here. If I need anything, I'll make her do it."

126

Cathy motioned to Laurie. "I've got it covered. Start digging in."

Mashed potatoes, gravy, green beans with almonds, turnip, squash, green salad, sunshine carrots, home made buns, and of course the turkey, this was the perfect meal. Charles couldn't remember the last time he was this happy. Is this what it would be like to live on the island? Living on Martha's Vineyard with Laurie and having Sunday night supper with Cathy and Keith? That seemed to be about as good as life could be. Other than the occasional, "thank you" and "yes please", the table was quiet while people passed dishes and fixed their plates. Charles cut into a homemade roll and it steamed as he pulled it apart. He hoped that no one noticed exactly how much butter he had put in it.

Keith reached his hands out across the table and Laurie and Cathy took them instinctively. The two ladies then reached for Charles. It took him a second before he realised what was going on. He took their hands and bowed his head with the rest of them.

Keith said grace. "For what we are about to receive and for our new friend, may the Lord find us truly grateful. Amen." The two ladies repeated the "Amen." Charles did not.

Keith cut into his plate and the rest of them followed suit.

"Catherine, you've out done yourself again." Laurie spoke with her mouth full of turkey. She tried to do it as delicately as she could but she swooned from the rapture of the homemade food.

"This is amazing." Charles did not speak with his mouth full. First time as a guest, his manners were out in full force.

"Thank you very much you two. Keith and I figured that since Charles didn't come down for Christmas, we would have Christmas now!" Catherine smiled at Charles.

"It was a wonderful idea. Thank you."

Laurie turned her attention toward Keith. "Keith, how did you know Bill Cunningham?"

Keith yelled out. "What time is it?"

Laurie and Charles were both startled. "It's ten to eight. Why?"

Keith turned to Catherine waving a finger. "I told you! I told you! You're doing the dishes!"

Catherine scrunched up her face. She was not happy. "You couldn't have waited eleven minutes? Damn! All right! All right! Get your finger out of my face, Keith!"

"Have you two completely flipped your lids?" Laurie stared at the two of them, her forkful of turkey frozen in mid-air.

"We had a bet." Keith was beaming. "We knew that you were coming over here because you wanted to talk about Bill Cunningham and Steve Christie. I said that you wouldn't even be able to wait until supper was over before you brought them up! Catherine had more faith in you. She said you'd wait until after supper and we were all in the living room with coffee. So we said eight o'clock. Whoever lost, had to do the dishes!" Keith turned toward Cathy. "And that's you!!"

"Yes, yes, don't be a jerk." Cathy was pissed. She took a swig of wine. "This is your fault!" She said to Laurie. "You're helping me!"

Laurie laughed. "Yeah, okay." They all laughed.

"But you're not talking about corpses over my dinner table. You can wait until supper is over. Pick another topic." Cathy mocked scolding them but everyone knew that she was serious in her sentiment. She topped up Charles' glass. "Charles, tell me about your family. You're from North Bay, right?"

*   *   *

"Bill Cunningham was an asshole."

"Keith!" scolded Cathy.

"Well, he was. There's no use beating around the bush now." Keith leaned back in his chair with his hands flat on the table.

"I know but you really shouldn't speak ill of the dead like that. It's bad luck."

"Fine. Can I say that I had no use for the man?" He called out to the kitchen.

"Oh, all right." Cathy went back to her dishes.

"Bill was all right when Virginia was still around but he took it badly when she left. At least, he kept up appearances. I don't know what he was like behind closed doors. We saw them in church but that was it. We weren't chummy or anything like that."

"They were here for supper once!" Cathy called out.

"They were? I don't remember that."

"Well, it must not have happened then." Her tone was pure sarcasm.

"What are you saying?"

"I'm saying that's enough scotch for tonight. That's what I'm saying."

Keith lowered his voice. "She's just pissed because she has to do the dishes."

"Oh, I should go and help her." Laurie started to get up but Keith grabbed her hand. "You'll do no such thing. You sit down. She'll just send you back out here anyway." Keith turned toward the kitchen and hollered, "Catherine, do you want the chief to come and help you out there?"

"No. Don't bother. I'm almost done anyway."

"See? Now, after Ginny left him. I guess he was no prize to live with or why else would she have gone? Am I right?"

Charles nodded in agreement.

"After Ginny left, Bill started drinking in public a lot more. He straightened up a bit with that. I think that's because of your sergeant there who's marrying his daughter, Marcie? Yeah, that's it. I think he keeps him in line for Marcie's sake. Well, he eases up on the drinking and finds himself working with the fishermen's union. He's up there fighting for the boys up in Washington. No one was more surprised than I was. I can tell you that. It goes to his head though a position like that. A sad man, no woman, lonely, he becomes a bully. Soon, even though he likes a good fight and that can work in some situations, soon he didn't have a friend on the island. I don't know anyone who would want to kill him though. There was a lot of

130

crap that he dealt with that no one else would want to. You know what I'm saying? These people don't want to leave this island for anything. Bill wanted to do it and they were happy to let him." Keith stopped speaking and sipped from his scotch.

"Did he know Steve Christie?" Laurie asked.

"Well, he would have had to, wouldn't he? He would know him through that contest. Christie was becoming more and more of a fisherman too. Originally, he was a government man."

"He was?"

"You bet. Now, that's going back some time. He used to work for fish and game. That was before Bill's time though. Christie had a much more pleasant demeanour about him. Probably just more educated."

"If they only knew each other through that contest. We have to get in there." Laurie started thinking.

"I'm in it." Keith said casually.

"What?" Charles said.

"I'm in it. I registered this year. I'm a good fisherman and frankly we could use the money."

"You're kidding!" Laurie was shocked. "Why didn't you tell me?"

"That I was in the contest? Why? What's the big deal, chere?"

"No, that you guys were having a tough time." Laurie was all of a sudden very awkward in her seat.

"We're not! We're fine. A little extra cash wouldn't hurt. That's all. Mon Dieu! You sound like we're poverty stricken." Keith grimaced at her.

"Sorry. That's not what I meant."

"I know. Don't you worry." Keith took her hand and squeezed it. "What I was going to say is this. Charles, why don't you join me on the boat?"

"What for?" Charles looked at him incredulously.

"You two want to get close to the contest. Laurie can't go because everyone knows who she is. Come on my boat. That will get you in there. Who knows what you'll find out?"

Charles stared at Laurie. She was speechless. "I'd love to!" He said.

"Really?" Laurie said.

"Yes. It feels right."

"I could use the extra hand. I'll just say that he's my friend, Charles, from Canada. It's not a lie at all really." Keith said.

"It'll be like I'm undercover." Charles smiled broadly.

"What's going on?" Cathy walked into the room carrying a tray of coffees. She took Keith's scotch away.

"Smarty-pants is coming on the boat with me tomorrow in the tournament."

"Oh! That's fun."

"Cathy, there's something going on at that tournament that has to do with the murder of Bill and Steve!" Laurie exclaimed.

"I see. Laurie, they're just going fishing. It's not like Charles is going to be alone in a dark alley looking for murderers and drug dealers. It will be in the middle of the ocean, in the middle of the day, with other boats. Keith will be with him the whole time." Cathy handed out the coffees and downed the remainder of Keith's scotch.

"Jesus Christ." Laurie ran her fingers through her hair.

16

Nursing a slight hangover, Charles stepped out of Laurie's police cruiser at the Monster Shark Fishing Tournament. The tournament had moved further up the harbour from its original spot but not far, just far enough to avoid contaminating the Bill Cunningham crime scene. The day was clear and bright. Under regular circumstances, it would be a beautiful day for fishing. Charles had never been a big fisherman but he loved being on the water, especially the ocean. Ocean storms were terrifying but if the weather was good, the ocean was beautiful. Before closing the cruiser door behind him, Charles reached down in front of his seat and picked up the bag that he had brought with him. In the bag was the lunch that Laurie had packed him. It was the last of the lasagne, apples, buttered bread, and homemade butter tarts that she had baked last night. She always baked when she was stressed and Charles going on this trip was upsetting her. Charles had also packed a change of clothes. He had never been deep-sea fishing before but he had seen a few videos on YouTube. He knew that there was a good chance that he could get quite wet. A dry change of clothes could be quite welcome. Toward that end, he had packed three pairs of socks. He hated wet socks.

Laurie got out of the car and looked at the tournament in front of them. "Did you pack sunscreen?" Her tone betrayed her worry. It was slightly higher than usual.

"Yes." Charles had to admit, he was a little worried too. He wasn't sure why. Now, in the sober light of day, he wasn't even sure what he hoped to learn on this trip. The two men had been connected by this tournament that was a fact. Learning how the tournament worked seemed like the only way to discover why someone involved might be killed. At least, it seemed like the only way at present. Charles and Laurie closed their car doors in unison and headed toward the docks. Keith would already be on board, waiting for them.

Charles listened to the voice coming over the microphone emanating into the harbour. It sounded vaguely familiar. "Who's emceeing the tournament now?"

Laurie shook her head. "I don't know. I'm kind of curious about that myself. I'd be a bit leery of taking that position. Kind of like becoming the drummer of Spinal Tap at this point."

Charles snorted in agreement. "Seriously." He picked up his pace and headed toward the crowd. He wanted to see the emcee's face. "He sounds familiar."

They walked across the street toward the crowd. Keith's boat would be in a slip, a little further up but Charles had to see this man. He made his apologies and wiggled through the crowd with Laurie in his wake. As soon as Charles saw him, he recognised him. He had seen him before, twice before actually. It hadn't occurred to him at the time. Charles leaned in to Laurie, "His name is Frank. I don't know his last name."

"How do you know his first name? I don't recognise him at all." Laurie strained to get a better look.

"I first bumped into him on North Water Street in front of an art gallery. His wife or girlfriend called him by name. She was admiring a painting; he was trash-talking it. I felt bad for her so I made a wisecrack. I thought I might get clocked actually." Charles kept watching Frank as he spoke.

"And the second time?"

"The second time, you were with me. We had just finished talking to Richard Brooker at The Golden Dragon. As we were leaving, he walked in. I wasn't really looking at him but now that I think about it, I heard Richard call him Frank when he came in. He told him to lock the door behind him."

"Oh yeah, I heard that too." Laurie grimaced. "So the two previous emcees are murdered and the business partner of the first victim is having private meetings with the man who takes their place? That restaurant needs another going over."

"Maybe I shouldn't go on this fishing trip."

"No, I think it's even more important that you go now. This tournament and that restaurant are connected somehow. You go fishing; I'll go to the restaurant. Unless I miss my guess, when you get back, we'll both have a lot of notes to share."

"I think you're right."

Laurie stretched up and kissed him. "We'll share them over our quiet dinner at home."

Charles moved in and kissed her back. "I'd better get out there so I can get back all the sooner." He grinned at her and then turned to start weaving his way out of the crowd. "We'd better find Keith and the Fascinating Rhythm."

*   *   *

The Fascinating Rhythm was Keith's sport fishing boat. When Charles had been there last year, he had only seen his professional trawler. This one was nowhere near as big but significantly more attractive. It looked newer. Whether it was or not, Charles couldn't be sure but it's pristine white fibreglass body gave it a new look that the other boat hadn't had. This boat had a long bow and what looked to be a roomy cabin. The cockpit was above it.

"Ahoy!" Laurie called out.

"I'd just about given up on you!" Keith looked up at them from his position on the deck of the Fascinating Rhythm. His blue eyes sparkled and his smile was broad under his Colonel Sanders moustache.

"Sorry. We got distracted at the tournament." Charles said. "Permission to come aboard?"

"Granted!" Captain Keith beamed. He was enjoying this.

Charles stepped down onto the boat warily looking for his sea legs. "Where should I put my bag?"

"Stow your gear on the bench in the galley. You'll see what I mean. It's just inside the door." Keith looked up at Laurie who was still on the dock. "You want to come with us chiefy?"

She grinned but her grin was worried and forced. "No thanks. Another time under different circumstances." She looked away from Keith as she could feel that she was getting emotional.

Keith watched her turn away and he knew exactly what was going on behind her stony exterior. His face softened and his voice lowered. "Hey...mon petite chou...I'll take good care of him, non?"

"I know." She still didn't look at him but rather looked across the harbour at the boats coming and going. The sea was calm; it was the perfect day for fishing. On the surface, there was no reason to worry.

Charles came out of the cabin and saw Laurie's face. He walked over to the edge of the deck and stood immediately below her. "You be careful out there. Who knows what you'll find at that restaurant. They seem to be messing with some pretty rough types."

"What am I going to tell Edie?" Laurie looked down at him. She looked at him intensely as if she were committing his face to memory. The boat started.

"Tell her I'm going fishing." He reached up and she took his hand. Keith's first mate untied them and

138

they started to pull out. He held on as long as he could but eventually Charles had to let go of her hand. He watched her get smaller as they pulled away, focussing on her as they manoeuvred their way out of Oak Bluffs harbour leaving a frothy, white, chevron wake. Keith's voice snapped him back on to the boat.

"Charles this here is Gavin O'Neill. He goes out with me sometimes." Charles was startled. He hadn't even realised that there was anyone else on the boat. He reached out and shook the man's hand. Gavin was stocky and his grip was strong. His toothy smile was broad and encased in a short red beard. He looked very Irish.

"Good to meet you Charles. You're a friend of Captain Keith's are ya? Surely you could have done better than that."

Charles laughed. The joke wasn't that funny but Gavin's thick Irish brogue made it all the more charming.

"Hey! Hey! We'll have none of that. Gavin you come up here and drive the boat while I get Charles sorted."

"Right away, skipper." Gavin climbed the ladder to the cockpit with an effortlessness that told Charles that he'd grown up on boats. When he was situated, Keith came down to the deck. Keith moved with the same familiarity but without the exuberance of Gavin's youth.

"Well, I'm not sure exactly what you and Laurie are looking for but we'll get a little further out to sea and I'll have you start chumming." He handed Charles a pair of work gloves. "If we're going to be out here, I'm going to try my damndest to win this contest."

"I'm chumming?" Charles looked at Keith with mild surprise. He didn't have any idea what he'd be doing but chumming hadn't occurred to him.

"Yes, chumming. Get that look off your face." He pointed to the large buckets that were stowed at the back of the glistening white transom. "Those are the chum buckets right there. There's a scoop on top of the bucket on the right. You'll do fine." He patted Charles on the back and then Keith disappeared into the cabin leaving Charles alone on deck.

The ocean was not rough by any means. The waves rolled continuously leaving the Fascinating Rhythm to heave and roll along with the punches. It seemed to handle masterfully. Charles looked up at the cockpit and wondered how much of the control was Gavin or the boat itself. Charles found that if he let himself go along with the motion, he felt better than if he tried to fight it. He wondered if that was what caused seasickness. He decided to look that up later. Charles had always been lucky when it came to motion sickness. It never bothered him. He remembered being surprised when he had discovered at quite a young age that some people couldn't even read a book in a car without feeling nauseous. That must be awful.

Charles looked out at the boats in his line of vision. There were sailboats out for pleasure cruises and there were several fishing boats just like this one. Charles was sure that they were out for the tournament. Most of them were out by themselves but a couple of them were clustered. That seemed odd to
140

Charles. Were they not in competition? Oh well, there was certainly plenty of reasons to be on the Atlantic, he thought. Maybe some of them weren't out for the tournament after all.

"All right Charles, start that chumming." Keith came out of the cabin with a large rod and sat in the centre chair. He looked at Charles and pointed down to the buckets.

"Um, yeah, okay captain." Charles put on his work gloves, walked over, and picked up one of the heavy buckets of chum. He set it down on the transom and using the scoop, he pried off the lid. The stench hit him hard. The chum was made of fish guts, fish oil, and blood. He had known that but he hadn't really thought it through. Charles gagged. In reflex, He whipped his head away. "Jesus!"

Keith looked at him and laughed heartily. "You'll get used to it."

Charles wasn't sure that he wanted to get used to it. He shoved his scoop deep into the barrel and hauled up a heavy mound of rotted fish. He looked down and a head stared back at him. This is bloody disgusting, he thought. Literally. He threw his load into the water and reached for a second scoop.

"Step back for a minute smarty-pants." Keith said.

Charles stepped out of the way and Keith cast his line.

"Thank you. Back at it now."

Reluctantly, Charles returned to his chum bucket.

The Fascinating Rhythm floated on the Atlantic uneventfully. The sun beat down on the deck and Charles was grateful that he had rubbed his head down with sunscreen. The three men didn't speak. There wasn't a lot to say. The ocean was hypnotic. It left each of them to their thoughts.

17

Keith's fishing rod pulled with a sudden jolt. Instantly, all three men were on alert. They stared where the line disappeared beneath the ocean surface. There was another downward yank. Keith strapped himself into his chair. Charles wasn't sure what to expect and had butterflies in his stomach but Keith seemed prepared and completely unfazed. With another pull, Keith's quarry was on the run. The line spool on his reel let out the heavy wire at an alarming rate. It whirred with a high-pitched buzz. Charles ducked as the rod swung toward him. Whatever Keith had hooked, it was fast, Charles thought. He scurried to get behind Keith and out of the line of fire. "Gavin! Stop the boat!"

Gavin put the boat in neutral and it slowed gently into the sea's pitch.

The angle of the reel switched but the tension did not ease up at all. The fish was rising. With an explosion, a large white marlin breached the surface. Charles was at once startled and amazed. He pressed his back up against the cabin and watched the fish in awe. He wasn't sure what he had been expecting but that wasn't it. He knew that marlins swam these waters but he had never seen one in real life. He had no idea that they were that big!

The fish crashed back onto the ocean surface and folded down into the dark water. It disappeared in an envelope of white froth.

"Are marlins always that big?" Charles asked Keith.

Keith shook his head. "No. He's a big'un all right." He shook his head. "Had to be eight feet. Two hundred pounds at least, I'd say." Keith stayed in his chair and let his rod follow the fish as it dived again. When it came back toward the surface, Keith reeled him in bit by bit, foot by foot. He kept the line taught.

The fish breached again. The long ridged dorsal fin was deep blue. His back glistened; it was almost black. His nose sliced through the air like a fencer's sabre desperately looking for its adversary. The marlin crashed back into the waves and disappeared once more.

Without warning, Keith flew backward. The tension dropped almost completely. He started reeling in quickly. The line whirred and clicked, as the rig got closer to the surface.

"What happened?" Asked Charles.

Keith just shook his head.

Charles leaned over the transom to get a better look.

144

"Get back here! Jesus Christ!" Keith yelled. Before he could explain or apologise, the marlin broke the surface.

The hook was still lodged in the marlin's mouth as firmly as it always had been. The marlin's nose stood perfectly vertical almost with pride and victory but there was nothing victorious here. The marlin's head was in tatters. Its body had been removed in a clean crescent bite. The fish's innards hung in a sinewy mass. Something had taken the eight-foot marlin. Something hungry.

"What happened?" Charles stared at the remnants of the fish as Keith reeled it in and lowered it onto the deck.

"You tell me. This is your area isn't it?" He looked at Charles with a keen and knowing look.

Charles' interest peaked and he stepped closer. The head of the marlin lay on deck, cold and bloody. Its large eye stared out not seeing anything. The flesh of the fish splayed out like tattered streamers after a party. Limp and past their usefulness. Charles got down on one knee and investigated the wound. "This was one bite!" Charles held up his arms trying to mimic the bite radius. "This marlin was taken from below. The body of the fish was consumed and bitten off like a person eats a Popsicle!" Charles leaned down closer to the remains of the fish. His face was almost buried in the bloody flesh. He took off his glove and dug his fingers into the head. He thought it felt like half-frozen rice pudding. The expression on Charles' face turned to one of surprise. He pulled hard, fell backward, but raised his hand with his prize. It was the serrated, triangular tooth of a great white shark. "Recognise this?" Charles looked from Keith to Gavin and then to Gavin again. His heart was pounding in his chest.

Keith nodded.

"We're not alone out here." Said Gavin.

"It's a big one too. Over fifteen feet easily, probably closer to twenty." Charles stared at the tooth. "You see... this tooth is about one point seven inches long, I'd say. Somewhere between one and a half and two inches long at any rate. If I multiply that by ten, that gives us the length of the shark in feet."

Keith smiled. "Still a smarty-pa-"

With a loud thud, the boat lurched. All three men were knocked from their feet. Something had hit them and hit them hard. As the three of them struggled to their feet, they were hit again. Charles fell a second time but the more experienced seamen stood their ground.

Keith turned his attention to the bridge. "Gavin! Get us moving again! This shark is far too curious for my liking!"

Gavin scrambled to the wheel, grabbed a firm hold, and thrust the gearshift into position. The Fascinating Rhythm pitched forward, moving quickly and cleanly through the waves. Charles stood and regained his footing. He turned to look back at their wake. He wanted to see it. He remembered his experience the year before. He needed to see it. He stood motionless and watched. He remembered the black triangular dorsal fin slicing the ocean's surface and heading toward him last year on the Fuller Street

Beach. Charles' heart was beating so loud that he was sure that his shipmates could hear it over the hum of the motor. He watched... There was nothing to see. There was just the sparkling blue Atlantic Ocean.

Keith followed his gaze. "Did you see it?"

Charles shook his head and there was a pause before he spoke. "No."

"Hey Gav'! You see anything from up there." Called Keith.

"No. Sorry captain. He must have dived right after he hit us. Just checking us out." Gavin shrugged. He glanced about briefly but for the most part, he seemed to have lost interest.

Charles' heart was still pounding. Even Gavin's Irish accent didn't make him smile. He continued to stare out into the ocean even though it did nothing but reflect the perfect blue sky. He stared at the spot where the Fascinating Rhythm had just been floating; the place where he could still see the traces of their initial wake. He stared at the white froth that slowly dissipated into the dark waters around it. No sign. No fin. No shark. "This might be a little too close to JAWS for me." He thought. As they sliced through it, the ocean sprayed his face. Charles hardly noticed.

Keith turned to look at Charles. "I don't want to hear one word out of you about needing a bigger boat!" His eyes twinkled and he winked.

Charles laughed a nervous laugh. "You got it."

*   *   *

The Fascinating Rhythm floated smoothly a mile from where they had lost the white marlin. Keith kept fishing but Charles had stopped chumming. The chum made him sick and as much as he had wanted to see the shark earlier on, the thought of a great white shark jumping out at him mid-chum was even less appealing. Truth be told, Charles was just about ready to pack it in. He didn't want to say anything to Keith although Keith could probably tell. Charles had never been good at hiding his feelings; however, Keith wouldn't say anything if Charles didn't. They both knew that he was out there for a reason and that reason had yet to surface. He needed to learn something about the murders of Bill Cunningham and Steve Christie. What exactly he had hoped to learn on this boat, he wasn't sure but it seemed at the time that the closer he got to the contest, the better chance he had of solving this case. That had been Charles' theory when he boarded the Fascinating Rhythm anyway. It was a theory that seemed more and more foolish all the time. Charles looked starboard at the Vineyard in the distance. A painting. The beach was a stroke of gold sand topped with a dab of green grass. It looked warm and inviting. He hoped Laurie was having better luck on land.

"Hey captain!" Gavin called out from the cockpit.

"What's up, young man?" Keith twisted in his chair on the deck to try and get a look at Gavin. The sun was bright behind the young Irishman and Keith winced to protect his eyes.

"There's a boat coming our way." Gavin pointed out to sea.

148

Charles and Keith both followed his finger off the port side of the boat. Sure enough there was another sport boat headed their way. In the bright sun, it was difficult to make it out but it didn't look too remarkable. At least, Charles didn't think so. The only thing that he noticed was that it was riding very low in the water. Maybe they needed assistance, he thought.

Keith stood up and Charles walked over to stand beside him. "Do you recognise them, Keith?"

Keith shook his head. "No...but that's not too surprising at this time of year. They must be off-islanders."

As the boat got closer, it was clear that they were headed straight for the Fascinating Rhythm. They were past the point where they would have veered away if they were planning on passing. They kept their course.

The boat was white and nondescript. The name, Flicka, was painted on the side. The Flicka was in good condition but not very clean. The sides of the boat were bloody. It looked like it had been through more than one successful day of fishing and rewarded with several big hauls. Either that or the owner didn't keep it in very good repair. That seemed unlikely to Charles from what he had seen on this island. Everyone on Martha's Vineyard kept their boats immaculate. Especially the white sport boats that stayed moored in Oak Bluffs Harbour. There were three men and a woman on board. They were all smiling as they pulled up beside the Fascinating Rhythm.

Charles looked at Keith. He looked wary.

One of the mates of the Flicka threw a bumper over and tried to grab the Fascinating Rhythm. Keith grabbed a long hooked pole and cut him off. Keith hooked their boat by the cleat. "Can I help you gentlemen?" His tone was one of authority. Using the pole he kept the Flicka close but at a couple of feet distance.

One of the men came forward with a broad smile. "Are you the captain?" He was tall and thickly built.

Keith ignored his question and did not return the smile. "What's your business here? Do you need assistance?"

The big man with the smile kept smiling. "Oh no, no. Well, not exactly. You see, we have been fishing this spot since the tournament began. We got kind of a late start to it today. We have some friends meeting us here. One in particular is kind of superstitious about lucky spots and all of that sort of nonsense. Even if he wasn't, we couldn't contact them now to negotiate a different location as it is. Anyway, I feel kind of foolish asking this but as one sportsman to another, would you mind if we fished this spot?"

Keith stared at him and didn't speak for a full minute. It seemed to Charles to last an eternity. Surprisingly, Keith smiled broadly. "You're in luck young man; we're just heading back to port. It's all yours."

"Really? That's really great! My name is Joe Zito. I didn't catch your name."

"I didn't throw it. Look, Captain Zito, you shouldn't just come up on another boat without radioing ahead to identify yourself and your intentions. It's just proper manners. They should have taught you

150

that in your nautical training. If you don't have nautical training, you shouldn't be out here. Furthermore, this is a big tournament, and an even bigger ocean. If I weren't heading in right now, you and your friends would have to go and fish somewhere else. Good luck to you, young man. I hope you fare well." Keith pushed them off with his pole.

Joe Zito's smile tightened slightly. It came across as less natural but rather frozen on his face. Charles watched Joe's light grey eyes narrow and become colder in their stare. His knuckles whitened in their grip on the side of the Flicka. "I didn't mean any offense sir."

"None taken. I've said my piece. Good luck in the tournament young man." He turned toward Gavin. "Get us home young Irishman."

"Yes sir." The Fascinating Rhythm revved her engines audibly and she slipped forward leaving the Flicka behind. Joe gave them a half-hearted salute as they left. Keith did not return it.

Charles watched as the Flicka passed them by. He looked over the crew one by one and stopped on the woman. She had been standing in the doorway of the cabin. Her eyes stopped on Charles. They recognised each other immediately. She was Frank's girlfriend.

18

Charles already had his hand on the door handle when Keith stopped his pick-up truck in front of Laurie's house on East Chop. He stepped out casually but deep down he couldn't wait to get inside, have a shower, and put this day behind him. He was tired and he smelled of chum and sweat.

"You did all right smarty-pants."

"You think so do you?" Charles gave him a limp half-smile.

"I do. 'A' for effort!" Keith grinned heartily at him from his position behind the wheel. Charles' opened his door and stepped out. He heard a creak and wasn't entirely sure whether it was the door of the truck or his back. He turned around and pulled his knapsack out after him. Keith spoke up again. "I'm sorry that you didn't really get anything out of it. I hope it wasn't too horrible."

Charles looked at his friend and smiled in earnest. "Not at all. It was very interesting. I'm not in any hurry to do it again but I'm glad I did." Charles reached into his pocket and pulled out the shark tooth that he had extracted from the marlin's head. "This alone was well worth the trip. Don't you think? How many people have a great white tooth almost the size of a shot glass?" He looked at it thoughtfully. "Especially from a shark that had considered attacking their boat! Anyway, thanks a lot for all your help." Charles thought for a minute before continuing. "Keith, are you planning on doing anything about the Flicka?"

"I should report them! *Tabernac!* The balls on them! Asking us to move! That's not a true sportsman's conduct, I can tell you that! Probably get them disqualified from the tournament! At the very least, they could get some points knocked against them."

"Do me a favour? Don't say anything...not yet anyway."

Keith looked slyly at Charles. "What are you up to smarty-pants? Did you learn more than you're letting on?"

"I'm not sure exactly. I need to talk to Laurie first. So for now, let's just let them do their thing."

Keith shrugged. "Whatever you say."

"Give my best to Catherine." Charles pushed hard on the truck door and it closed with a heavy crunch.

"I shall do that. Give my love to Laurie. Catherine will be expecting you two for supper again soon."

"I'd love it." Charles waved as Keith started to pull away. He watched him drive up the road until the truck disappeared around the bend. Walking up to the grey shingle home, he dug his hand into his bag looking for the spare house keys that Laurie had given him back at the station. By the time he needed them, he had them out and poised to open the door.

So that guy, Frank, was the emcee of the tournament and his girlfriend, at least Charles assumed it was his girlfriend, was on the Flicka. That was worth looking into. Not to mention that they had asked them to move. Why the hell would they do that? What would they possibly have to gain? It is possible that they were meeting someone but they could have been a couple of hundred yards off and they would have been seen. Sailors did have a reputation for being superstitious. Was there such a thing as lucky co-ordinates? Seemed ridiculous to Charles but who knows... They didn't seem to Charles to be very experienced sailors, at least that Joe Zito didn't. They didn't look like sailors. They looked like businessmen in a boat. Just like weekend warriors didn't look like real hockey players. Charles didn't trust Joe Zito and neither did Keith. Charles couldn't wait to tell Laurie. He also wanted to tell her about their experience with the shark! There was a good-sized Great White out there. Surely someone in the contest would find that out. Charles had visions of the posse in JAWS going out to hunt the shark. He hoped that didn't happen. At

154

least Great Whites weren't on the list of acceptable quarry for the contest. That shark had been a considerable size too. A fisherman in these medium sized sports boats might think twice about trying to catch him. That might be enough to keep the shark alive. When the shark had bumped their boat, Charles had been pretty freaked out but he certainly didn't want to see any harm come to it. Like Gavin had said, he was probably just checking them out. That was the last they had seen of him.

"Hello?" Charles called out as he set his bag down on the floor of the front hall. There was no response. He walked back in to the kitchen and looked out the window at the back deck. There was no one home. Laurie was probably at work. Charles pulled out his iPhone and called the Edgartown Police Station.

"Hi sergeant. This is Charles Williams. Is Chief Knickles in?"

"Yes, she is Mr Williams. I'll put you through." He said.

"No! That's fine. Don't bother her. Can you just pass on a message for me, please? Tell her I'm home, I'm making supper, and ask her to call me when she's on her way."

"Got it. No problem. I'll give it to her right away."

"Thanks." Charles pressed 'end' on his phone and walked back out to the front hall. He opened his bag and pulled out the dry set of clothes that he had brought with him. He felt them thoroughly; they were still dry. That made him smile. Charles stripped down in the front hall and stuffed his wet clothes into his bag. His damp bare feet left prints on the dark

155

hardwood. Collecting his dry clothes, he went upstairs to have a shower.

Laurie's house was quite classic in its exterior design but the interior was very modern. The upstairs bathroom was no exception. The walls were done in large white ceramic tile that co-ordinated with the floor. There was a mosaic of decorative smaller tiles around the room at chair rail height in a mix of light greys. The fixtures were chrome with a stylized industrial look. Instead of the standard showerhead over a built-to-fit bathtub, there was a glass shower stall that was completely open on one side. The slight slope in the floor ensured that the water would drain properly. The tub was a modern take on an antique claw-footed tub. It was sleeker and straighter in its lines not rounded like a classic tub. It was on legs but they were sharp angled blocks not animal feet. The faucet stemmed from the floor and poured into the side of the tub instead of the more common foot. The window was large and bright and the curtains were gauzy, white, and delicate. They almost looked antique and they softened the modern room. White towels had been rolled and stacked on their ends in a large natural wicker beach basket. Charles didn't consider himself a decorator by any means but it seemed to him that Laurie had excellent taste.

Charles stepped behind the glass partition that made up the shower stall and turned the double handles. Water cascaded down on him from an over-sized rain showerhead. It felt good. The day had been interesting but stressful. It was amazing to him how restorative showers could be. He stood there motionless until all of his stress was gone.

When Laurie called, Charles was in the kitchen, chopping broccoli. The sound of her voice energized him. "How was your day?" He asked.

"Interesting...yours?"

"Mine was interesting but it was more exhausting than anything else."

"That's not too surprising. Yet, I hear that I have supper waiting for me?"

"Possibly...If you play your cards right." He was sure that she could hear his grin over the phone.

"I'm not sure I have any cards left. What if I picked up some new cards? Will a bottle of wine get me a hot meal and a foot rub?"

"I don't know that seems a bit on the cheap side. It's a pretty sweet meal and I'm known far and wide for my foot massages." He bartered.

"Two bottles of wine?" Laurie sounded hopeful.

He paused before answering. "That sweetens the pot. You have yourself a deal." He smiled like she could see him.

"Great!" She sounded good, really good. "You might not be cheap but I'm sure glad you're easy."

"Laurie?"

"Yes?"

"Hurry home."

There was a brief silence but they both understood it. "Okay."

Charles put down his iPhone and returned to his food preparation. He rinsed the broccoli when he was done and started washing the baby carrots. Charles hated carrots with a passion. He had discretely avoided them at Keith and Cathy's and wouldn't have made them again but he knew that Laurie liked them, especially sunshine carrots. They had been so popular in the eighties. He would make them for Laurie but no amount of sugar and orange juice would ever make carrots palpable for Charles. There was broccoli and cauliflower for him. There was a spinach and kale salad too. Actually, there were roasted potatoes in the oven with the prime rib. Charles began to wonder if he had made too much food. Oh well, who doesn't like a Thanksgiving type dinner with all the fixings? He smiled to himself and reached for his glass of Kim Crawford Sauvignon Blanc. He took a generous mouthful. The wine filled his cheeks and rushed over the back of his tongue. It was tangy, crisp, and delicious. It tasted of green apples but it was its herbaceous undertones that betrayed its New Zealand origins. It was Charles' favourite wine. It was a great cheese wine. Toward that end, Charles set down his Bordeaux wine glass and picked up a hunk of very old white cheddar. He bit off a piece. The combination was almost too much...almost.

Charles opened the oven door and checked the roast. It was browning beautifully. He stuck his thermometer deep into the centre to confirm. Yes, he thought, it is done. He turned the oven off, pierced a potato with his thermometer, and stole it out of the pan. Too hot to eat, he plopped it onto a small plate on the counter and closed the oven door. All that was left to do was steam the broccoli and cauliflower and dress the salad. Charles cut into the potato and blew on it before popping a morsel into his mouth. The crunchy skin gave way to a soft almost creamy interior. The rich flavours absorbed from the meat, olive oil, and rosemary filled his mouth. Charles loved potatoes. He could eat an entire meal of them in any size, shape, or form. He was convinced of it.

"I'm home!" Laurie called out from the front hall. "Hey! You left footprints all over the floor."

"Sorry!" Charles called out. He walked over to the cupboard and got out a clean wine glass. He poured her a glass and set it on the counter.

Laurie walked into the kitchen and set her bags down on the island. "No problem. For future reference, there is a mop in the hall closet. It's one of those Swiffer Wet Jet things. I keep it up there for exactly that reason."

"Got it." Charles pointed to the glass of wine he had just poured.

"Is that for me?" She asked. "Yummy!" She picked it up and took a mouthful. She pulled two more bottles of Kim Crawford out of her bag and put them in the fridge.

Charles smiled when he saw the wine. "My kind of girl. That's my favourite wine."

"I know." She winked at him. "So, what's for supper?"

"Prime rib and potatoes, spinach and kale salad, broccoli, cauliflower, and sunshine carrots."

"Holy crap!" Laurie's eyes widened. "Who's supposed to eat all of that?"

"So, we'll have leftovers. Who doesn't like leftovers?"

"True enough." Laurie opened the oven and leaned in to peak at the roast. "Amazing." She inhaled deeply. "...And you made carrots? You hate carrots!"

"Yes, you're on your own there." Charles chuckled.

"With pleasure." Laurie closed the oven and looked at him fondly. "You're spoiling me Mr Williams."

Charles moved closer. He took away her wine glass and put his arms around her. "I don't think so."

"No?" She looked directly into his eyes.

"No." Charles returned her gaze. He was happy to be with her. "Spoiling to me implies that someone is getting more than they deserve. You, chief, deserve everything I can give you."

Laurie whispered. "I don't know if I deserve you..."

"You do." Charles leaned down and kissed her deeply. His tongue pushed its way into her mouth. His hands rubbed her back and then made their way forward. He began to unbutton her shirt. He found her bra.

"I'm not showered..." Laurie pulled from their kiss.

"I don't care." He pushed back in. He un-tucked her shirt from her pants and undid her belt.

"What about supper?" She leaned her head back as he moved down her neck. He was inhaling her scent.

"It'll keep."

*   *   *

Charles cut into his slice of beef and put another piece on his fork. He was devouring his meal. It turned out beautifully if he did say so himself. He had turned the oven off at just the right time and even with their unexpected delay, the roast and the potatoes were perfect. He kept chewing and reached for his wine. He took just a sip. Just enough wine to add to the beef, not take away from it. He looked at Laurie; she was beautiful. After they had made love on the kitchen floor, she had gone upstairs for a quick shower and to change into her Lululemon yoga wear that she always wore around the house. She looked fresh and bright. She looked happy. Charles supposed that it could have been the meal but he liked to think that wasn't entirely true. She looked at him and smiled knowingly. No, he didn't think it was entirely true at all.

They had plugged Charles' iPod into the living room stereo and at the moment, Fleetwood Mac's album Tusk was playing in the background. It was one of Charles' favourites. It wasn't playing very loud and every once in a while they could still hear the waves of the Atlantic rolling into Laurie's private beach.

"Pass the salad, please." Laurie reached out her hand and Charles passed the wooden bowl full of leafy greens, pears, blue cheese, pecans, and red onion. "Thank you. Jesus, everything is delicious, Charles. You've really outdone yourself."

"I'm glad you like it. Really, it's a very simple meal to make. There's nothing to it. There's a lot of chopping but other than that, it's pretty easy. The oven does all the work." Charles shrugged.

"I disagree. There's something to it. There's a knack." She shook her head. "I don't have that knack." After dishing herself up a second helping of salad, she placed the bowl on the table beside her.

Charles nodded his head in dramatic humility. "Well, thank you ma'am." He took another sip of wine before he spoke again. "So, what did you discover today?"

"Oh! Isn't that something? I almost forgot!" Laurie exclaimed wide-eyed before grinning ear-to-ear and narrowing her eyes. "I can't imagine how I got so distracted..." She kicked him under the table.

Charles blushed and laughed. "Enough! What did you learn?"

"Okay, okay. So, that guy who is emceeing the tournament now? His full name is Frank Zito. He owns a seafood wholesale company on the mainland."

"Frank Zito? His name is Frank Zito?"

"Yes. Why is that so remarkable?"

"Keith and I met a really weird guy today out on the ocean by the name of Joe Zito."

"That's his brother. They own Zito Seafood together." Laurie stopped eating. She was too focussed. "What do you mean that you met him on the ocean? How the hell do you meet someone on the ocean?"

"Well, it was weird. We were out fishing- boy do I have a fish tale for you- and this boat called Flicka starts coming directly toward us. When they got close enough, they put up a fender and tried to raft themselves along side us. Keith wouldn't let them. He kept them at distance with a hooked pole. I thought it was impressive actually. Couldn't have been easy

162

manoeuvring it like that. Anyway, the captain of the boat came forward and was trying to be charming but he came across as smarmy, unpleasant. He said his name was Joe Zito." Charles took some more wine.

"What did they want?"

"That's the weirdest part. They asked us to move!"

"Move?" Laurie stared at him incredulously.

"Move." Charles nodded. "He tried to pass off some obtuse story about having to meet a superstitious friend in that particular spot as they had been fishing there since the tournament started but neither Keith nor I bought it."

"So why do you think they wanted that spot?"

"I have no idea." Charles shook his head. "Can't figure it out."

"Is that it?"

"No. That woman whom I said I had seen with Frank on North Water Street? She was on the boat."

"It's probably Frank's wife, Kim."

"Well, now that we know that Frank and Joe are brothers, that's not such a big deal." Charles looked at his now empty plate. He was full and glad that he had decided against making dessert because he would have forced it in anyway. "How did you find out who Frank and Kim were?"

"Well, when we saw Frank, he was on foot. When you saw him on North Water, he was on foot. I knew he wasn't an islander so I started checking the hotels and inns in the immediate area. I figured he wasn't at The Edgartown Inn or you would have seen him. I checked registration and found him at The Hob Knob.

Nice place, that. Turns out there aren't that many Franks around and he fit the description." Laurie pushed her plate away and reached for her wine glass.

"That's awesome. Well done." Charles picked up his glass and they clinked them together. "You said they own a seafood wholesale company on the mainland?"

"Yep. Boston."

"I wonder if that means anything." Charles thought for a minute. "They wouldn't be trying to supply anyone here on the island would they? I mean that doesn't make sense- coals to Newcastle and all of that. Any islander would use someone local like Larsen's. Wouldn't they?"

"I agree. I have quite a few friends on the force in Boston. I called in a favour and asked someone to see if they could get their hands on Zito Seafood's customer list. I would like to learn a little more about their business. I want to keep it quiet too. I don't want them to know that we're looking around. They might not have anything to do with anything but I have a feeling..." Laurie's voice tapered off.

"Me too." Charles looked around. "Let's get the kitchen cleaned up." He stood.

"Oh, let me do it! You made this incredible meal and besides, you barely left any mess as it is." Laurie got up from the table and collected their plates.

"I admit I like to clean as I go. It comes from living alone, I think." Charles picked up the salad bowl and the remaining carrots.

"Well, whatever the reason, it sure is convenient. Now, set those down on the counter and go sit down in

164

the den." Laurie pointed in the direction of the sunroom that faced the beach and the ocean. "This won't take me a second to clean up."

"You know, considering services rendered, I think that I should be the one getting the foot massage..." Charles grinned at Laurie.

"Oh you do, do you?" She chuckled and handed him an unopened bottle of Kim Crawford. "Here, take your wine."

19

Charles woke up in Laurie's master bedroom alone. Not in any hurry to go anywhere, he just lay there...thinking. It was early. Charles couldn't see the sun directly but he stared absently at the light leaking in the window. Quietly at first, dripping over the crisp, white window frame, down the periwinkle wall, and across the richness of the dark wood floor. As the sun rose, the room brightened. The light flooded in, bringing out the natural beach tones in the sand faux-suede furniture, ocean blue walls, and sea froth white trim. The watercolours over the fireplace were of small birds on delicate branches. Charles looked them over carefully. He was pretty sure that the birds in the first picture were male and female goldfinches while the second painting was of grackles. They were framed in dark wood to tie in with the floor. The only other wall fixtures were bamboo roll-up blinds and an oval mirror in a heavy gold frame that hung over the head of the bed. Charles loved the room. He found it comfortable and warm. It was a good place to think but he had lain there long enough.

Charles threw back the blankets and planted both feet on the floor. He sat for a minute on the edge of the bed before walking over to his clothes and putting on his NHL boxers and a worn JAWS t-shirt. They were the ones he had brought the day before to change into after his fishing trip. At some point in the day, he would need to go back to The Edgartown Inn and get a fresh change of clothes. He decided to shower there as well. His shaving gear was there and he would feel better slipping on clean clothes if he had just stepped out of the shower rather than off a bus. Charles knew that it would be a lot more practical to be living in one place but he just didn't feel like it was the right thing to do at this point in his relationship with Laurie. He loved spending time with her and when he wasn't with her he was thinking about her but he just didn't think it was time. When they both thought it was time, it would be right.

As he went down to the kitchen, the stairs creaked in the otherwise quiet house. The ocean could be heard in the distance. Its roll seeped constantly and rhythmically through every open window and every door jam but the house itself was silent. Laurie was at the station. Mumbling, half asleep, he had offered to go with her but she had assured him that she was going to be catching up on paperwork all day and that she would get more done if he wasn't there. Charles hadn't argued. In fact, he was happy to spend some time alone. There were a few people who Charles enjoyed very much but for the most part, he was a loner. He always thought that there were two types of people, those who recharged their batteries by being out with other people and those who recharged their batteries by being alone. Charles was definitely in the latter category.

The kitchen window was full of morning light. The room was bright and cheery. Charles went directly to the fridge and pulled out the eggs, a tomato, a green pepper, onion, and hot sauce. He would make a quick vegetable omelette and then be on his way. He had to figure out what he was going to do all day. There were a lot of sights that he hadn't taken in on this trip. In fact, there were quite a few that he hadn't taken in last time either. He could rent a bicycle and tour around. He wouldn't mind making his way over to the Gay Head Lighthouse. The red cliffs were beautiful. He hadn't spent much time this trip in Vineyard Haven either. Somehow, he knew that at some point, he would end up back at The Monster Shark Fishing Tournament. It wouldn't be the most pleasant way to spend the day but there were still so many unanswered questions. Charles thought that if he spent some time down there, he might just see what the Flicka was catching. They had wanted to fish in a specific spot for a reason. Everybody does everything for a reason. Charles would like to see their haul.

Charles took one last look around the house to make sure that he had everything. Not that it was that big of a deal if he didn't but he liked to be organised. It wasn't like him to put things down anywhere other than his gym bag, that way he was always together.

168

This time seemed to be no different. Charles put on his running shoes, picked up his bag, and left the house, closing and locking the door behind him.

It was a beautiful morning and time was on his side so Charles decided to walk to the bus in Oak Bluffs. He figured it was two miles maximum. Back in Toronto, Charles did ten miles a day for cardio. This would not be a problem, especially with the ocean on his left and the Vineyard rising up on his right. He couldn't imagine a more pleasant walk.

Stepping out of the shade of the porch roof, Charles took the four steps down to the lawn briskly. He cut across the grass that separated the house from East Chop Drive and headed east to the centre of Oak Bluffs. Laurie had neighbours on both sides and across the street as well but the properties were well secluded, separated by tall pines, untamed scrub oak, trimmed hedges and split-rail fences. It was a lovely part of the island. The downside was that you really needed a car to make it work. Living out here was a far distance from any grocery or convenience store. Charles was used to the convenience of the big city where everything was within a short walking distance. The houses out here were invariably built in the island tradition of weathered cedar and white trim. Charles wondered how long it took from the time the houses were built and the cedar was fresh to take on that weathered grey colour. He made a mental note to look that up later. The homes on the ocean side of East Chop Drive, the ones that Charles could see anyway, the ones not hidden behind extensive yard work, were made up of just as many windows as they were cedar planks. Their decks were expansive. Both features designed to take full advantage of the ocean and private beaches. Charles decided that it was a small price to pay for having to drive to the closest store for bread and milk. A little further on, behind a short white picket fence and a sign that read 'Telegraph Hill' stood The East Chop Lighthouse.

The original East Chop Light had been built in 1869 by a sea captain named Silas Daggett. It burned down in 1871 but it was replaced in 1872. In 1875, that lighthouse and the property on which it stood was purchased by the United States Congress and they removed all of the existing buildings and built the existing lighthouse in 1878. Why government was always doing foolish things like that was far beyond Charles. Waste of money if you asked him. He was glad that they did replace the lighthouse and not just remove it altogether. It was one of Charles' favourites on the island. It was the final of the five lights on the island to be built. The first was the original Cape Pogue lighthouse but that was long gone. When Charles had come to the Vineyard as a child, the East Chop Lighthouse had been a reddish-brown colour. People referred to it as the "chocolate lighthouse". Some locals still did. It had been scheduled for destruction in the eighties but an historical group called VERI had saved it along with the Gay Head Light and the Edgartown Light (Charles' other two favourites). The group had saved them with a federal petition. Charles loved that. He couldn't even begin to imagine the Vineyard without those three lighthouses. That was one of the best things about the locals.

Everything about the islanders said, "Don't mess with our Vineyard! Leave us alone!" and for the most part, people did just that. Charles stopped for a minute to look at the lighthouse. It was magnificent, classic. Forty feet in height, white with a black lantern, and with a light range of nine nautical miles. How could anyone consider tearing down such a structure? Now the lighthouse was safely in the hands of the Martha's Vineyard Museum. That thought made Charles smile. The museum had even re-opened it to the public on Sundays. Charles would love to check it out. It had been closed up for fifty-five years after the government had automated it in 1933; however, the museum had put some money into restoration including the exterior guardrail and the elevated lighting room inside. That would be cool to see, thought Charles. At this point, like a lot of things, Charles had only read about it. He carried on.

Newer houses had been squeezed into smaller lots on the ocean side the way greedy developers do. Blue and pink hydrangeas had been planted around each home. They were a motherly flower thought Charles, warm and kind. As the road wrapped around the bend of the chop, the land became too narrow on the waterfront even for the most zealous of builders. The only homes in sight were large century homes with wrap-around porches and expansive lawns. They were magnificent. Gardens of ornamental grass and short scrub oak planted around the occasional street lamp looked antiquated and charming. Charles thought that other than the paved road, it had looked like this out here for a hundred years, maybe more. The same sounds of waves delicately reaching the shore and the same call of the omnipresent gulls. This was why people came here and this was why the locals were so protective. If it works, he thought, don't fix it.

Charles continued along East Chop Drive with no company except the short, whitewashed, reflective posts across the street. The Chop dropped off beyond the posts and the waves rushed in below. When the land broadened enough to be sellable again, the posts stopped and the fences and manicured lawns started once more. He was getting closer to Oak Bluffs Harbour.

After Charles turned the final corner on East Chop and headed down toward Lake Avenue, he left the residences behind him. On his right was hilly, wild greenery. Charles figured that it was state property. Across the street, on his left behind a chain link fence, was the harbour. The Oak Bluffs Harbour was always busy and today was no exception. The sun was getting warmer the higher it rose in the sky. That kind of weather coupled with the tournament ensured that the harbour traffic would be in full swing. Charles watched the goings-on with a fascination that could only be felt by someone who did not live by the sea. The fishing boats headed out from the tournament docks. Sailboats of every colour filled with families and friends ignored the tournament and set out for their own day of recreation. The water was criss-crossed with wakes making it choppier than it otherwise would be. Everything sparkled.

The street traffic at Lake Avenue and East Chop was just as hectic as it had been when Charles had been there a couple of days ago in Laurie's squad car. It was much easier to navigate on foot. As he passed, Charles looked into the tournament. He didn't actually make his way into the melee but watched for any familiar faces in the crowd and thought of his plan for the rest of the day. Charles was also kind of half-looking for Chief Jefferies. He was probably in there somewhere. He decided that later, when the boats would be coming in, he would make his way down and watch the catches. With any luck, he would be able to see what the Flicka was bringing in. For now, he headed to the bus stop up at Ocean Park where he could catch the bus back to The Edgartown Inn. Charles needed to shower, change, and maybe even score one of Edie's breakfasts. He'd see how he felt when he got there.

20

"How was your fishing trip?" Chief Jeffries asked when Charles picked up the phone.

"How'd you know about that?" Jeff hadn't said hello but Charles recognised his voice right away.

"I was talking to Laurie this morning; she filled me in on what's been going on. I hear you had some excitement out there." Jeff sounded distracted like he was working while talking. Charles guessed from the background noise that he was at the Oak Bluffs Police Station.

"Yes, I suppose I did." Charles stood in his room at the Edgartown Inn, drying himself off with one of Edie's plush white towels. "We learned a few things. Did Laurie fill you in about Zito Seafood? About the Zito brothers?"

"She did. She is putting in her call to Boston as we speak. Calling in a couple of favours from what I understand. I'm curious about that boat. What was its name? Flicker?"

"Flicka." Charles corrected.

"Right, the Flicka- weird name for a boat. I wonder where they got that?"

"It's a horse." Said Charles.

"A horse?"

"A horse. There was a novel written in the early nineteen-forties called *My Friend Flicka*. It was very successful. There was a trilogy of them, I think. They all took place in Wyoming. They made a movie and a TV show too."

"How do you know all this?" Jeff asked in disbelief.

"Honestly? I have no idea. Read it somewhere, I guess."
Charles said dismissively.

"Crazy... Well, if the Flicka was so hot to have that spot, I want to know what they're catching. I'm going to head down there in a bit. I thought that you might want to come with me. Are you interested?" Jeff sounded more focussed on their conversation as he waited for an answer.

"I am actually. In fact, I was planning to do the exact same thing today. I was going to head down there shortly. Want to meet me there?"

"Why don't you give Jack Burrell a call? He's right behind the Inn and he's headed down to the tournament today to help me control the crowd. That Jack, he doesn't mind working; I'll give him that. He can give you a lift here to the station in Oak Bluffs."

"Alright, that sounds great. Do you have his number?" Charles went over to the desk and as Jeff dictated it, he wrote down Jack's cell phone number on a small white pad of paper. "Got it, thanks." He hesitated for a moment before speaking again. "Hey Jeff..."

"Yeah?"

"Have you seen Jack lately? I mean since all of that business with Bill's murder? The last time that Laurie and I saw him, he was pretty rough." Charles was wondering about Jack's ability to return to work. He had been really out of it.

Jeff chuckled. "Laurie asked me the same thing. He must have made quite an impression. I saw Jack yesterday and he was fine. Good to go. With Bill gone, there is no longer any issue with him working the crowd at the tournament so he was eager for the extra hours. I can't say that I blame him. That wife of his is a piece of work. All she talks about is money. At least, that was what she was like when I was around her. Have you ever met Marcie?"

"No, I haven't. She was in bed the time that Laurie and I were at the house. She was pretty tight with her dad from what I understand." Charles was getting more and more intrigued about the enigmatic Marcie Burrell.

"Well that's certainly true. They were thick as thieves those two. Well, a lot alike anyway. What is it they say, 'Daddy's girl and Mama's boy'? I'm sure she loves Jack. I'm just glad I'm not married to her... for lots of reasons." Jeff laughed. "I'm sure she's a nice girl. I don't know why I'm telling you all of this."

176

Charles pulled fresh clothes out of his suitcase and set them on the bed. "I don't know either. It's all very interesting though. Maybe I'll tell Jack that I'll just walk up to the house and meet him there. If she's home, I'd like to meet her."

"Good luck with that. Call Jack. I'll see you when you get here." Jeff hung up the phone without saying goodbye.

Charles ended his call and then dialled the number that he had written down on the pad. It rang twice before Jack's distinctly youthful voice answered.

"Sergeant Burrell speaking!" He seemed back to his usual self.

"Hi Jack. This is Charles Williams. How are you doing?"

"Mr Williams! I'm fine. Thanks! What can I do for you?" Jack always spoke like he was in the middle of a workout- energetic and slightly winded.

"I just got off the phone with Chief Jeffries and he told me that you were heading up his way soon. He suggested that you give me a lift. Would that be alright?"

There was a pause on the other end. "Oh, sure. You're going up to Oak Bluffs? What for?" Jack's tone seemed less enthusiastic than it had been a minute ago.

"I'm going to take a look at the tournament with Chief Jeffries." Charles wasn't sure if he was imagining the shift in attitude or not. It was difficult to tell over the phone. "Is that a problem Jack? I can take the bus if need be. It's okay really."

"Oh! No! It's totally fine. I can take you. Yep. That's no problem at all. When did you want me to come and get you?" Jack's tone seemed to be back to normal but still there was something underneath it.

"Actually, I bet it would be a lot easier if I just walked over to you. It would be faster that's for sure. Too many one way streets in this town."

"You're going to come here?" Jack asked. Charles thought the tone was back.

"Yes. When are you leaving? Shall I be there in an hour? Does that give you enough time?"

"Sure Mr... Charles. That would be great. I'll see you around eleven." Jack hung up without saying goodbye too. Maybe it was an islander thing, thought Charles.

Charles finished getting dressed. With any luck, he'd be introduced to Marcie Burrell when he got out to the house. He wasn't sure why he felt that he needed to meet her but he did. Charles felt that if he was going to be on the field, he should know all the players. It would only take five minutes to get to Jack's house. That left him plenty of time to have one of Edie's breakfasts complete with homemade toast and coffee cake.

*　　*　　*

Charles walked down Simpsons Lane and turned the corner onto Peases Point Way. The Burrell house was only a couple of houses down from the corner and he could see Jack's cruiser in the driveway. As he got closer, he saw that Jack was sitting in the car waiting for him. Charles was disappointed; it looked like he wouldn't be going in to meet the missus after all. Jack stuck his hand high out of the open car window and waved to make sure that Charles saw him.

"I hope I haven't kept you waiting!" Charles sat down in the passenger's seat and put on his seat belt. He closed the cruiser door.

"Not at all! I was just finished getting ready and I can play games on my iPhone out here just as easily as I can inside. I play 'Flow'. You ever played 'Flow'? It's so cool! I'm addicted to it! Do you know it?"

Charles smiled and shook his head. Jack seemed to be back to business as usual. "I don't know it. Sorry."

"You should totally download it! It's free. There are all of these different coloured dots. Well, there are two dots of each colour and you have to connect them without crossing the paths made by the other colours! Get it? It sounds stupid probably but it's not. It's really cool! The patterns keep getting harder and harder as you progress. Oh! And you can't leave any blank spaces either. The whole board has to be filled in."

"Jack?" Charles smiled at the young officer with genuine affection.

"Yes?"

"We should probably go."

"Oh, right! Yes. On our way!" Jack turned the key in the ignition and started backing out of the driveway.

"How's Marcie making out?" asked Charles. Jack's face changed noticeably. His energy seemed to stumble on its way out of Jack's body.

"Oh...Marcie's okay. You know, it's a lot to take." Jack spoke without looking at Charles.

"She up and about more or is she still spending most of her time in bed?"

"Huh? Oh, right. No she's up and about now." Jack nodded his head and stared directly ahead of him, his eyes on the road. "Thanks."

"Well, that's probably a good sign then. Sounds like she's coming around. I'm glad to hear it." Charles looked at Jack. "I'm glad you're back at work too. Laurie is too."

"It feels so good to be out of the house! I hate sitting and stewing about things all the time. I don't think it's healthy, you know what I mean? That's what my mom always says anyway. Besides, I like being out around people! But not even that, I really love my job too. I miss it when I'm not there."

Charles smiled at Jack and then turned his gaze toward the ocean. They were leaving Edgartown behind them and heading up along State Beach. This was still Charles' favourite drive on the island. The day was sunny and warm so the beach was busy. It was good to see.

"Charles?"

Charles turned around to Jack with a start and a guilty expression. He hadn't heard a word that he had said. "I'm sorry Jack, what did you say? I got lost in the scenery."

"Oh! That's okay. Pretty isn't it? I love that beach. It might even be my favourite beach on the island, my favourite one for swimming anyway. I like walking on South Beach but sometimes it gets too
180

rough to swim. Lucy Vincent Beach is pretty fantastic though! Have you ever been to that beach Charles?"

"Didn't you have something to ask me Jack?" Charles asked.

"Oh! I did... I don't remember what it was though. Must have been a lie!!" Jack laughed at his own silly joke. "Oh! I remember! It was nothing major really. I was just curious as to why you were going back up to the tournament? I didn't think that it was your thing at all."

"Very astute of you. You're right- it's not. I don't really know. I guess I'm hoping that I will know it when I see it. All of the connections between the two dead men seem to lead to this tournament. I keep thinking that I need to learn more about it if I'm going to figure out who murdered them." Charles stared out at the Atlantic Ocean but this time he didn't see it. He looked past it, lost in his own thoughts. "I'm hoping to start to see more of what the boats are hauling in." Charles was thinking of the Flicka specifically but perhaps he wouldn't notice anything special about their haul until he compared it to the hauls of the other boats.

"What will that tell you?" Jack asked.

"I don't know." Charles said absently. "Maybe nothing." Sadly, that was true. If they didn't learn anything from the hauls of the boats then they would be at square one. They wouldn't know anything about their victims' deaths and their killer could be long off the island. Actually, he or she could be long gone already. "It's like having a big puzzle in your head, Jack. There are big holes and there are a lot of little pieces. None of which makes any sense until you figure out how they all fit together." Charles continued to stare out his window as he spoke. Not even the JAWS Bridge could get him out of his own head right now. "It's frustrating really."

Jack drove past Ocean Park and the ferry terminal and pulled up in front of the Oak Bluffs Police Station. The building was long, low, and finished in greyed cedar shingles. It was almost a bungalow but the roof was gabled. It looked like it had a half of a second floor. The entrance was centred on the front of the building under a small peaked roof that completed a brick porch. The roof read 'Town Of Oak Bluffs' in big black letters. Hanging just beneath it was a sign that read 'Everett A. Rogers Municipal Building'. The roof, the brick porch, the large, heavy, white wood door were all held together by two Greek revival columns. The building was modest but charming.

Jack parked just to the left of the facade. The spots right in front and to the right were reserved for taxis. "Have you ever been here before?" Jack asked as they got out of the car.

Charles shook his head. "No. No, I haven't."

"That's kind of cool. This is your first time! It's not as big as the Edgartown Police Station but it's nice! I like it! I could totally see myself working here. Not that I'm not happy working in Edgartown with Chief Knickles! I just mean that this would be cool too." Jack led the way to the front door. When he got there, he opened it for Charles.

Charles stepped inside to find that it was exactly what he had expected. "It's very nice," he said almost to no one in particular. White walls, wood desks, and an American flag on a pole that was just tall enough to keep it off the floor. Plaques on the walls commemorated the department for a variety of achievements in the community. Charles would have stepped closer to read them but as soon as he got inside, Chief Jeffries stepped out of his office to greet him.

"Charles! Hey! You've never been here before have you?"

"No, actually I haven't."

"Well, it's pretty much what you would expect. The building is pretty straightforward but the people are great. That's the important part. I'll have you meet them at some point." Jeff looked around with an obvious sense of pride. He turned back around and opened the door that Charles and Jack had just walked through moments before. "Shall we?"

"Whenever you're ready, Chief."

"Lead the way." Jeff turned briefly to the desk sergeant. "I'll be down at the shark tournament if you need me."

The two men stepped outside into the sunny day. Oak Bluffs was busy with tourists of all sorts. Charles found it fascinating. There were tourists in Oak Bluffs that he never saw on any other part of the island. He expected that quite a few people came over on the ferry and never left Oak Bluffs. Charles wondered how many of them were day-trippers from the mainland. Their ferry would dock in Oak Bluffs and they could shop, party, swim, and eat all in Oak Bluffs. Then they could take the last ferry home. It was obvious to Charles that Oak Bluffs was the only community on the island designed with tourists in mind. As soon as you disembarked from the ferry at the terminal, beaches, cottages, hotels, restaurants, bars, and shops surrounded you. There was everything that the tourist could need and or want.

"Let's grab a coffee before we go down there." Jeff turned left down Oak Bluffs Avenue towards downtown Oak Bluffs. When he turned left again onto Circuit Avenue, Charles knew exactly where he was leading him.

"What's with you guys and Mocha Mott's?" Charles laughed.

"Why? What have you got against Mocha Mott's?" Jeff looked at him with a smirk.

"Nothing at all. I quite like it actually. Their cappuccino is amazing." Charles said quite seriously.

"So I don't need to drive you to Starbucks?" Jeff laughed. "Hey, it looks busy bud. You want to wait out here while I just slip in? It will probably be faster that way. Unless you want to come in?"

"No, I'm good. I'll wait. Let me give you some cash." Charles reached into his pocket for his wallet.

"Don't even think about it. You pull out any money and I'll arrest you for trying to bribe a police officer!"

Charles laughed. "Ok. Thanks. One Cappuccino, please."

"You got it. I'll be back in a minute." Jeff turned and disappeared behind the trees that separated Mocha Mott's from Circuit Avenue. The street was bumper-to-bumper with seasonal traffic and the sidewalk was equally busy. Charles did his best to stay

184

in the sidelines but finding a spot to stand still without being in someone's way proved to be a challenge.

Charles thought about what lay in store for him again that day, more of The Monster Shark Fishing Tournament. He wasn't really looking forward to it but he was looking forward to getting some insight into their investigation. Really, they were nowhere. Charles suspected that the next couple of steps would be big ones. They would know in which direction to head when they found out a couple of things. When Laurie came back with some information about the Zito Seafood business and he and Jeff figured out why Joe Zito had been so hell bent on having the Flicka fish in that particular spot, they would be much further ahead. If they didn't have anything concrete soon, they would have to actually sit the Zito brothers down and question them. Looking into the Zito brothers without their knowledge seemed like the best way to go, at least for the time being. If they knew that they were being investigated, they were likely to destroy evidence or at the very least, change their activities. This way, Charles and Laurie would have a better chance of learning what was going on. For now, it was business as usual as far as the Zito family knew.

Jeff came out of Mocha Mott's with two large cappuccinos in paper cups with plastic lids and two paper bags. He handed a cup and a bag to Charles. "What's this?" Charles peered in the bag. He couldn't believe his eyes.

"An apple fritter." Said Jeff. "I love them."

Charles laughed. "Yes, I used to love them too."

21

Charles and Chief Jeffries slowly made their way through the crowd that had collected on the docks. The tournament attracted quite a diverse crowd, thought Charles. Families of all ages were out to witness the spectacle of nightmarish beasts bloodied, dying, and dead right before their very eyes. At least, that's how Charles imagined that they saw it. It was like the witch burnings of Salem or the beheadings at the guillotines of Paris. People wanted to see their monsters up-close and personal in the safety of a controlled environment. More than that, they wanted to see their monsters destroyed. They wanted to feel the strength and security that comes from having the upper hand. They wanted to feel warm in their beds, secure in their imaginations, and in this case - safe on their beaches.

The smells were the same as they had been when Charles was there the other day, the tang of boat gas, the salt water, and fish oil. Not entirely a bad smell. It smelled like vacation. Actually, Charles had always loved the smell of boats. That distinct mixture of gas, water, and wood oil was a very singular smell. It reminded Charles of the cottage in northern Ontario and of being on the dock listening to a cedar strip boat rocking in its slip. Smell was a big memory trigger for most people. More than they usually realised.

Once again, the boat unloading was the Hot Wave. With a rope tied around its tail, the prize shark was hoisted above the dock and pivoted over to the scales. This one was a porbeagle shark. It had always been one of Charles' favourites. It was a beautiful fish with such elegant lines and rich, dark colour. The porbeagle was part of the mackerel shark family; therefore, it resembled the great white shark quite a bit. Like other mackerels, the porbeagle has two dorsal fins; the first is tall and rigid while the second is minute. Its snout is pointed and its gills are gigantic compared to those of other sharks. The tail was large and crescent shaped. All of these characteristics made the mackerel Sharks the fastest sharks in the ocean. Their speed was even more impressive when you considered their exceptional girth. These were big sharks. In fact, because the great white shark was in this clan, Charles was sure that these were the sharks that the general public pictured when they pictured sharks at all. So, it was only fitting, thought Charles that they had been given some of the largest teeth in the ocean. These sharks were predators. Strong swimming, spindle shaped, smooth, and elegant, Charles loved them.

This one was bloodied, jabbed, hooked, and gored. Just like the mako had been when Charles had been there the first time. There was no movement in its gills. This one was dead. Charles couldn't help but imagine it as it once was, swimming gracefully through the sea. Minding its own business. Charles had a terrible habit of anthropomorphising. He was far too sentimental at times. He tried to look at the shark for what it was now. It was just meat. The thought made him gag. He would never, could never, eat a shark.

Charles took a deep breath. He was letting his emotions get the better of him. He needed to stay detached and focused on solving the murders - the murders of the humans, not the sharks.

"We have a 361 pound porbeagle for the vessel, Hot Wave! Let's have a round of applause for the Hot Wave my friends! That's a good catch! Well done! That's an excellent size for a porbeagle by any standard! That's a good eatin' shark!" The crowd responded to Frank Zito's booming announcement with boisterous applause and whistling. Off the dock, past the barricades, each cheer was met with an equivalent boo. The protesters were out in full force.

The same signs were held high above the angry crowd that Charles had seen on his previous visit. "Save Our Sharks", "Killing Sharks Is Killing Our Oceans", "Catch And Release Only", and "The Only JAWS Here Is The One Eating Money" all bobbed up and down in a wave. Charles really wanted that last one on a T-shirt.

"Catch and release only!!" Charles instantly recognised the voice of "Ginger" the redhead girl from

188

the other day. She was easy to spot standing with her tall, tattooed friend, "The Illustrated Man", as Charles had dubbed him.

Charles turned toward Jeff. He had to tap him on the shoulder to get his attention in the crowd. Jeff leaned in. "Do you know those two protesters?" Charles tried to motion inconspicuously toward Ginger and The Illustrated Man.

Jeff watched them for a minute and then shook his head. "I remember them from the other day but outside of this tournament, I've never seen them before. They've gotta be off-islanders. Why?"

"I'm not sure. They seem very intense to me. Focused."

"If you think they're worth checking out, I can get one of my men to look into them. It shouldn't be too hard to find out where they are staying. They don't exactly blend in."

"No but that's almost their saving grace really. It's been my experience that the people who are really worth worrying about are the ones trying to disappear in the crowd." Charles said.

"Agreed but it's not too much of a stretch to think that these murders were committed by an overly zealous protester."

"No. No, it's not."

Jeff watched them for a moment longer before turning away. "I'll have them checked out. It would be worth it to rule them out. I don't like discovering things in hindsight. Let me know if you see anyone else noteworthy."

Charles nodded his head but turned his attention toward the docks once more. The next boat had come in to be a contender for the catch of the day. It wasn't long before Charles could see that it had been a bad day for porbeagles.

The second boat to pull up with its catch was The Green Machine. It, too, had caught a large porbeagle shark. Charles could tell just by looking at it that this fish was larger than the Hot Wave's catch. The Green Machine pulled into its slip. It was indeed green. Charles didn't know enough about boats to know what kind of boat it was but it had a wrap around deck and a centre console. It seemed logical to Charles that such a feature would come in extremely handy for deep-sea fishing. Two men working the tournament helped the crew of the Green Machine tie the rope around the tail of the large porbeagle and start to hoist it over the docks. The shark, like the one before it was shiny, gun barrel grey, and sleek; however, this one was much larger.

"This is an impressive catch for the Green Machine! This should help them make up for missing a catch yesterday." Frank Zito talked into his microphone with a voice that was much more pleasant than his predecessor's. Charles had to give him that at least. He was a good emcee; he just needed to find a better venue.

Once hoisted up in its entirety, the shark was swung over the scales and lowered. Charles watched as one of the men slipped on the wet dock but regained his balance. There seemed to be a lack of any real safety precautions at this tournament. Charles wondered what the insurance was they had to carry.

"411 pounds! That's enormous! Well done, Green Machine! That blows the Hot Wave out of the water – if you'll excuse the pun!" Frank laughed at his own joke and there were some chuckles and groans from the crowd. Frank was smooth. Charles didn't trust him. "These anglers will be hard pressed to beat this *fako!*"

Charles turned to Jeff again. "What does he mean '*fako*'?"

"Local word amongst our fishermen for a porbeagle. It means 'fake-mako'. They get mistaken for makos regularly."

"Oh." Said Charles. He couldn't see himself making that mistake but he could see how someone else might. Actually, a lot of the differences between the two were ones that were not really that obvious either from a distance or on a shark that is fighting for its life in the open ocean. Their teeth were different and their tails were different but Porbeagles did look like fat Makos in a lot of ways. Charles was used to looking at sharks in books where they were still and posed. It was a far cry from watching them in the open water. On the other side of the competition set up, the first Porbeagle was being measured and filleted almost out of sight from the audience. Charles watched briefly as the Massachusetts State Marine Biologists checked reproductive organs, size, age, and anything else they could think of before the carcass was removed and sliced into steaks. Charles watched as the fishermen who had hauled in the shark, disembowelled their catch. It was all in a day's work for a fisherman, he thought.

"Give Captain Lawrence Zerner and his crew a big round of applause ladies and gentlemen! That puts them in first place so far today!" The crowd applauded enthusiastically. Not only were there people filling up the docks but also there were spectators in small rubber dinghies floating around the harbour watching the day's proceedings. They got as close as they could without getting in the way. Each one manned by someone sitting at the stern with his hand on the outboard, ready to shift out of the way at a moment's notice.

The Green Machine captain pushed off and the crew hauled their catch to the sidelines for measuring and cutting. The slip wasn't empty long before the Flicka eased smoothly in. Charles felt his whole body tighten as he focused on Joe Zito's boat. He wished that Laurie were there with him right now. She would want to see this. He wanted her to see this. The more eyes there were watching this crew, the better. They moored expertly and turned to retrieve their haul for the weigh-in. Charles strained his neck to get the best vantage point possible. He needed to know why they had been so adamant on fishing in that spot. The only way he could think to figure it out would be to see their catch. What could Joe Zito and the crew of the Flicka catch in that spot on the ocean that they couldn't catch in any other?

The two men who had been working hauling up the sharks for the contestants began to tie up the tail of the Flicka's shark but then stood and motioned over to another tournament employee. The third man ran over and grabbed the rope on the hoist. The three of them then began to hoist. They pulled with all of their might. The strain was clear in the scrunching of their eyes. It was clear in the baring of their clenched teeth. It wasn't long before Charles could see why.

Joe Zito's team caught the biggest Porbeagle shark that Charles had ever seen. It was difficult to tell if it was longer than the one that the Green Machine had brought in but it was certainly fatter. Porbeagles were quite thick through the middle but this one was just a big shark. There were audible gasps from the audience as it was pulled high over the wooden docks and swung toward the scales. It swayed uneasily with the combination of the swing and its own considerable weight. There was a spray of blood from the shark's mouth as it moved across the stage. It looked like this shark had put up quite a fight. Its mouth was quite bloody. There were several hook and spear marks around its head. Hanging over the scale, the shark did look like the stuff of nightmares. The fish hanging there was the reason for this entire tournament, thought Charles. "Look at what man could conquer!" It screamed. This beast of the depths had been mutilated and killed. It hung now as an omen to all other sharks and beasts that crossed the path of man. Charles was sickened. At that moment, Charles hated this place and everyone involved with the tournament. He needed to leave.

"475 pounds!! I've never seen a Porbeagle shark of this size ladies and gentlemen! This might be one for the record books! Brought in by my own brother! Let's hear it for Joe Zito and the crew of the Flicka!" Frank bellowed with pride at his brother's catch.

The crew of the Flicka stepped out onto the docks and the crowd cheered. Charles watched them all carefully. They were a motley looking crew although he had to concede that after a day at sea, no one looked their best. The one who caught his eye was the woman. She was the woman that he had seen on North Water Street with Frank. Of that, he was sure. Charles already knew that though. He had figured that out when they had crossed paths out at sea. He was struck by the way she seemed to be trying to hide her face. She shrunk back from the crowd. She should be waving like the rest of the crew. Cheering at their accomplishment but instead she looked as if she couldn't wait to get out of there. She looked up briefly into the crowd and her eyes stopped on Chief Jefferies. She seemed to freeze in her tracks. Charles looked at Jeff who had done the same thing. He was motionless. His mouth hung open. He seemed to stare in a combination of disbelief and confusion. It was that look that people in movies had when they were standing outside their trailer in their bathrobe and they saw a U.F.O. Charles looked back toward the docks in time to see the woman scurry off the dock and tear through the crowd. In an instant she was gone. The audience seemed to swallow her whole. She vanished. Chief Jefferies stared at the spot where she disappeared. He still looked dumbfounded.

"Jeff...what the hell was that all about?" Charles stared at his friend and waited for an answer. "Who was that woman?"

194

Jeff didn't respond right away. The time seemed to go on forever before there was a sign that Charles' question had registered at all. Finally, Jeff cleared his throat. He sounded dry when he spoke. "That was Marcie Cunningham."

It took a minute to sink in. *"Jack Burrell's wife?"*

Jeff nodded still staring at the point in the crowd where she had disappeared. "Jack Burrell's wife."

22

Charles and Chief Jeffries walked into Seasons Pub in Oak Bluffs. They had left the fishing tournament in search of something to eat and to try and get Laurie on the phone. Charles had been in Seasons Pub the summer before and it was pretty much as he remembered it except that it was a lot brighter. When he had been in last, it had been evening and quite dark. Too dark for eating supper, he remembered thinking; however, now, with the sun shining in, it was a great place for lunch.

"Anything yet?" Jeff motioned toward Charles' phone as they sat down in an empty booth.

"No." He shook his head. "I'll send her a text. I hate leaving voicemail. Drives me crazy. I don't even know if she checks them or not. It wouldn't surprise me if she didn't. It's not her work phone."

"Who doesn't check their messages?" Jeff looked at him incredulously.

196

"I don't." Charles stated in a matter-of-fact tone.

"You don't check your messages?"

"Nope." Charles shook his head and unconsciously pursed his lips and raised his eyebrows to emphasise his statement.

"Never?" Jeff couldn't believe it.

"Never. If I leave them long enough they clog up my voicemail so people can't leave me any messages anyway."

"Then why do you have voicemail?"

"Good question. I tried to cancel the service but it would have cost me money. I don't understand that at all. Why would it ever cost money not to have a service? Ridiculous."

"Ridiculous is not checking your voicemail! What if it's an emergency?"

"Who would call me in an emergency? Friends? Family? They would all text me or just keep calling. They know that I don't check messages."

"I've never heard of such a thing." Jeff sat back on his bench shaking his head.

"Well, I'm pretty sure that Laurie doesn't check her private messages either. Maybe it's a Toronto thing..." Charles shrugged.

The waitress came over to their table. She was middle aged, redhead, and her nametag read, "Blanche". That made Charles smile. It was such a great waitress name. She began to set down menus but Charles stopped her.

"Do you need a menu Jeff?"

Jeff sat up straight. "Oh! No, I suppose I don't." He looked at the waitress. "Hi Blanche! How are you? How's George?"

"I'm just fine chief. Thanks. George is fine. Business is good, so that keeps him happy. Keeps him out of my hair too, so that keeps *me* happy!" Blanche laughed at her own joke. The two men at the table smiled at her politely. "You boys must be working on that Steve Christie & Bill Cunningham business, are ya? Terrible shame that. Personally, I never had much use for that Bill Cunningham- I don't think too many did frankly. Steve was a good sort though. Always seemed to be there when the community needed someone. Good to have those types around. He'll probably be missed. Anyway, what can I get ya's?" Blanche looked from one to the other waiting to see who was going to go first.

Chief Jeffries spoke up first. "I'll have the banquet burger with fries and a coffee please and thank you Blanche."

"My pleasure chief." She turned and looked at Charles, "and for you Mr Williams?"

Charles was taken aback at this total stranger calling him by name. "Christ," he thought. "This really is a small island."

"Don't look so surprised. You made a hell of an impression last year on my good friend, Edie. You're staying up at her place again this year I think."

Charles' face relaxed once more. "That explains it then." Charles could see it too. Blanche and Edie being friends. They had the same sort of demeanour. Edie was a lot more refined but Charles could see that

198

they probably had the same sense of humour. That was everything in a friendship. "I'll have the same please Blanche except make my coffee a Guinness if you don't mind." He grinned mischievously at Jeff. "I'm not on duty!"

"Sure! Rub it in why don't ya?" Jeff grumbled.

Blanche laughed. "You know chief, I can pour something in that coffee of yours if you like..." She winked at them both.

Jeff laughed. "No thanks Blanche. Nice of you to offer; however, I haven't reached that point yet...I don't think. I don't exactly work Manhattan vice!"

"Ok chief." She grinned. "Two banquets coming up. I'll be right back with your drinks boys." Blanche walked away with a strong stride but without hurrying.

When he was sure that Blanche was out of earshot, Charles leaned into Jeff. He spoke in a low voice. "Are you going to try and call Jack Burrell?"

Jeff shook his head right away. "No. For starters, he's not my cop. What ever happens has to come from Chief Knickles. I can't interfere. Even if he were my cop, I have no idea how to proceed. Technically, we haven't seen Marcie do anything wrong. We haven't even seen the people she's hanging out with do anything wrong. They're a bit shady but if we ran around arresting everyone for being shady, where would it end?" He shrugged with his shoulders and his hands.

"No, I know. I'm not even sure that I would want to notify him anyway." Charles said. He was staring off into nothing like he did whenever he was deep in thought.

"What do you mean?"

"Well, what I mean is maybe we should just see how it plays out. Is Marcie going to pretend like nothing ever happened? Is she going to confess? Maybe Jack already knows what's going on and he's been stringing us along the whole time."

Jeff furrowed his brow. "No way. I don't believe that."

Charles' face was clinical and unemotional. "Why not? You don't even know what you don't believe yet."

Jeff's furrowed brow ran the risk of becoming more of an angry glare. He leaned into Charles and spoke quietly. "Yes I do. You're asking me to entertain the idea that one of our police officers, one who up until now has had an exemplary record, is up to something involved with or connected to the murder of two locals. Isn't that right Charles?" Jeff took a breath but did not back down. "I really like you and consider you a friend and you know I have a great respect for you as an investigator, Charles. When dealing with a fellow officer, before you go asking a bunch of questions that are going to get all of the tongues wagging on this island, I am going to ask you to remember that he is completely innocent until proven one hundred per cent guilty. Okay?"

Charles realised that he had inadvertently touched on a sore spot; more like kicked a sore spot actually. "Of course Jeff. I'm sorry. I didn't mean anything by it. I like Jack Burrell a lot truly and I don't know him as well as you. I'm sure that Laurie feels the same way." The two men were tense and awkward.

"Chief, I think that you really should have a beer with Mr Williams. I saw you from the kitchen; you are way too serious! It's lunch time, lighten up!" Blanche returned with their beverages. "Anyway, I put some extra pickles on the side of your plate. I know that you love them. They're those full sour dills. We get them in from New York. Jar says they're kosher. I don't know why Jews make such good pickles."

Charles picked up a pickle from his plate and inspected it. "Kosher dills are full sour pickles and tend to be crunchy. They are kosher but that just refers to the brining procedure. If the brine is emulsified with polysorbates that are made of animal bi-products, they have to come from cattle slaughtered in accordance with Jewish law. If the polysorbates come from pigs or animals not slaughtered in accordance with Jewish law, the pickles can't be called kosher. Some say that kosher dills have a full more robust flavour to them but really the question of whether or not they are kosher has nothing to do with the flavour. It's just a marketing ploy."

Blanche and Jeff stared at him blankly until they looked at each other and burst out laughing.

"Relax hun!" Blanche said. "It's only a goddamn pickle!" She patted Charles on the shoulder and walked away still chuckling.

"That was awesome." Jeff grinned. "I don't know where you come up with this stuff. It's amazing." He picked up the ketchup and lifting the top bun from his burger, squirted it from the squeezable bottle onto his patty. He then passed it to Charles and reached for the mustard. "Anyway, as I was saying. As soon as Laurie

201

gets back to you, get her to meet us. Then, we'll sort out how to proceed."

"Sounds like a plan." Charles took each condiment in turn as Jeff was finished with them. He was thrilled that Blanche and his pickle tutorial had broken the awkwardness at the table but his mind was still on Jack and his wife, Marcie. How much did anyone really hide from a spouse? Somewhere, spouses always knew what was going on at least to a certain extent. Charles believed that most marriages relied on suspension of disbelief. Husbands and wives, they always knew; they just selected not to know. Charles would talk to Laurie about it privately but eventually, they were going to have to talk to Jack Burrell. Charles picked up his phone from the table and just as he did, a text came through. It was Laurie.

"Where are you?" It read.

23

Once Charles told Laurie where they were, it didn't take her long to come and meet them. Charles was on his second Guinness and Jeff was on his fourth cup of coffee, when Charles motioned out the window at Laurie's cruiser driving slowly through Oak Bluffs. The two men presumed that she was in search of a place to park. She drove out of sight and before long, Laurie walked into the restaurant and spotted them immediately. It was mid-afternoon by this point and the restaurant had emptied out accordingly. They were between the lunch and dinner rushes. There were still a number of people dining, some of whom Laurie nodded to as she walked by but most were out-of-towners and unknowns.

Even though she had been sitting at her desk all day, her uniform looked as fresh as it had early in the day. Charles wondered what fabric had been used to make it. The shirt looked like cotton but maybe it was a little too heavy. The slacks were definitely a polyester blend of some sort. How the police wore them all day without sweating right through them was a mystery indeed, thought Charles. When she got to the table she turned toward the bar and motioned to Blanche. With one hand, she mimed holding a coffee mug while with the other she mimed pouring a pot. Blanche gave her a thumbs-up indicating that her message had been received and Laurie sat down on the bench beside Jeff, across from Charles.

"Gentlemen." She acknowledged, looking from one to the other. "How was lunch?"

"Excellent, actually." Charles said with an exceptionally pleased look on his face. "Jeff ordered the banquet burger and he ordered it with such conviction that I knew it must be a good one so I followed suit. I love a good burger and it didn't disappoint." Charles raised his Guinness in a toast to Jeff and took a deep mouthful of the dark stout.

"Glad you liked it." Jeff raised his coffee cup in mock salute and took a sip. He grimaced at the tepid beverage and put the cup down with distain.

"They do make a good burger here. That's for sure." Laurie looked around the restaurant, smiling. She took a deep satisfying breath. "It smells good in here."

"That warm bread, butter, and cheese smell that most restaurants have." Charles had noted it upon entering.

"Is that what that is?" Jeff shrugged. He tilted his head back and inhaled deeply but his nostrils found no satisfaction. He'd been sitting there too long.

"Exactly!" She grinned. "And garlic! These places always smell like garlic bread with cheese! I think that's how they rope you in off the street."

"It's a good smell." Charles nodded.

Inhaling again, Jeff looked disappointed. "I can't smell it anymore."

Laurie looked up as Blanche came around with a clean cup on a saucer in one hand and a pot of black coffee in the other. The pot was full so Charles surmised that it was probably very fresh.

"Hi chief." Blanche set the cup down in front of Laurie and poured the steaming beverage until it filled her cup. "Chief Jeffries would you like a refill?"

He shook his head. "I think I'm good Blanche maybe a glass of water when you have a minute. I'm going to get the shakes pretty soon." Jeff grinned. "No hurry though."

"You got it." Blanche winked at him before turning to look back at Laurie. "Are you eating, hon? Do you want a menu?"

"No. I'm fine. Thanks, Blanche." Laurie smiled appreciatively.

"Ok. Say, you expecting any more chiefs today? You know what they say, it's never good when the chiefs outnumber the Indians!" Blanche laughed at her own joke again as she walked away. Laurie laughed too but her laugh was an incredulous one. She laughed more at Blanche than with her.

"Was that racist?" Charles laughed when Blanche was out of earshot.

Jeff and Laurie shook their heads, chuckling, and answered in unison. "I'm not sure."

"Did you hear from America regarding the Zitos?" Jeff asked Laurie.

Charles grinned bemusedly at the term 'America' being used for the mainland. Islanders were so detached. He thought it was great.

"I did actually. I'm not sure if I found out anything or not." She looked pointedly at Charles. "You're not going to like this."

Charles' head jerked back. "Okay," was all he said.

"The Zitos operate a seafood market. We all know that and for the most part, it seems that the family and the market are both on the up and up. They're not exactly seen as pillars of the community but the cops don't have them on their shit list either. There are some parking violations, some drunk and disorderly charges that were dropped, even one or two minor health code violations but I gotta figure that every seafood market hits one of those now and again. They were corrected immediately so they don't hardly count. The only thing that is a little shady maybe is that their market sells shark fins to Chinese restaurants in the city, five of them to be exact. Now, that's not illegal-"

"It should be." Charles interjected.

"I agree, it should be but it's not." Laurie tried to continue.

"So, why is it shady then?" Asked Jeff.

"Let me finish!" Laurie glared at them both. "Jesus, you guys!"

"Sorry, go on." They said in unison.

"What's suspect is that no one seems to know exactly where they are getting their shark fins *from*." Laurie put the emphasis on 'from' indicating to Jeff and Charles that there was more to the story and that was the key. "Selling shark fins in Massachusetts is not illegal but shark-finning is."

"So?" Jeff asked.

"You think they are shark-finning while they're out fishing for the contest?" Charles' tone was one of mild disbelief. This hadn't occurred to him. A lot of things had run through his mind over the course of the last couple of days but shark finning hadn't been one of them. "How do you suppose they are doing this undetected?"

Laurie shook her head. "I have no idea. I'm not even saying that they are shark-finning but it's a possibility." She paused and took a mouthful of coffee. "There's a lot of money involved in shark fins."

Jeff balked. "Enough to make it worth killing for though?"

"It's a billion dollar industry in the states alone." Laurie stated. "I checked and the Boston markets, Zito Seafood included, sell shark fins for about five hundred dollars a pound, I'm sad to say."

"Jesus!" Said Jeff. "I had no idea."

"Me either. Now, all of the other markets that I checked have a record of getting their fins from Asian distributers. The Zitos do not. If they were supplying their own fins, that would certainly increase their profits, probably by about double I'd bet. Getting $500 per pound over $250 would well be worth a good season. Let's say they were able to bring in five hundred pounds of fins. That would be a quarter of a million bucks. I'm sure that five hundred pounds is a conservative estimate too. How many sharks would that be Charles?" Laurie noticed for the first time since she had started on the subject that Charles didn't look so hot. He looked peaked. "Charles?"

"I'm okay." Charles rolled his eyes. "Sharks kill five people a year and for that, they are labelled "*Monster Sharks*"! Seventy million sharks are killed annually for their fins. I can't comprehend that level of stupidity. Commerce over environment every time."

"It's shitty, we get it but you can't let that be your focus here. Until it's illegal, we will be focusing on the murdering of human beings. Is that alright with you?" Laurie's sarcasm made it perfectly clear that her patience for his soapbox was wearing thin.

Charles took a sip of his Guinness and looked at his friends. "Of course...I'm just sayin'..." He grinned to reassure them that he was fine. He grinned partially to reassure himself too. He took a heartier mouthful of Guinness and then swallowed quickly. His eyes widened. "The Flicka!" Charles exclaimed when his mouth had cleared.

"Yes?" Laurie asked. "What about it?"

"The Flicka?" Jeff turned to look at Charles and could tell he was bursting.

"When I went out with Keith! The Flicka was sitting extremely low, unhealthily low in the water."

"Yes? I'm not getting it." Laurie stated.

"There was blood all over the stern! It was filthy." Charles continued. "What if The Flicka had been arranging a pick up/drop off of fins? What if it was full of fins at the time? Their haul could have been what was weighing them down. That would explain why they needed that spot. They had arranged to meet someone at those co-ordinates! What else could it be?"

Jeff and Laurie looked at each other and then back at Charles. He continued.

"I really don't think that they are doing the finning themselves, not the Vito brothers anyway, it's too risky and time consuming; however, they could have people working for them and they collect a haul at a certain time and place."

Laurie nodded as Charles paused. "I'll buy that but it still doesn't explain why they needed to murder Steve Christie and then Bill Cunningham. That doesn't fit at all yet. There's nothing to tie any of this to the murders. The Zitos are entered into the contest on the Flicka which is presumably the boat being used to collect all of these contraband fins but it would be a stretch to even call that circumstantial evidence!"

Charles nodded in frustrated agreement. "It's true." Charles kept thinking. "Well, at the very least, can we have the Flicka put under surveillance? From a distance would be best. Can we try and catch them connecting with another vessel?"

"Absolutely. I can put Jack on it right away." Laurie stated confidently.

Charles and Jeff looked at each other warily. "Oh crap." Charles said. "I forgot."

"So did I." Said Jeff. "We're going to have to put someone else on that detail at least for the time being."

"What? Why? What's going on?" She glanced back and forth but focussed on Chief Jeffries. "I'm not going to like this, am I?"

"I'm not jumping to any conclusions yet but the fact of the matter is that Charles and I saw Marcie on the Flicka this afternoon."

"What? Aw shit. Why are you doing this to me? Aw shit." Laurie grimaced. "You're sure Jeff?"

"Absolutely." He nodded guiltily.

"She's also the woman that Keith and I saw out on the water when we ran into the Flicka and the woman I saw in Edgartown on North Water Street with Frank Zito."

Laurie sat and said nothing for quite a while. She stared at her coffee cup and saucer but did not see it. Her brow was furrowed and her face slightly flushed. It was impossible to tell whether her cheeks were red from stress or just too much coffee. Her breathing was calm.

Charles sipped his pint. He tried to focus on the goings on outside the window, the tourists shopping on Circuit Avenue but Laurie kept drawing him back into the restaurant. Jeff drank his water and crunched on ice cubes. He fidgeted with his glass. None of them spoke while Chief Knickles absorbed this new information. Eventually, she cleared her throat and lifted her head into the sunbeams that were making their way through the window. The sun was lowering in the afternoon sky.

"Jeff, do you have someone who could keep an eye on the Flicka for us?" Her voice was quiet and so delicate that both men found it more than a little unsettling. The way freshly blown glass is, you daren't breathe in its presence. You knew it could shatter at any moment. Explode into tiny little shards.

"Yes ma'am." He nodded. "Sergeant Peter Barton is a good man. He could take care of that for us. Don't you think?"

"I do. Thank you." Laurie slid out of her place at the booth. When she stood, she turned to look at Charles. He could see little beads of sweat across her forehead. Her lips were tight. "I'm going to get the car. Meet me out front."

Charles nodded. "Alright. Where are we going?"

"*I want to speak to Sergeant Jack Burrell.*"

Charles winced. He was sure that he had just heard the shattering of blown glass.

24

Laurie stormed out of the restaurant with Charles trailing behind her. She pushed through the front door leaving it to slam back in Charles' face with a force for which he was unprepared. With both hands he braced the door before it hit him. Charles winced as he half-expected the glass in the window to shatter. "Hey!" He stammered.

Laurie looked back briefly but did not lose her stride. "I don't know if you should come with me right now, Charles."

"That's *exactly* why I *should* come with you!" Charles pushed his way out of the restaurant door in a much calmer fashion than his partner had. He found bad tempers irritating and was always annoyed and disappointed in the people around him when they displayed such behaviour.

"What the hell is that supposed to mean?" She snipped.

"I don't want you to say anything that you will have to apologise for later. Don't get in that car!" Charles' heavy lunch and several pints were telling him to slow down or he'd regret it.

"You're not my damned shrink. I was doing just fine here as the police chief long before I had the benefit of your infinite wisdom and psychobabble. *Thank you very much!*"

Against his better judgement, Charles ran until he caught up with her. He reached her just in time to force his body between her and the driver's side door of her police cruiser. He tried to grab the keys from her outstretched hand but she was too fast for him. Instead, he grabbed her by the shoulders gently but firmly. "Don't get in this car yet." He stared at her with both eyes.

"You're pissing me off." Laurie huffed.

"You were already pissed off. I had nothing to do with it."

"Well, you're not helping."

"I disagree." He said calmly. Charles continued to stare at her without flinching. His green eyes locked directly into her blue ones. They were both breathing heavily, more from the stress and anxiety of the situation than the physical demand of the near run to the car. They were both in very good shape. Their stand-off continued for what seemed like an eternity but in reality could not have been longer than two or three minutes. "Look, you can still go after Jack and you should. I just want you to calm down and organise your thoughts first. That's all. Sitting in this car is not going to do anything to deplete your energy."

Laurie glared at him and then expelled a deep breath. She broke her gaze and looked over his shoulder. Her shoulders dropped and her posture weakened. Charles let go. "What did you have in mind?"

"Let's go for a walk in the campground. It's pretty, it's handy, and we can talk this over before we find Jack." He watched her face. He could tell that she thought it was a good idea but she didn't want to come out and say it. He smiled at her. "Fifteen minutes- that's all I'm asking."

Laurie looked at him. He was smiling from his eyebrows to his chin. His eyes were twinkling. She tried not to smile back but was not entirely successful. "Fine."

"You're acquiescing to my request?" Charles' grin broadened even further.

"Oh, shut up." She walked ahead of him just far enough that he couldn't see her own grin.

*　　*　　*

The Martha's Vineyard Camp Meeting Association or Wesleyan Grove was first organised in 1835. It amazed Charles that it had been around since before the American Civil War. The history on the island was astonishing. The campground had started as a religious organization where churches from the mainland would come and pitch large 'society tents', each tent holding the congregation of a visiting parish. By the end of the civil war, in 1865, the organisation had become largely Methodist. There had been all-day
214

religious services day in and day out. It was still a religious organisation although now, with the tabernacle standing as the epicentre of the campgrounds goings-on, the services are more ecumenical in flavour.

The end of the civil war also marked the removal of the societal tents and the construction of the first of the permanent, ornate and colourful, gingerbread cottages. The area was famous for them. There had been about five hundred cottages and about three hundred of those remain. They were small for the most part. Brightly painted, wooden structures of blue, pink, yellow, purple, and green all stood in rows with very little real estate between or in front of them. Most of them were adorned with small porches just big enough for two porch rockers. The gables, windows, and eaves were all invariably trimmed with white 'gingerbread'. Elaborate wooden carvings painted white and attached to the trim of every cottage. Charles found them charming and he was certainly not alone. The cottages had made their way onto thousands of postcards celebrating Martha's Vineyard. They were so unlike the rest of the island. All of the other homes were so uniform with their sea-weathered, grey shingles, white trim, and pastel hydrangeas. The rest of the island was so simple and pure. Yet, if you turned the right way in Oak Bluffs, you stumbled into this magical campground that was quite unlike anything else. It was certainly unlike anything else Charles had ever experienced. Even the tiny size of the cottages made the whole thing very surreal. Charles thought that he could quite easily slip an entire cottage into his townhouse in Toronto. Most of the cottages were only a floor and a half in height and they couldn't be more than fifteen feet across on the outside. They were so delicate they were almost impossible. Yet here they were, all of them standing around the Martha's Vineyard Campground Tabernacle. By comparison, the tabernacle was quite large. Charles had read that it had been renovated and upgraded several times over the one hundred and fifty years that it had been standing. That wasn't really too surprising at least not to Charles. It seemed to him that religious groups were always raising money to renovate their places of worship. This one seated four thousand people at present. Charles could not recall how many people it had housed at its inception but he'd bet a pay cheque that it hadn't been four thousand.

Charles and Laurie walked in silence down the narrow pathways lined with the gingerbread cottages. The trees towered over them and filtered the sunlight into a flecked and fluid pattern. Persistent rays of sunshine forced their way through the leaves and danced on the faces of the cottages and pedestrians alike only to disappear again in an instant. It reminded Charles of the sun sparkling on the sea. Unfiltered, on the ocean it was the unending motion of the water that made the sun dance. Inland, it was the motion of all other living things that gave the illusion of rhythm and spirit on the solid ground. If you stood still and watched long enough, no matter where you were, thought Charles, the magic of nature would find a way. He looked at Laurie. Her face had relaxed. She looked the cottages over and watched the vacationing children run in and out of the screen doors. The doors smacking shut behind them. It was such a summer sound. The expression on Laurie's face betrayed the fact that she could feel the magic of this place too. He could tell. It had calmed her as he had sincerely hoped it would.

"I love it here." Charles said.

"What's not to love?" Her voice was soft. Her smile was delicate and fine. "It doesn't seem possible, this place." She looked around, walked backward for a few steps, and turned back around.

Charles thought for a brief moment that she looked just like the little girl he had known growing up. He could almost see the barrettes, the pink halter-top, the matching terry shorts, and the scuffed running shoes.

"You knew what you were doing bringing me in here, my friend." She didn't look at him but rather kept watching the neighbourhood kids. "Freaks me out sometimes how well you know me."

Charles liked that but he also knew exactly how she felt. Having an old friend was like knowing the great and powerful Oz. No matter what you said or did, they always knew what was going on behind the green curtain. "Heads and tails of the very same coin."

She looked at him then. "Indeed."

"So, where do we go from here? What do we know and what do we need to know?"

She sighed and looked around at the sweeping trees and the delicate cottages. It was like a fairy tale, Hansel and Gretel maybe. "That's the problem with

217

coming into a place like this, you never want to leave." Laurie nodded her head in thought. "You're right though. Let's start walking back." She turned on her heel and Charles followed suit. After a few steps, she spoke again. "I want to speak to Jeff now. I'm glad that we took a moment. I'm still angry but I'm angrier at the situation than I am at him. That's probably a better focus anyway. I'll get more accomplished that way. But what the hell was his wife doing with the Zitos?"

"When I saw Marcie and Frank Zito together on North Water Street, they certainly struck me as a couple. It's a distinct possibility that Jack doesn't even know that there is a relationship there at all. You might be blowing his marriage apart with this little morsel of information."

"Oh shit! I didn't think of that!" Laurie looked stricken.

"Well, it's the most likely scenario wouldn't you think? I don't believe that Jack could be dishonest if he tried. I don't know the man that well but I just don't think that he has it in him." Stated Charles in a matter-of-fact tone.

"Agreed."

"Furthermore, if I know anything about him at all, it's that his job and your approval mean everything to him. He's been a little odd lately and a little awkward but doing a good job is still all he talks about. I can't see him consciously doing anything that would put that at risk. It just doesn't make sense to me."

"Well, all of this speculation is useless. Let's go and find him and sit him down for a delicately worded talk. I'm more worried about him than anything else... the stupid little shit." Laurie stopped in front of the driver's door of her police cruiser. She pressed the button on the automatic opener on her keychain. It beeped, the car beeped, and she slipped inside.

Charles laughed, "nice." He opened his door and sat down on the passenger seat. It was warm from being out in the afternoon sun. Charles remembered getting in this car for the first time the previous summer. It had been at State Beach. Out of curiosity, Charles had stepped off the bus at the crime scene Laurie had been investigating. That young boy had bumped into the half-eaten corpse of Karl Bass while jumping off the JAWS Bridge. That had been the beginning of what Charles now called 'The JAWSfest Murders'. He still thought it would make a great book. He looked at Laurie as she put the car in drive and pulled out into the summer traffic. "So where do you want to start?"

"I think the only place to start is the Burrell house. If he's not there, we'll head to the police station and see what's what." Laurie looked pensive for a minute. "Actually..." she reached down to the police radio and called the desk sergeant. "This is Chief Knickles, do you have a 10-20 on Sergeant Burrell?"

"Last I heard chief, he was at the Christie house." The voice of the desk sergeant crackled over the two-way radio.

"The Christie house? What the hell for? Did he say?"

"No chief. I'm sorry. He didn't. Do you want me to call him?"

"No I don't. In fact, I want you to keep this conversation to yourself until further notice. Understood?"

"10-4 chief."

"Thank you. Chief out." Laurie hung up the radio and glanced at Charles briefly before returned her gaze to the road. "Change of plan. We're going to the Christie house."

Charles nodded. "Alright, the Christie house it is."

25

Laurie and Charles pulled into the drive of the Christie house at Edgartown West Tisbury Road and Main St to find it much as they had left it. White cedar, black shutters, gabled windows and manicured lawn, a pristine setting for the bloated rotten corpse floating in the pool out back. Charles knew that the pool had been drained and the corpse long shipped out but in his head, it was all back there. It would always be there, waiting. Those images made the otherwise inviting presentation of the house seem threatening. That sickly sweet smell of death mixed with the chemical smell of the pool was still firmly asserted inside Charles' nose. He doubted that it would ever leave completely. Even the pale blue hydrangeas could not convince him with their alluring beauty. To Charles, they hung like bait.

There was no car in the drive. If Jack had been here, it seemed to Charles that he was long gone. He tried to strain his neck to look for signs of life in the house. "I don't see anyone."

"No, me either. Let's take a look though. Maybe we can see why he was here in the first place. Our team should have been long finished with this place." Laurie strained her neck looking around the property. "Even if Jack isn't here, there should be a guard here of some sort." Laurie got out of the car and gently closed her door behind her. Charles followed suit. He wondered if she had not wanted to alert anyone inside of her arrival. If someone had been alerted, there was no sign. In fact, there was still no sign that there was anyone to be alerted. Everything was still. There wasn't even a wind, not a trickle. The air held the stagnancy of a long sealed mausoleum, not the life flow of an open field or the freshness of a spring forest but the malodorous calm of mould and rot. With each blink, Charles saw the pool out back as it had been the day that they had discovered the dismembered Steve Christie floating in it. He shook his head violently as if that would jar the images from him. It helped a little.

"Are you alright?" Laurie looked at him with concern.

Charles nodded. "I'm fine." He looked a little sheepish. "I am having a surprisingly difficult time with the memories in this house. I'm not sure why."

"Well, get a grip." Laurie smiled at him.

"Don't worry, I'm good."

"I'm not worried."

Over the doorknob hung a lockbox. Laurie entered the combination, removed the keys, and opened the front door. With a push, it swung open easily. She stepped into the dim calm of the front hall.

As Charles approached the threshold, an overwhelming sense of foreboding told him not to go in. A dread. He felt scared and stupid all at the same time. There was no body, there was no one at all. Even if there was a body, there was nothing to be afraid of but nonetheless, Charles could feel the hairs on his arms stand up. There was gooseflesh on his neck. In disgust, he took a deep breath, walked inside, and closed the door behind him.

Laurie hadn't moved that far in. She was in the living room. Charles had spent quite a bit of time in the living room when they had been here before. Laurie was at the desk. She picked up the papers that were still there from the day before. They had all been photographed, bagged, and catalogued by the police. Charles turned toward the kitchen but before he had left the room Laurie called to him.

"Charles, look at this!" She exclaimed.

He walked back toward her and stood in front of the desk beside her. The light was good here, best in the room. The late afternoon sun shone indirectly in the large front window. They hadn't turned on the lights for there had been no need. "What?"

"Remember when I said that Boston P.D. told me that Zito Fish Market sold shark fins to five Chinese restaurants in the Boston area?"

He nodded. "Yes. You said that there was no documentation on the Zitos receiving the fins just delivering them." Charles peered over her shoulder to see what she had in her hands.

"Right!" She turned to face him. *"These are the restaurants!!"* Laurie held up the police bag of brochures that Charles had discovered the last time they had been at the Christie house. "I don't know why it didn't occur to me before now. I was distracted by everything else that was going on I guess but these are definitely them: Pink Pagoda, China Pearl, Chang Lee's, House of the Orient, and Hong Kong Cuisine. I remember the name *Pink Pagoda* in particular. What the hell is a *Pink Pagoda* anyway?"

"It's a multi-tiered tower. They're common in Oriental architecture. You know those buildings that you always see in Chinese restaurants that have roof on top of roof on top of roof each smaller than the one under it?"

"Yes." Laurie nodded, interested.

"That's a pagoda."

"Oh." She looked back at the menus. "Oh look there's one on their menu...and it's pink!"

"Of course it is. Anyway, why does Steve Christie have the menus for the same restaurants where the Zitos are selling possibly illegal shark fins?"

"I don't know but that proves that this is the connection to the whole crap shoot. Don't you think? If Christie knew about illegal shark fins and about the money involved in selling to these restaurants, he just might have wound up dead because of it." Laurie looked around on the desk. "Didn't he write all of the names down on a pad somewhere? You did your little etch-a-sketch trick and recovered the list remember?"

Charles was deep in thought. "If he was approached and refused to have any part of a scheme,

224

they would have to remove him from the contest before they were removed themselves; however, it still doesn't tell us why they needed to be in the contest at all."

"No...no it doesn't. It doesn't tell us why Bill Cunningham was killed either." Laurie pursed her lips and furrowed her brow. "It does give us enough suspicion to talk to the Zitos though. Maybe even put them in dry dock. At least long enough to remove them from the contest."

"Laurie? Can you do that?"

"I can do anything; I'm the chief of police." She looked at him mischievously.

Charles grinned. "Nice one." How could he not love a girl who could quote JAWS to him?

"Come on, I want to see the backyard." Laurie put the menus back on top of the pile of papers and they walked through to the kitchen. The kitchen table was clear except for one pad of paper. The house was darker toward the back. There wasn't as much light at this time of day and generally speaking the windows were smaller. The only good-sized window was over the kitchen sink and the one in the back door wasn't bad but they were the biggest in the room. Laurie took the handle in her hand and twisted it. Pulling it in, she opened the door and the room lit up a little more.

"This is that pad of paper with the list on it." Charles said. He motioned toward the pad on the kitchen table. "What's it doing in here?"

"That doesn't make any sense." Laurie turned back into the room and looked at the pad.

Charles reached into his pocket and pulled out his iPhone. He took a photograph of the pad on the table.

"Thank you." Laurie said. "Don't touch it. I'm going to dust it for prints once more. You never know. I'll have to get my bag from the car."

"You still want to see the backyard again?" Asked Charles.

She nodded.

They walked out along the path toward the pool. There wasn't much to see.

"Did they empty- *damn it!!*" Charles tripped on a patio stone and lunged forward. Nearly landing on Laurie. *"Jesus H Christ! I did that last time too!"*

"What is with you and this house? I've never seen you so jumpy."

"I'm not jumpy!" Charles was pissed off mostly for making himself look like an idiot...again. "I'm just clumsy, apparently."

"Apparently." Laurie agreed before turning back toward the pool.

Regaining his composure, Charles walked out to the pool behind her. It was empty. What's more, he noticed that it still smelled quite strong if he got close enough.

Laurie stood still and just took it all in. Charles watched her and then did a complete turn, taking in the entire backyard as he did. There was nothing to see. To Charles, at least, it would seem that the police had done a good job with the clean up. "Anything?" He asked.

Laurie shook her head. "No. Let's go back in. I'll dust that pad and we'll go over to the Burrell house and see if anyone's home."

"Ok." Charles led the way back in. This time minding where he stepped, he followed the stone path to the back door and opened it. Charles walked into the kitchen and just inside, stopped dead in his tracks.

"Charles let me in!" Laurie punched him lightly on the lower back. He stepped aside for her. "What's the matter with you?" Laurie walked in and followed Charles' gaze. The pad was no longer on the kitchen table. Charles pointed at the kitchen closet. The door was wide open. It had been closed when they were in there five minutes ago. Laurie looked at Charles. She took her weapon out of its holster. "Stay behind me. We're heading toward the front door."

Charles nodded but said nothing.

With purposeful steps, they made their way out into the living room. It was empty. Charles pointed at the desk almost immediately. The desk had been cleared of all bagged paperwork including the pamphlets to the Chinese restaurants. The front door was wide open. Charles looked at Laurie, "I closed that door behind me. I heard the latch click."

"Get in the car now."

26

Charles sat in the car waiting for Laurie to come out of the house. He wasn't sure what she was doing exactly but he assumed that she was doing a complete sweep and wanted him safely outside. He had to admit that he was more than happy with that. It was a very creepy feeling knowing that someone had been in the house watching and listening to everything they had said and done. He tried to think if they had said anything in particular that they would not want anyone else to know, official or otherwise. He couldn't think of anything. Charles had not wanted to go into the house from the get go. Now he knew why. He firmly believed that people should always listen to their first instinct. He believed it was the human survival instinct. Leftover from a thousand years ago when people actually did need it to survive. Every once in a while, it still reared its head and people should always heed its warning. It indicated that there was something important going on of which they should be well aware but weren't. It told them that they weren't paying attention. Some people were blindly unaware of its existence at all. Charles wasn't sure why that was. What type of person was less in tune with himself than another? He was sure that some scholar had studied this in minute detail. It was just the sort of thing that academia loved to focus on. He made a mental note to look that up later. For now, Charles sat in the passenger seat of the squad car and thought about what had just happened. He was a little disgusted with himself. This time it had been him who hadn't been aware. Charles hadn't been paying attention. Had the closet in the kitchen really been closed all the way or had it been open a crack to give the intruder a slivered look at what Charles and Laurie were doing? Had the intruder been in the closet since they drove up or had he stealthily made his way into his hiding spot while they were still in the house? More importantly, Charles thought, who was the intruder? In a way, he thought that the goings on inside probably cleared Sergeant Jack Burrell of any wrong doings. Certainly made him less of a person of interest anyway. A police officer wouldn't have bothered to steal the physical evidence from the crime scene. A police officer would know full well that everything had been documented unless of course the photos ended up disappearing or sabotaged in some way back at the station. As long as they were intact, things looked pretty good for Jack. That made Charles happy. He liked Jack a lot.

Laurie came out of the house with a solid stride and a serious face. She walked across the lawn and pulled her door open on the cruiser. "There's nobody in there now." She said as she slid into her seat.

"Any thoughts about what is going on?" Charles asked.

"Not a god damned clue." She tapped her fingers on the steering wheel. "You?"

"Not exactly." Charles said.

"What does not exactly mean?" Laurie said a little too sharply.

"Well, not exactly do I have an idea what's going on but rather I think it gives us an idea about what's not going on. I think that it's obviously not the work of a police officer." Charles thought that this news might lighten Laurie's mood.

She stared out the window for a moment as she took this information in. "That's true. A cop would know that this was a waste of time. I'm going to need to confirm that all of the photographic evidence is present and accounted for at the station."

"Exactly what I thought." Charles was pleased that she had followed his line of thinking.

"Well that's something at least." Laurie's face didn't lighten. She continued to stare out the front window... seeing nothing except what was happening in her head. "I'd really like to know why there was no guard on the house. That's what I'd like to know. I called the station; someone's coming right over. We're going to sit here until they arrive."

"That sounds fair." Charles adjusted in his seat as if he needed to get more comfortable if they were going to be there a while; however, the second cruiser showed up almost immediately.

230

As soon as it did, Laurie leapt out of the car. "Stay here." She said.

Charles watched in the rear-view mirror as Laurie interrogated the sergeant in the driver's seat of the other cruiser. He couldn't hear what was being said. At least, he couldn't hear actual words. He could hear Laurie barking noises that were a hybrid of the adults from Charlie Brown cartoons and a Doberman Pincer. It was an unpleasant sound. When he had heard enough, Charles reached down and turned on the radio. MVY Radio was playing The Animals' "Don't Let Me Be Misunderstood". He turned it up. It was probably his favourite song of all time. Charles was a big Eric Burdon fan. He sat and he thought.

What did they know for sure? Two people had been murdered in correlation to the Monster Shark Fishing Tournament. They had been killed to get Frank Zito in position as the emcee and co-ordinator of the whole show. Frank's brother, Joe, was up to something out on the high seas with, amongst others, Sergeant Jack Burrell's wife, Marcie, in tow. Marcie also happened to be the daughter of one of the deceased, Bill Cunningham. That was what they knew. Somehow, all of this tied into the fact that the Zito brothers were illegally catching and/or possibly smuggling shark fins into America to be sold at their fish market. That was what Charles and Laurie needed to know. If you had hundreds of pounds of shark fins that you needed to sneak onto the mainland and into your markets, how would you do it? More to the point, how would you use a fishing tournament to do it?

Movement in the rear-view mirror caught Charles' eye and he refocused on what was going on behind him. The second squad car started to reverse and Laurie began walking back to her own squad car. Charles straightened in his seat and turned the radio down but not off.

"Alright." Laurie slipped into her seat and put her key in the ignition. The engine turned over smoothly. "Apparently, there was a schedule misunderstanding. Everyone agrees that there should have been someone on duty but no one agrees on which someone that should have been exactly. I'll never get to the bottom of it and I'll just drive myself crazy trying. All I can do is make everyone's life miserable for the next couple of weeks to make sure it doesn't happens again." As soon as the other cruiser had cleared the drive, Laurie backed up and turned first onto Edgartown West Tisbury Road and then sharply onto Main Street. In the rear-view mirror, Charles watched the second cruiser pull back into the Christie's drive.

"Where are we going?" Charles asked.

"To go see Jeff about heading out to sea again."

"Oh." Charles visibly shrunk. "Great."

27

The Great White shark swam through the shallow water with an inhibition and air that only comes naturally to a creature that knows no predators. An animal that has never known threat. Her black eyes seemed to simultaneously have no distraction and no focus. All they had was black. Her mouth was open and water flowed smoothly in and through her gills. She wasn't very close to shore but the water was shallow here a long way out. She had eaten two sharks yesterday but she was still hungry. All of the blood in the water kept her appetite revving. Her instinct was to eat when the eating was good and to eat well. The sharks she had eaten had been bleeding and sinking. Not dead but well on their way. Their mouths gulped for water as they sank toward the bottom. She had slipped underneath them and they had slid into her gullet. The first one hadn't actually slipped. She had torn through it, missing pieces as she did. Bits floating away for scavengers to eat in her wake; however, the other had slid right down. Neither of her prey had been a large shark by any means but she was just so big. There had been entrails as well. Innards floated in the sea. Stomachs, intestines, livers- all suspended flotsam waiting for her to take in easy gulps as she swam along. This was not normal even she knew that. She took it hungrily.

All of the blood in this part of the ocean made it difficult to hone in on anything with too much accuracy but there was one spot she could sense, not too far away, that seemed to be particularly thick with blood and fish oil. She could feel the thrashing of distress from other fish. Her crescent tail swept harder and her nose shifted down. Her pectorals pulled back and she became a torpedo firing through the water. All of the other sea life gave her a wide berth. She could feel that urgency in her stomach. It was all consuming. In reflex, her mouth gave a bite at the empty sea. The fact that she found no satisfaction only heightened her desire. She felt a primal lust prickle down her back. The skin around her mouth retracted briefly. Her jaw extended. Her triangular serrated teeth flashed and then disappeared. She was the creature from which nightmares were made. She was just a fish. When she got like this and instinct took over though, she became more than that. She became death. Black finned, white bellied, and beautiful.

28

The Oak Bluffs police station was alive like a beehive in a bush fire. Laurie and Charles walked in and were almost bowled over by a worker bee that had no time for pleasantries. They pressed their bodies against the wall just in time to let him race by. Exchanging incredulous glances, they made their way toward the desk and asked the desk sergeant if he knew where Chief Jeffries was. Without looking up, the sergeant replied, "He's in his office... You're gonna have to wait."

Laurie scowled. "Sergeant, is this how you always greet people who come in here requiring the service of the Oak Bluffs police department?"

Frazzled, the sergeant looked up and opened his mouth to speak. Whatever shovel full of words he had been compiling, he caught just before they were heaved out, burying him in a hole from which he would have found very difficult to climb out. "Chief Knickles!"

"Your deductive powers do you credit. Really, it's like watching Sherlock Holmes at work." Laurie took a deep breath. "Sergeant, what the hell is going on in here? This place is jumping like a virgin at a hillbilly family reunion! And where the Christ is Chief Jeffries?"

"The sergeant reddened. "Yes ma'am. Ma'am, Chief Jeffries is in his office, I just put a call through to him and he picked it up. There is a lot going on and I think it would be better coming from the chief if it's all the same to you."

"That's fine. Thank you. Sergeant, I realise you are busy but let's not lose sight of the reason that we're really here. All right? You wouldn't want to find yourself spending the summer directing traffic at five corners would you?"

"Yes ma'am. I mean no ma'am." The sergeant looked truly confused and more than a little frightened at the validity of Laurie's threat. "Sorry ma'am."

"No sweat." Laurie turned to Charles and spoke with her back to the sergeant but still at a more than audible level. "Do you want to come back with me or wait here with the traffic cop?" Laurie winked at Charles.

Charles watched as the still red sergeant ran his hands worryingly through his sweaty hair. "No, I'll come with you."

"I thought as much." Laurie led the way down the white corridor.

When they were out of earshot, Charles looked at Laurie. "*A virgin at a hillbilly family reunion*? Where the hell did you get that little gem?"

"Oh shut up." Laurie grinned.

"There. That's more like the clever repartee that I'm used to coming from you." Charles chortled. "...and Sherlock Holmes? Jeezus..."

"Would you shut up?"

"What are you going to do? Put me on traffic duty?"

"I can do much worse than that. You don't work for me. You're a friend- I can kick you 'til you're dead. What's more, anyone who knows you wouldn't blame me a bit."

"Nice." Charles rolled his eyes.

Halfway down the hall, Laurie stopped and knocked on a closed door.

"Come in!" Charles recognised the bark as Jeff's.

Laurie reached for the doorknob, twisted it, and opened the door.

"Oh hey you guys! Come on in." Jeff was on the phone. "I won't be a minute. Sit down." Jeff motioned to the two office chairs that faced his desk. Jeff's desk, noted Charles was exactly the same as Laurie's. He imagined that all of the police furniture on the island was the same. Some a little older and some a little newer but there was probably standard issue on these things. Charles wondered if it was state wide or just local. Not that it mattered he just found it interesting.

Charles tried not to listen to Jeff's conversation but it was impossible not to overhear. He politely looked around the office pretending to find the generic art on the walls interesting, paintings of Martha's Vineyard lighthouses and one of the ferry docking at Oak Bluffs ferry terminal; however, Jeff's voice was loud and he had asked them to sit down. How private could the conversation be? The WASP in Charles told him that the conversation was none of his business and good manners dictated that he should at least act like he didn't hear a word. Phrases like, "Where are they now?" and "Just get out there and tow them in. Take McBride with you." Settled in Charles' brain although they meant nothing to him. When Jeff hung up the phone, Charles turned his focus to the two chiefs. He got the impression that Laurie had not tried to detach herself from the conversation but quite the opposite. She had been trying to figure it out.

"Who was that?" She asked almost immediately.

"Bill Randolph." Jeff stretched back in his chair. He pressed his arms up and arched his back in that way a man does who's been sitting in a chair for far too long. "He and Tom McBride are heading out to rescue a fishing boat that ran out of gas and then bring a bunch of kids who are day sailing back to port. Seems nobody had any parental permission and there are minors involved, so now we are too. Honestly..."

"Damn." Laurie said.

"What?" Jeff didn't understand.

"I think we were hoping to commandeer one of your boats, Jeff." Charles said.

"I still have one boat."

Laurie shook her head. "I'm not going to leave you with no boats."

"What's wrong with your boats?" Asked Jeff.

238

"Yours are much closer to where I want to go. I want to bring in the Zitos."

"On what charge?"

"Well, we don't have a charge yet but we certainly have enough to question them. At least to bring them in on suspicion of importing and selling illegal goods." Laurie's lips smacked like she had just bitten into a rotten salmon. Charles could tell that she didn't like the way the words sounded coming out of her mouth.

"Laurie, if they are connected to the murders, that will only alert them and send them back to Boston. Then we're screwed."

"What do you suggest?" Laurie snapped at him. "We have nothing else to go on. Nothing. This goddamned tournament is over tomorrow and they'll be leaving anyway. If we bring them in for questioning, we might be able to tell them not to go anywhere for a couple of days. That would give us a little bit of time." She stopped herself and looked a little sheepish. "I'm sorry. I shouldn't be yelling at you, Jeff."

"That's cool. I get your frustration but I think we're better to wait. What do you think Charles?"

Charles sat quietly. His elbows rested on the padded arms of the chair, his fingers tented in front of his face. "Why does anyone enter a tournament like this one?"

Jeff and Laurie looked at each other and then back at Charles. "What do you mean?" Jeff asked.

"The only thing that we know about the Zitos, if indeed it is the Zitos behind all of this, is that they were willing to do anything to get into the contest.

Why?" Charles asked. "Why does someone enter this contest?"

"To catch sharks?" Jeff offered.

"Exactly. To catch sharks."

"So?" Laurie said.

"So, the sharks that the Zitos caught, how did they do?"

"Actually, I happen to know that they're doing real good." Jeff said. "They've brought in the prize shark every day so far."

"That is interesting. Where are these sharks now?" Charles moved his hands and met Jeff's eyes.

"I believe that they're in the refrigeration unit at the Oak Bluffs Marine."

"Can we go take a look at them?" Charles raised his right eyebrow.

"Sure. I don't see why not." Jeff said. He turned to Laurie, "what do you think?"

"It's fine with me. I don't know why though. They were already seen when they were brought in and they were weighed in front of a whole crowd. We were in that crowd!" Laurie exclaimed.

Charles looked at them both. "If two men had to die so that the Zitos could get into the contest, I want to see what it is that they were so desperate to catch."

"That's a good point." Laurie said. She stood up. "You coming Jeff?"

"Sure thing." Jeff stood up and grabbed his black police windbreaker. "I would love to get this mess off my desk."

*　　　*　　　*

The refrigerator at the marina was quite large and exactly what Charles had anticipated. He smelled it before he saw it. It smelled of fish and grease. It was obviously old. How old Charles wasn't sure but the industrial stainless steel was dented and the large door was on runners like a sliding closet door you see in apartment bedrooms. More modern refrigeration units, at least the ones he had seen back of house in hotels and restaurants had doors on hinges. They pulled open with a latch like an old fridge and they all had a safety latch on the inside. This one looked like it slid open and shut like a tomb- cold, dark, and permanent. The fact that there was no one around only added to the mausoleum feel. The marina hadn't been re-opened since the murders. The marina employees had to work out of a makeshift office up the harbour and the members had to do without their clubhouse, at least for the time being. No doubt that Jeff was getting plenty of grief about that on a daily basis.

Led by Chief Jeffries, the three of them made their way toward the fridge. At the door, he pulled a key out of his pocket and opened the padlock attached to the handle.

"How do the contestants get their catches in here?" Asked Laurie.

"At the end of the day when they've all been weighed, Joe Zito and two officers bring them in here. We really have no choice. It's the only place big enough to store them."

"Joe Zito, eh?" Charles raised an eyebrow.

"They're his catch. He has to be there. I know what you're thinking but what can he do under police supervision? And before you say anything, no it is not always the same officers and I refuse to believe that my entire police force is on the take my friend." Jeff spoke pleasantly but only half joking. He meant what he said and Charles and Laurie both knew it. Jeff pulled the sliding door open with a rumble. Charles could see by the effort Jeff used that the door was heavy and the tracks on which it slid needed tending. For a moment, the three of them stood staring and assessing. From their vantage point, there was nothing to see except unending black but there was no doubt that the fridge contained fish. To Charles it smelled like boathouses and fishing cabins at the cottage in Northern Ontario. Jeff stepped inside with his arm reached out. When he found the chain, he pulled it and the light came on with a hum and a flicker. There were sharks, a lot of them. All hung from the ceiling on hooks. Most of them hung by the tail but some hung from the mouth. Charles wondered why. It probably didn't matter.

"Ok. How do we know who caught which fish?" Asked Charles.

"It should say on each one. They will be tagged." Jeff walked over to the shark closest to him and turned it on its hook lodged in its tail. He found a yellow tag and holding it up, read it out loud. "See? Vessel: Green Machine. Captain: Lawrence Zerner."

"So we're looking for shark toe tags." Charles grimaced.

"Ya kinda." Jeff looked at Charles. "Sorry."

"Why are some of the sharks hung by their head and not their tail?" Asked Charles.

"I don't know. I've never seen that before. Have you Laurie?" Jeff looked at Laurie who was reading her first identification tag.

She shook her head. "No. This one belongs to the Hot Wave, Captain Rob Dyer." Laurie moved to the next fish.

Charles moved into the closest fish that hung by its head. He tentatively put his hands on the shark. It was cold, heavy, and leathery. He twisted it until he found its tag. "Hey guys! I have a Joe Zito original here." He let go of the shark and it twisted back into its original hanging position.

"Christ it's big." Stated Laurie. "Is this big for a porbeagle Jeff?"

Jeff nodded. "It is. It's not particularly long but it's thick...really thick."

"So now what?" Asked Charles. "Why weren't these sharks carved up? I saw some being sliced and diced at the proceedings. Why weren't these?"

"I don't suppose they have to be. After they're weighed, you can do what you want with them I guess although these haven't even been gutted. That's weird." Jeff motioned to the other sharks. "See, these others have had all of their entrails removed. They're just meat now. But this one is intact."

"So is that one." Charles motioned to another shark. It too hung by its head.

Laurie walked through the fridge inspecting all of the sharks. When she was finished, she returned to the shark that the two men were holding. "How do we get this thing down?"

"There's a crank on the wall over there. Why?"

"Because every shark hung by its head is still intact and they were all caught by Joe Zito and the Flicka. I want to know why."

"So what are you going to do?" Jeff asked.

"I'm going to cut the son of a bitch open. That's what I'm going to do."

"Alright." Jeff walked over to the wall and flicked the corresponding crank to the chain holding the shark in suspension. The fish lowered smoothly. "I'll go get a knife. There must be something in the marina kitchen that will do." Jeff walked quickly out of the fridge.

"Are you sure that you can do this?" Asked Charles.

"Absolutely." Laurie said.

"What are you hoping to find?"

"I have no idea but you said it yourself, what are they catching out there? Well, here it is." She kicked the shark lying on the metal floor. "This is what they're catching. So far all I see is a fat shark. You can catch those anywhere can't you?" She stared at the dead fish like it was going to start giving her hints. "All the other sharks are open and gutted. Let's see why he didn't gut this one...or any of those ones for that matter."

Jeff returned with a butcher knife worthy of the job. It was big and it looked well used. He knelt down in front of the animal and looked up at Charles and Laurie. "I'm assuming that of the three of us, I'm the one with the most experience in cutting open big fish."
244

"That's probably a pretty safe bet. You can have the honours." Said Laurie.

Charles crossed his arms over his chest and took a step back. "Please do."

Jeff stuck the knife in the shark's lower abdomen and started to pull the knife toward its head. He stopped almost immediately. "This doesn't feel right."

"What do you mean? What's wrong?" Asked Laurie.

"Well, it's too easy." Jeff stared at the belly of the shark with the knife handle sticking out.

"Did you find the alimentary canal?" Asked Charles.

"What the hell is the alimentary canal?" Asked Laurie.

"The digestive tract." Jeff said. "I should have."

"Should have?" Asked Laurie.

"It doesn't feel like its there." Jeff reached down and took the knife handle again. Charles watched, as the knife slid with what even he thought was greater ease than he would have imagined possible. When he had pulled the knife about four feet along, adequately opening up the belly of the fish, Jeff pulled the stiff skin down to reveal the guts. Clear plastic bags of shark fins fell out onto the gun barrel grey flooring. Jeff fell backwards in stunned silence. Long gone were the entrails of the shark. The stomach, liver, intestines had all been removed to make room for the porbeagle's precious cargo. Jeff stood and picked up one of the bags. "This is fifty pounds- easy."

"If the Zitos could sell those in their market for five hundred dollars a pound," Charles said grimly, "that would be a twenty-five thousand dollar bag of fins you have there."

"Jeff, get the rest of these sharks down." Laurie said quietly.

"No kidding." He set the bag down and walked over to the wall. One by one, as he figured out which lever corresponded to which hook, he lowered them to the floor.

"These sharks are all mules." Said Charles without a hint of amusement.

"So it would seem." Laurie said. "So it would seem."

29

Chief Jeffries, Chief Knickles, and Charles walked as fast as they could up Oak Bluffs harbour without breaking into a run. They had left their findings in the fridge with a new pad lock from Laurie's squad car. A lock for which there was only one key. That key that was on Laurie's belt. When they reached the goings on of the tournament, Jeff made his way into the crowd in search of one of his officers. Laurie and Charles waited for him on Lake Avenue. It wasn't long before Jeff re-emerged from the throngs of onlookers. Once reassembled, the three of them continued up the harbour.

"Well?" Asked Laurie.

"I told one of my guys that the marina was off limits. They were going to have to figure out another place to store today's catch, temporarily at least."

"Did you tell him why?"

"He asked but I told him it was none of his business. That was the end of it. He was caught sleeping in his cruiser last month and it ended up on Twitter. He wasn't on duty and he had been up all night with his sick four year old but of course no one said that part in the tweet. Anyway, he's not asking too many questions these days. He is more than happy to do what he's told and keep his head down."

"Gotta be Ted White." Said Laurie.

"You saw the picture?" Jeff frowned.

Laurie nodded. "I think some of my guys rode him pretty good over that pic. Someone put it up in the lunchroom. I took it down but other than that, I stayed out of it. I figured it would go away faster that way."

"Good call." Jeff nodded in agreement.

"Uh Jeff, where's this boat you said that we had at our disposal?" Charles interjected.

Jeff turned his attention to the slips in the harbour marked with signs that read, 'Reserved for Oak Bluffs Police Department'. They were all empty. They expected some of them to be gone but Jeff had assured them that there was still one at the ready. Jeff's face showed that he was just as shocked as the others were.

"Son of a bitch!" Jeff punched at the air.

"Where is it?" Asked Laurie.

"I have no idea." Jeff looked embarrassed by this statement.

"What do we do now?" Laurie threw her hands up in exasperation.

"Laurie..." Charles said.

"What?" She turned to look at Charles. He was pointing into the harbour, into the thick of the boats. She followed his finger. Keith Hurtubise and Gavin O'Neill were in the harbour on the Fascinating Rhythm. Just coming back in from being at sea by the looks of things.

"Can't Keith take us out?" Charles asked.

"They can at least get us out to a police boat! Good call. What do you think Jeff?"

"What choice do we have?" Jeff said with a matter of fact tone.

Laurie ran out to the end of the police dock and waved them in. Gavin saw them immediately and Charles watched as he yelled something inaudible at Keith who turned toward them. Laurie beckoned at them with big sweeps of her arms and when Keith pointed, Gavin turned Fascinating Rhythm in their direction. Jeff and Charles walked out to the end of the dock where Laurie stood and waited. When Gavin had her close enough, Keith slid up to the bow of Fascinating Rhythm with surprising grace for a man of his size. He threw Laurie a rope. She caught it and looped it over one of the wood posts on the dock.

"Everything alright chiefy?" Asked Keith as he grabbed a cleat on the dock.

"Keith we need a boat. All of the police boats are out and we need to get out to our friends the Zitos and bring them in. Can you help us out?"

"Bringing in that S.O.B. that smarty pants and I bumped into the other day would be a pleasure! Climb aboard!" Keith grinned happily.

"I hate to burst your bubble captain but I'm going to get you to take us to a police boat and we'll take it from there." Laurie stated.

"Well that's no fun! Always a bridesmaid, never a bride. Climb aboard anyway. It's a pleasure to serve." He laughed and held out a hand to help Laurie climb aboard, Charles followed, and then Jeff. "Jeff tell your dad that he still owes me eighty bucks!"

"Ok." Jeff smiled. "What for?"

"Poker." Keith grinned and his blue eyes twinkled.

Jeff laughed. "I *will* tell him."

"If he feigns ignorance, threaten to tell your ma! That'll jog his memory sure enough!" They all laughed at that. "Now that that's settled, you said something about a police cruiser. Where is it?"

"They should be about fifty miles out about halfway between Nantucket and the wildlife refuge, Keith." Jeff said, leaning back on the transom and grabbing a cleat for balance.

"You get that Gavin?" Keith bellowed.

"Got it captain! Fifty miles due east." Gavin pulled out of the harbour slip and turned the Fascinating Rhythm to navigate his way out of the busy harbour.

Leisure boats of all sorts travelled in every direction. Each one peopled by vacationers and islanders alike, all of whom were completely oblivious to the serious task ahead of Charles Williams and the police department. Two murders down, hundreds of pounds of contraband shark fins, and the perpetrators yet to be apprehended. Charles was more than a little concerned. He had no idea what to expect. Up until now, neither Joe nor Frank had given them any trouble. Charles could tell by watching Joe the last time he saw him that he was capable of more than he was letting on. There was a darkness behind his eyes. He was too ingratiating, overly friendly. It didn't take a genius to see that it was a mask. With people like that, the brighter the mask, the darker the reality. His crew hadn't looked like the most upstanding citizens either. The one he was most curious about was Marcie Cunningham. Had she really been mixed up with these men when they killed her father? By all accounts, Marcie and her father had been thick as thieves. Charles had not actually met either one of them but surely patricide had to be a pretty infrequent crime. Matricide, from everything that Charles read, was far more common and even that wasn't exactly happening every day. Maybe it wasn't more common at all. Maybe Charles had just seen Psycho too often. Poor old Norman Bates.

Charles leaned on the leeward side of the boat watching the Atlantic Ocean open up in front of him. It was beautiful. Broad, sparkling, and magnificent. There were a few clouds in the distance but for now... blue meridian. Charles thought it was probably his favourite thing on earth. People were always trying to get him to go see the Pacific Ocean but the warm, tropical image that the Pacific portrayed did not appeal to him like it did to others. He liked the cool, crisp, intellectual feel of New England over the hot, languid, and slow feel of the South Pacific. Among his friends, Charles was alone in this position. Laurie walked across the deck and stood beside him. She had been standing on the windward side of the boat and was quite wet because of it. The spray was cool but it didn't seem to bother her in the warm air.

"Hey." she said.

"Hey." he smiled at her. Charles thought about putting his arm around her but decided that the official nature of the trip made it a bad idea. The only people on the boat were Jeff, Keith, and Gavin but she was still in uniform and acting in an official capacity. He would wait. He would wait until she was in her Lululemon yoga pants, in her family room, drinking wine, and watching the ocean hit the beach. He would wrap his arms around her then and take in the smell of her, the feel of her. This trip had been more business than he had expected. Charles imagined that it was more business than she had expected too. Dead bodies and Martha's Vineyard were starting to go hand in hand for Charles but that fact hadn't quelled his love for the place.

"I was thinking that when we find Sergeant Barton, you should go back in with Keith and Gavin." Laurie spoke quietly so that only Charles could hear.

"Why?" He looked at her surprised. Not really sure what his response should be.

"We don't really know what these guys are capable of. When we get the other police boat there will be three officers; that should be more than enough to bring them in. It will be safer to get you out of the way. I might be able to justify you staying if it was just you but with Keith and Gavin there are just too many civilians to keep track of. I don't need that." She looked at him earnestly. "See my point?"

Charles met her gaze. "I must admit I do. While I'm a little relieved, I also find it a bit anticlimactic. I'm not really sure how to react."

"It doesn't matter. It's settled then. I'll feel better knowing that you're at home making me dinner." Laurie smiled up at him. She looked quickly around the boat to make sure that they weren't being watched and then pressed up and forward, kissing him deeply but quickly. "Thank you."

"Thank you!" Charles chuckled. Jeff walked over to them and the couple stepped apart. They grinned sheepishly at their friend like high school kids. He smiled a broad and mischievous smile.

"Don't let me stop you!" He jabbed playfully.

"I think we're good for now." Charles said. He was trying to be nonchalant but he was still blushing.

"There's a boat on the horizon; probably our boat." Jeff said.

"How far out is that?" Asked Laurie.

"Oh, I don't know. Still pretty far out I guess."

"It's about three miles." Charles said matter-of-factly.

"How do you know that?" Jeff asked him. He was getting used to these statements from Charles and sounding less astonished and less questioning, just curious.

"If you're looking out over water, the horizon is always one point one seven times the square root of the height of your eye over the water's surface." Charles said.

Jeff stared at him blankly.

"Oh, for Christ's sake, Charles." Laurie said. "What the hell does that mean?"

"It's basic geometry. Jeff is just over six feet. I added a couple more inches for the height of the boat deck. I figure the square root is about two point five. Multiply that by one point one seven and you get three miles...approximately."

"Wow! That's cool!" Jeff said.

Laurie looked sceptical.

Gavin called down from the bridge. "Hey you guys! Captain, we have a cruiser coming up about three miles out!"

Charles looked at Laurie and started to laugh.

"Geometry sucks." Laurie shook her head and rolled her eyes. "Jeff have you tried to raise him on the radio?"

"No. I'll do that now." Jeff entered the cabin but came out in a matter of minutes. "I'm not getting any response."

"You couldn't have tried for very long." Laurie said sounding like she was very much still his chief.

"Relax, I'll try again in a minute or two. Keith says there might be temporary interference. It happens." Jeff calmly stood his ground.

There was nothing they could do but wait. They watched as they approached the boat on the horizon but that was becoming more and more difficult to do with the naked eye. It was still a dot and hardly discernible at all under the best of circumstances. Now the weather was changing. Clouds came in with the wind and the boat got harder and harder to see. In

254

fact, a distinct horizon became harder and harder to see. If it wasn't for Gavin and his electronic instruments on the bridge, thought Charles, they might have lost the boat altogether but they stayed their course. Charles kept regular visual checks on Keith and Gavin. He figured if neither one of them seemed phased by the weather then there was no need for him to be concerned either. Neither of the men seemed to even notice it at all. The same wind that brought in the cloud coverage caused the sea to roll in heavier and higher waves. They weren't stormy but they were big enough to hit a white cap occasionally. The Fascinating Rhythm heaved and surged but still cut cleanly through the Atlantic. The sky darkened. The hot summer air was cooling off quickly. Charles could tell they were in for a storm. Perhaps it would go around them, he thought. With any luck they would just get the edge but there would be a storm.

Keith came out of the cabin where he had been cleaning bits of machinery that Charles did not recognise. They looked like parts of a boat engine but he couldn't be sure. "Backwind came up." He said. Keith looked Charles in the eye and grinned. "Just going to be a bit of rain Smarty, nothing to worry about. If you don't want to get wet, the sea's no place for ya. That's what I always say. Don't I always say that Gavin?"

"Don't ask me old man. I stopped listenin' to ya a long time ago." Gavin turned his head back far enough to make his thick Irish accent heard by everyone on deck. It wasn't actually that funny but the accent made it hilarious. There was laughter from everyone but the captain.

"Boy has he got your number!" Laughed Laurie.

"Ya hear the way he talks to me? You can't get good help anywhere." Keith looked up at his first mate in disgust.

"That's shite an' you know it. I'm the best there is." Gavin looked down and winked. "Besides, you know I'm just takin' the piss."

"And that's another thing! 'Takin' the piss'? Who the hell says that? Speak English would ya? *Tabernac!*" Keith hollered back at him. Jeff, Laurie, and Charles broke up at Keith's ridiculous statement and even Keith couldn't help joining in.

Gavin went back to his instruments and steered the boat five degrees port before holding his course again. Charles watched him as he pulled up a pair of binoculars and focused them out in the direction of the cruiser. He brought them down again, looked out to the horizon, and promptly brought the glasses back up. He stared long. His face was squinted up in concentration, his brow furrowed, and his lips pursed above his thick red beard. The Irishman turned toward the deck and the captain, "Captain!" He called. Charles noticed that he always called him by title when it was something official, something nautical. Keith turned immediately.

"What's up?" Keith asked.

"That cruiser isn't a police boat at all." Gavin stated. "It's Zito's boat. It's the Flicka."

"Shit." Jeff said.

Laurie stared intently out to sea. She could see nothing. The sky was still dark. The wind had disappeared which meant the clouds weren't going anywhere and the quick drop in temperature had brought on a mild fog. The sea calmed a bit; that was something. She stared out anyway where she knew the Flicka was floating, rocking in the waves. Charles went up and stood as close as he could beside her. Without thinking, he put his arm around her. She didn't shrug it off. "I guess you're not going back," was all she said.

30

Gavin pulled the Fascinating Rhythm up alongside the Flicka with an ease and precision that betrayed the fact that he had been doing it all his life. The darkening sky and sea seemed of little consequence to him. That amazed Charles. Charles expected nothing less of Gavin or Keith but he always found talent impressive. Charles had noticed as they approached that the Flicka was once again sitting low in the water. Being side by side with the Fascinating Rhythm only emphasized it. Both boats were approximately the same size but the Flicka was sitting a good ten inches deeper. In fact, Charles thought that if the sea got any rougher, they might end up awash.

Joe Zito stepped forward with the same broad and mechanical salesman's grin he had worn on their last meeting. His crew of two men held back on the other side of the boat. They looked nervous, wary. If being visited by the police was indeed the joy and honour that Joe Zito's smarmy grin made it out to be, the crew was not aware of it. The dichotomy made Charles antsy.

"Captain Hurtubise again! Quite a pleasure." Joe's eyes surveyed the boat. When they flashed over Charles, he felt like prey being outlined by an African cat. "You've brought friends, the police. I don't believe I've had the pleasure." Joe used the same tone that a school bully used when approaching kids on a playground. It was posturing, a dance, instinctive circling before the attack.

Laurie stepped forward. "Joe Zito, my name is Chief Laurie Knickles of the Edgartown Police. I'm working in conjunction with the Oak Bluffs Police Department represented here by Chief Jeffries. We'd like you to follow us back to port please. We have some questions we'd like to ask you and your crew."

Joe's face tightened. His eyes narrowed almost imperceptibly. From this distance, they looked black like they were all pupil. His broad smile didn't falter. "This sounds official. Can we not answer your questions here or wait until the day is over? We have the tournament to consider and I think my crew and I have a good chance."

Jeff spoke up. "Unfortunately, I am removing you and your crew from the tournament Mr Zito, my sincerest apologies."

Zito's smile fell immediately and his face reddened. "My crew has worked hard in this tournament! They've earned the opportunity to see this through to the end!"

"I'm sure they have but our situation takes precedent. I'm sorry."

"On what grounds?"

"Suspicious conduct." Jeff said. "That's all for now. That's all I need."

"My brother-"

"-is running the tournament, yes we know but he must answer to the law. We'll collect him on our way to the police station."

"So am I being charged with something?" Joe asked. He maintained a level voice but it was deepening along with the colour in his face.

"We don't have to play it that way but we can." Laurie said.

"I think you need to have an arrest warrant if you want me to come with you. If you don't have one, I don't have to come with you. My vessel is like my home. It's my property. You can't come aboard and I don't have to leave it." Joe's expression was one of triumph.

"Chief Knickles?" Charles spoke up from behind them. Laurie turned around to face him. "May I speak to you for a moment?" She eyed him briefly and decided that he wouldn't have interrupted without a good reason. She walked over, out of earshot from the others, listened to what he had to say, and returned moments later.

"I don't believe we've met friend, at least not officially." Joe looked Charles over carefully. "You were out here with Captain Hurtubise and his mick the other day. Who are you?"

Charles looked up at Gavin at the Irish racial slur. Gavin was chuckling, amused.

"He is a special deputy and that's all you need to know." Laurie spoke perhaps a little too quickly, exposing too much emotion.

Joe's grin returned but with a little more menace. "Sure he is."

In the shadows of the dark sky, Charles thought Joe's teeth looked sharp almost pointed.

Jeff stepped forward and put one foot up on the port side of the stern abutting the Flicka. "Permission to come aboard, Captain Zito."

Looking back at his crew, Joe laughed but they did not join in. "Denied!!" Joe Boomed.

Jeff hadn't been expecting this refusal and was not sure what to do next. He was about to step down when Laurie stepped up beside him.

"That's alright Jeff, we don't need his permission." She stood beside Jeff and looked Joe Zito directly in the eye. "Captain Joe Zito, Chief Jeffries is boarding your vessel. We have the authority to do so if we suspect that it is a crime scene. You know, for your own safety." Laurie's expression was strong and authoritative. Joe's look of triumph had been washed away. "As of this moment, we do. I would like to ask you to step back with your crew and leave him to his search. At the end of his search, regardless of his findings, you will be towed back to port for further questioning. Am I understood?"

Joe stood his ground. His neck was livid and purple.

"Joe, I can arrest you for interfering with a police investigation, cuff you here and now, and we will just tow it all in. Is that what you want?" Laurie stepped forward and looked up at him, unflinching. If she was intimidated or even impressed by Joe Zito, it did not show.

Charles watched as Joe clenched his fists and then, after a moment, stepped back. He went back and stood with his crew at the stern of his boat.

Jeff stepped forward and down onto the deck of the Flicka. He landed on the wooden deck with an earthy, *'thunk'*. It reminded Charles of grave robbers landing on unearthed coffins in movies.

Laurie looked back at Charles, "I hope you're right."

Charles stepped up beside her. "Me too."

Jeff circled the deck and then motioned to two trap doors in the flooring. "Open these please." He motioned to the crewmembers that had remained motionless and quiet. They looked at their captain for instruction. Dourly, Joe nodded his approval. They lifted the doors exposing nothing but pumps and engine parts. The spaces were big enough for a deck hand to reach in and work on the mechanics but nothing else. They were certainly not large enough to have anything stowed in them.

"Perhaps if you told me what you were looking for I could help you find it? If it exists, that is. We could save ourselves a little time? You've already kicked me out of the tournament. I'd like to get this over with. I have fish already caught that I could be packing and sending home to Boston. I am in the seafood business; freshness is everything." Joe said flippantly.

"We know all about your previous catches Mr Zito." Laurie said.

Joe whipped around to face her and the tension was visible as it coursed through him. He wanted to hit her and hit her hard.

"We have them in safekeeping. Perhaps that shines a little light on the situation for you." Laurie grinned the same smarmy grin that Joe had given her not ten minutes ago.

Jeff turned to the cabin, grabbed the handle, and swung open the door. A single gunshot hit him in the chest. The force of the bullet pushed him back. He lost his footing and did a complete about face. The crews of both boats watched in shock as Jeff staggered across the deck and off the stern of the boat. He hit the water in an almost comical dive. He disappeared beneath the surface briefly and then came back up. Jeff floated facedown in the water. A halo of blood circled his head and neck. His body moved fluidly with the movement of the sea. There was no other movement. His feet dipped under the surface, weighed down by his boots. They did not kick. His head bobbed but did not come up for air.

Without hesitation, Gavin dove into the water from the cockpit platform. He came up right beside Jeff and flipped him over. Gavin slid his arm around Jeff's neck propping his head up to clear his breathing passages and swam over to the Fascinating Rhythm. Laurie and Charles scrambled across the deck to meet them. Gavin reached up and grabbed the boat with one arm and pulled Jeff by the collar with surprising strength. Jeff was limp and weighed heavy in the water but Gavin was able to lift him high enough to be reached by the others. Charles and Laurie stretched over the side of the boat and each of them grabbed Jeff under an arm. The dead weight of their friend was almost impossible to manage but Charles was a big man and Laurie braced her foot against the transom. They pulled. Unconscious, Jeff slid up the side of the boat like a net full of dead squid.

Keith ran across them with a rope, put a fender up, and tied the two boats together in a reef knot. He then went for Gavin. "Son of a bitch! Get the hell up into this boat!"

Charles and Laurie got Jeff flat on his back. His shirt was dark with blood. The bullet had gone right through his chest on the upper right side. He was bleeding pretty badly. Charles was grateful that it hadn't been his heart. If he could stop the bleeding, he was sure that Jeff would be all right eventually. Surprisingly, he was breathing. Short, shallow, wheezing but he was breathing. Charles looked at Laurie, "I've got this. Get over there." Charles began to unbutton Jeff's shirt to get a good look at the wound. With no argument, Laurie got up and jumped across the stern of the Fascinating Rhythm onto the Flicka. When she landed, her gun was out and trained onto the Flicka's cabin door.

"GAVIN!!!" Keith's screams to Laurie's right made her turn her attention from the Flicka's crew.

"Holy shit!" Said Joe Zito.

264

Laurie turned and watched the swell of ocean lift behind Gavin. The water propelled by long, cylindrical blackness. The sharp, shiny triangular dorsal fin sliced through the water's surface like a branding iron through skin. The shark's black nose crested the surface. There was a brief flash of white as the shark's jaw opened. Serrated white teeth. It shut like a bear trap and there was an explosion of red froth. The shark sunk below the surface taking Gavin with it. There was nothing but red between the two boats. No one moved. Keith hung helplessly over the side of the boat. Everything seemed to be in slow motion. The red sea slopped up Keith's arms leaving them wet and stained.

Gavin exploded through the water with a deep and gurgling yell. His red hair and beard streaked and blackened as fresh bloodied seawater left his mouth in a spray. Keith grabbed a fresh hold of him and pulled him toward the boat. Laurie jumped down to help him but Keith reached down and pulled him up like he was a one-pound bag of sugar. The fin breached the surface twenty feet away. The back breached next. The great white shark headed toward the boat.

Joe Zito reached under his stern and grabbed a rifle. He aimed and hit the shark with a single shot in the back. The shark didn't react. It didn't flinch. Nothing.

The shark's nose breached. Empty black eyes crested the surface. Its teeth pulled apart and all of its pink and muscled jaw slid alongside the forward of the Fascinatin' Rhythm. Aiming to take the rest of its prey. Keith grabbed Gavin by the belt buckle and hauled him in. His remaining leg flailed almost ridiculously above their heads. The other leg had been removed mid-thigh. Shredded and gone. Gavin's bare white skin exposed under the remaining shreds of denim. The shark missing his quarry, slid back into the ocean with an eerie hiss.

"Get a tourniquet around it!" Charles yelled at them. "Use his belt!" Charles knelt over Jeff stuffing his wound with gauze from the first aid kit and taping it off. Deciding that Jeff could hold his own for a minute or two, Charles slid across the deck to assist with Gavin.

Gavin sputtered and shook. His lips were blue and his already Irish pallor was paling. Keith had him by the shoulders. Gavin shook and panted.

"Lie him down." Charles said. "Prop his hips up! Elevate his legs higher than his head."

Laurie helped Keith get him down as instructed and placed two flotation cushions under his hips and leg. Charles pulled Gavin's belt out of his pants and strapped it tightly around his thigh. The blood slowed to a minimum. "Keith do you have a clean towel, a garbage bag, and some duct tape?"

Keith got up with the agility of a man half his age and disappeared into the cabin. He reappeared a couple of minutes later with all three items. "Here you go, Charles."

Charles registered the use of his given name for the first time by Keith. It sounded good even though it denoted worry and desperation. Charles folded the towel neatly and tightly over Gavin's open stump and wrapped it tightly in place with the duct tape, fastening it tightly to Gavin's bare upper thigh. Charles

266

covered the whole mess with the garbage bag and knotted it. He looked at Laurie and nodded. The salty sea air was now filled with metallic bloodiness. The deck of the Fascinating Rhythm was red.

Laurie leapt up from her position on the deck and with a stabilizing step on the stern landed on the deck of the Flicka with her gun out and pointed at the cabin. "Whoever you are, open that door slowly and kick that gun out on the deck. Come out with your hands up. I won't ask twice." She looked at Joe Zito. He was still carrying his rifle in both hands. She turned her gun on him. "Drop your weapon Zito- now!"

Joe hesitated but did as she requested. He set the rifle at his feet and then kicked it across the deck.

Keith knelt over his first mate. He looked at Charles, "I'm going to grab another towel." He disappeared inside.

"You! In the cabin! Out!" Laurie held her gun on the cabin door. It eased open and a handgun slid across the deck. Marcie Cunningham stepped out. Laurie lunged at her. Marcie screamed as the full force of the chief's body weight and her own drove her face into the cabin wall. She slid down the wall with the chief on top of her. Laurie cuffed her and yanked her to her feet. Marcie grunted as she tried to find her footing. Dragging her by the cuffs, Laurie pushed her over the edge of the Flicka. There was a brief moment where it looked like she might fall into the ocean but she tipped just far enough forward and they all watched her fall onto the Fascinating Rhythm. She landed with a scream and a thud. Laurie stood up on the transom of the Flicka and loomed over her. She sunk into her hips to leap at her again.

"Chief Knickles!" Charles yelled.

Laurie caught herself and stopped before jumping in after the girl. Laurie stared at Charles. Her breathing was heavy and her eyes wild. Charles looked at her with a warm stare. He inhaled and exhaled with dramatic exaggeration. Laurie followed suit and took a deep breath. She turned to face Joe Zito. "We're going to tow you in now. This is over."

Joe looked at her. He looked tired for a moment but then he straightened. His toothy, broad, mechanical smile was back. His eyes were piercing and sparkling. "No."

31

"What do you mean, '*no*'?" Laurie gawked at him incredulously. Her patience was thin. Charles was still tending to Gavin and Jeff. Keeping pressure on both of their injuries, making sure that they were both as comfortable as possible. Jeff was still out cold but breathing regularly. There wasn't much more that Charles could do for either of them but he did his best. All the while, he was listening to the exchange between Laurie and Joe intently. Joe's monosyllabic response hung heavily in the air like the pop of a champagne cork. He could still hear it.

"Exactly what I said...no." Zito stood tall on the deck of his craft. His crew of two still cowered behind him. Marcie sat whimpering where Laurie had tossed her on the deck of the Fascinating Rhythm. "The way I see it, there's only one way out of this."

"What way is that exactly?" Laurie asked angrily.

"You go in to port and I go home to Boston or wherever I see fit." Joe sounded quite pleased with himself at this scenario. Charles looked up at him with contempt. He was sure that he knew what Joe was thinking but he was also sure that he was the only one who had figured it out. Even Joe's crew looked at him like the last of his cheese had slid off his cracker.

"What could possibly make you think that I would allow that to happen? You're not that stupid Joe." Laurie said.

"I don't want to be arrested. You need to get your friends into the vineyard to get proper medical attention and you need to do it soon. That mick has lost a lot of blood. Chief what's-his-name has a while yet but Redbeard there is definitely on a timer. You have the sharks and their contents and you have Marcie so you're not going home empty handed. She did shoot your friend. Who's to say she didn't commit the other murders too? You could wrap this case up rather nicely without me... and save your friends. Everyone wins."

"What do you mean you *have* Marcie?" Marcie's attention had peaked at this last statement. "What the hell is that supposed to mean Joe? Frank's not going to like you talking about me like that!"

"*Frank's not going to like you shooting a goddamned cop either! You stupid bitch! Who the hell told you to do that?*" Joe yelled.

"He was going to go inside! He was going to find-
"

"*Would you shut the fuck up!*" Joe Zito yelled so loud that his neck swelled and pulsed.

270

Charles winced. He was sure that the windows behind him rattled.

"What is it with women?" Joe continued. "They never know when to shut up! Fuck!"

"What were we going to find Marcie?" Laurie turned her attention on Marcie. Jack's wife.

Marcie looked at Joe. He glared at her violently, threateningly. He may have overplayed his hand and there wasn't much he could do about it now. "Joe?" She asked.

"Come on Marcie. I would have figured out a way to get us all out of this. You know that." Joe sounded nervous for the first time.

"You were going to leave me Joe." She stared at him like a wounded deer.

"That's right Mr Zito. You were." Laurie turned to Joe once again. "Besides, what other murders were we going to pin on her? How did you know that murder was even involved? I didn't mention any murders. Neither did any of my counterparts. What are you talking about? Who did Marcie apparently kill?"

"Nobody!! I never killed nobody!" She exclaimed from her position on the deck.

Laurie turned and kneeled down in front of Marcie. She stroked stray hairs out of her face. "Marcie, Joe was going to leave you to take the rap for this whole mess. I don't believe that you are responsible but it doesn't look good. You just shot a police officer; Joe's right about that. You need to think about yourself now. Help me Marcie. Help me get you out of this. You need to trust me." Charles listened to Laurie talking to Marcie. He remembered the first time he had heard that tone. It was the tone that she had used to talk to Charles' friend, Mike when his brother had been murdered last summer. Laurie had used that voice to get Mike to focus on that bench in front of The Kelly House. She had used it to get information. It was a calming and soothing voice. It was manipulative and effective. "Who does he want me to think you killed Marcie?" Laurie asked with a softer tone.

Marcie looked at her, weighing her options in her head. She looked at Joe and spat her answer. "That nice Mr Christie. That's who. They said that he had to be killed to get Frank in place at the tournament. I didn't like it..."

"Marcie what about Jack? How could you do this to Jack?" Laurie asked pointedly.

Her eyes welled up and she hung her head. "I don't know! I love Jack!" She shook uncontrollably. Her head hung low and she tried to reach for her face pathetically with her elbows and shoulders but gave up. "He was never home. I was so lonely. Frank was so nice at first. He bought me nice things. I don't know how all of this got started but once it did, it seemed impossible to stop. Frank seemed all right until his brother showed up." She looked up quickly at Laurie with a sudden realisation. "Jack doesn't know anything about all of this. I think he thinks I'm having an affair but nothing else. God I wish that's all there was. Jack never asked me but I know that's what he thinks. He's been acting all funny. Jack's a good man, Chief Knickles. You have to believe me."

Laurie stared at her with sadness. "Marcie, what about your father?"

272

"What do you mean?" Asked Marcie.

"Well, there's a distinct possibility that he was murdered by the same person who killed Mr Christie. It was a very similar m.o."

Marcie looked at Laurie quizzically. She stared at Laurie's face as she tried to unscramble Laurie's words in her head. She had been handed a Rubik's Cube and been told to sort it out. Her brow furrowed. "Daddy wasn't killed." She said finally.

Laurie and Charles exchanged glances and then both looked at Marcie. "Marcie... your father is dead."

"I know. It was a fishing accident. Jack told me and mom that it was a fishing accident... He identified the body and everything... A fishing accident... Jack told me. *He told me!*"

Laurie stared at Marcie with an ache that she had never felt before. Charles watched her and saw the colour drain from her face as she realised what had happened. Jack, not wanting to upset his wife or her mother more than necessary, had told them a lie. A white lie but a lie nonetheless. No wonder Jack had been acting so oddly lately. He suspected his wife of having an affair and he was lying to her at the same time about the violent nature of her father's death. He was protecting her. Standing here, now, Laurie was going to have to rip that cold comfort away from her and Marcie's father was going to die all over again.

"I'm sorry Marcie but that's not true. I think Jack was trying to spare your feelings." Laurie took a deep breath. "Your father was murdered, Marcie. There's no question about it."

Marcie looked at Laurie and then at Joe. She even looked at Charles. She was trying to find anyone who would back up her side of the story. Someone who would tell her that it wasn't true. Her mind was reeling behind her clouded, red eyes. Her chest heaved. Her glare became fixated on Joe. "You killed my daddy? Just because they put him in charge of your stupid tournament?"

"Marcie, no. I didn't kill anyone. You know that. Marcie..."

"Then you had him killed! You or your goddamned partner or your brother!" Marcie began to stand shakily. Not an easy feat with her hands cuffed but she managed. "You goddamned bastards killed my daddy!" She hissed. "I told you that he had been killed in an accident. Your brother consoled me for Christ's sake!! Did he kill him Joe? Did he kill him and then hold my head while I cried on his goddamned shoulder? You sick goddamned bastards! Hey Chief Knickles! I have a few stories for you! Let them go! You'll have enough to put them away for a long time when I'm done! How about that Joe?"

The force that hit the Flicka was a strong one. It came from below. The Flicka lurched sideways into the Fascinating Rhythm. The two boats hit each other with a deafening crash. Joe Zito lunged forward and grabbed the rifle lying on his deck. He came up quickly and aimed at Marcie. He shot and hit her in the chest. He hit her left of centre. He hit her high. Her body pushed back. Her head snapped forward and then back. Out of reflex, Marcie pulled at her hands for balance but the cuffs were tight. Her eyes rolled wildly unable to comprehend what was happening. Her feet couldn't find their ground and she fell over the starboard side of the Fascinating Rhythm. She fell away from the Flicka. Laurie and Charles watched her go. They couldn't turn their back on Joe, certainly not when he was armed. They were helpless.

Keith emerged from the cabin, crouched, and low. He grabbed Gavin by the shoulders and dragged him inside. Keith re-emerged and placed his hands delicately around Jeff's shoulders. Gingerly, he pulled him inside. Once safely inside, he reached up and closed the cabin door behind them.

The shark hit the Flicka again. Joe looked at the deck as he heard a crack. The boat was already sitting dangerously low and now it was taking water over the side at the stern. It wouldn't be long before the boat was awash. Joe fired again but this time the shot went straight in the air. Three inches of water filled the deck and there was more coming all the time. The boat was filling too fast for it to be just the water they could see flowing over the corner. The boat was filling from below deck. Joe lost his footing and landed on his back. There was another crash from below as the shark hit their hull again. Joe's gun went off. He hit nothing.

Laurie tried to aim at him but the boats were tossing too heavily and a clear shot was impossible.

The Flicka's crewmembers half-ran, half-waded across the deck, through the water, and jumped for the Fascinating Rhythm.

"Sit down and shut up!" Laurie ordered them. They did as they were told. She turned back toward

Joe and then turned back to them. "Actually, get Marcie out of the water!"

The two men stood and turned to look into the ocean for their former partner in crime.

Charles stood and watched Joe Zito try to regain his footing on a boat deck that was now covered in over a foot of water. Various bits of garbage swirled in a circular motion as the deck filled. He was going down fast. The shark must have done serious damage to his hull, thought Charles.

"Joe! Get rid of the gun and come aboard!" Laurie shouted.

Joe stared at her wide eyed and terror stricken. His once livid, purple, angry face was now white. He looked down at his feet. He was more than knee deep in water. The boat was pounded hard again from below. The port side went under. The corner of the stern disappeared completely in a gurgling, sucking noise.

Keith ran to the stern of the Fascinating Rhythm and untied them before the Flicka pulled them down together.

Wood creaked as the Flicka began to break apart. It twisted as one twisted a dishrag. Joe fell face first into the water and lost his grip on the gun. It hit the water and sunk. Joe lifted his face and gasped for air. His eyes stayed shut as they stung with the salt water. His hands moved in a dog paddle and his feet tried to kick away from the sinking vessel. The Flicka was sideways in the water now. Water rushed into the windows and door of the cabin. It was capsizing quickly. Soon it would be completely upside down.

In a single explosion, Joe was ejected from the water. He came up in a bloody froth, held tightly in the mouth of the Great White. The shark breached up to his gills. He seemed to almost hover in the air with his trophy. Joe hung out of both sides of the shark's mouth as torrents of bloody seawater ran down his legs and head. The force of the impact had knocked the wind out of him and all Joe could do was cough and hack up blood. There was no screaming. Charles stood motionless in horror and watched this man that he loathed being dismembered in front of him. He could actually see where each gleaming white tooth had torn into Joe's torso. In some parts the flesh had torn and there were gaping red holes. They peeked into Joe's entrails. Charles thought he might throw up. The shark slid back under the tumultuous red sea and Joe was pulled under with it. No screaming, just coughing. Just coughing, then silence. Charles and Laurie rushed to the side of the boat and waited for him to come back up. He didn't. Not even parts of him came back. They stood there staring at the dissipating redness of the ocean. They watched as it returned to the black topped, stormy sea that one would expect. Soon there would be no sign that anything had ever happened. Joe was gone. The Flicka was gone.

Keith had started up the motor from inside the cabin. The Fascinating Rhythm was turning around.

Laurie turned to look at the remaining crewmembers of the Flicka. "Where's Marcie?"

They both shrugged their shoulders. "She wasn't there. She was just gone."

Laurie turned to look at Charles. He was standing, propped against the wall of the cabin. "That shark couldn't have eaten Gavin's leg, Marcie, and Joe, could it? I mean... she must have sunk."

"She couldn't have sunk. Bodies don't sink right away." Charles looked into the sea. His gaze followed their wake. He watched where they had been as they slowly headed into port, picking up speed as they went. "That was a really big shark... seventeen feet would be my guess."

"That shark ate two people and a leg?" Laurie exclaimed.

"Nobody really knows how much a shark that size can eat. There just haven't been enough studies."

"Why did it attack the Flicka like that?"

"You saw it. It was soaked with blood." Charles turned to face the two crewmembers sitting on the deck. "Did you guys have a full load of shark fins on board?"

They looked at each other and then back at Charles. The bigger of the two spoke up. "Yes sir."

Charles looked back at Laurie. "There you go – one load too many. Like Ahab being killed by the great white whale or Quint being killed by his own Great White shark." His eyes trailed back to the ocean and their wake. He found something calming about watching the wake. It was good to know where you've been. "I guess there really is something to poetic justice after all."

Keith stepped out of the cabin. "I called the emergency services. There's an ambulance waiting for us at Oak Bluffs harbour."

Laurie smiled. "Thanks Keith. That's awesome. How are the boys doing?"

"They're both out. That worries me but there was nothing I could do about it. Jeff came around briefly and Gavin held on as long as he could. He's a tough little bugger. With no painkillers, it seems like a bit of a godsend to be unconscious really. Their heartbeats are regular. Pulses are good if a little weak. Christ, I don't know what I'm doing in there. I'm not Florence Nightingale!"

"They'll be okay." Laurie said.

"I'll tell you one thing though…the pirates knew what they were talking about!"

"What do you mean?" Laurie looked at him quizzically but Charles laughed knowingly.

"Pirates said that it was bad luck to have a woman on board!"

Laurie laughed in spite of herself. "Very funny, old man!"

Keith winked at her and went back inside to bring them in.

Charles moved closer to Laurie. He reached out and put his arm around her tightly. She pushed into him like she wanted them to be one person. She needed to feel close and warm. He could feel a tremble deep inside her. "What are you going to tell Jack?"

"I have no idea. The truth I guess." She rubbed her hands up and down his forearms.

"You don't think he was involved at all do you?"

"Oh shit, no. I really can't see it."

"Me either." Charles paused. "I really feel badly for Marcie. I know she was as sharp as a bag of wet mice but she just got mixed up with the wrong people and then..."

"She shot a cop, Charles!" Her body stiffened under his arm. "I don't feel sorry for her at all. She got what she deserved."

"Fair enough." Charles knew to let it go. Neither one of them said anything for quite a while. The sun was starting to sink and the sky was turning red. There would be a beautiful sunset over Menemsha that night for sure. Soon they could see Oak Bluffs harbour. As they got closer, they could make out the ambulance and beside it stood Jack Burrell. His energy was palpable. He almost bounced with stress.

Laurie spoke first. "Do we have wine at home?"

"Tonnes."

"Good. I'm gonna need it."

32

Keith slid his boat into the first slip on the pier. An ambulance was waiting with two paramedics and Jack Burrell. The three men looked ready to pounce at the Fascinating Rhythm. Only the light from the open doors of the ambulance lighted them. The sun was setting quickly. The sky was volcanic in colour. Reds and yellows erupted from the horizon before dissipating and cooling into the night sky.

As soon as the boat was secure, the two medics jumped aboard and Charles directed them to Jeff and Gavin. Neither Jeff nor Gavin looked very good. Both men were carried from the boat on stretchers and set down in the ambulance. Vitals were taken and intravenous drips set up immediately.

Laurie used the ambulance radio to call the police station. She called in to have two officers arrest Frank Zito on the suspicion of smuggling, fraud, and complicity to murder. When she was finished, she stepped out of the ambulance and Keith jumped into the front seat she had just vacated.

"Where are you going?" Asked Laurie.

"I can't leave Gavin like this. I'm going to the hospital. I'll let you know as soon as I hear something." He said. He tried to shut the door but Laurie stopped him.

"Jeff's a cop. I have to go."

"There's nothing you can do for them. You're needed here." He looked up at the wide-eyed and obviously shaken Sergeant Jack Burrell.

She closed the ambulance door. "You're right, I am. All right old man, you win but I want hourly reports whether anything changes or not with either one of them. You got it? I'm out on East Chop and I can be at that hospital in two minutes if I have to be."

"I know you can. I'll call Catherine to bring me some supper. If you're lucky, I'll get her to bring you some too. You take care of that boy and then you go home with Charles. They're both good boys and they both need you right now." He kissed his hand and then placed it on her cheek. "Take care of yourself too, chére."

Laurie smiled. "I will." The ambulance drove off with sirens blazing and left Laurie to walk over to Sergeant Jack.

He looked fragile, scared. His short muscular body seemed small and his face was younger than ever. He watched the ambulance disappear into Oak Bluffs and then turned to Laurie. "I...um...I don't know what's going on." He trembled. "Chief, I can't find my wife. I can't find Marcie. I'm sorry. I'm really sorry. I've

282

been trying to keep my private life and my professional life separate but it's not working out so good. That's why I haven't been myself lately but I... Marcie has a boyfriend at least I think she does... I can't find her now. Marcie's gone. She's just gone. You and Mr Williams, Charles, were out in the boat looking for someone and nobody would tell me who or why. Am I being fired?"

Laurie placed a hand on Jack's shoulder. "Jack you are a really good cop. I'm not going to fire you."

He looked at her with his innocence totally exposed. The kindness was almost too much for him to bear. "Then why won't anybody tell me what's going on? *How am I supposed to be a member of this police force? What did I do wrong?*"

Charles watched the two of them uncomfortably. He didn't feel like he should be a party to this. It really wasn't any of his business. This was between Jack and his boss, his mentor. "I'm going to get a cab home. I shouldn't be here for this."

"*Be here for what?*" Jack was almost manic.

"Jack, you and I are going to have a talk right now. When it's over, we will start to make things okay." She spoke soothingly to him but stern. "Charles, I'll see you at home at some point this evening. Thank you." Laurie led Jack to a bench at the end of the pier and Charles walked down the harbour making his way into Oak Bluffs central. The city was well lit and there was a lot of movement. Enviously, he watched the patrons on the deck at Nancy's restaurant watch the sunset over the harbour. Wine glasses in hand, laughing, and enjoying lobster dinners. Maybe he and

Laurie would go there for supper tomorrow night, he thought. As he suspected there was the usual line of taxi vans along Lake Avenue between Central Avenue and Circuit Avenue. The line of white vans stood in front of the bike rental and Slip 77. Slip 77 was such a great store. If the circumstances had been different, Charles would have gone in. He never passed it without a quick peek but tonight he was tired. Body and mind were exhausted. He just wanted to make his way onto East Chop, to Laurie's house. Have a hot shower and pour some of the wine he knew was chilling in the refrigerator.

A young kid wearing a white T-shirt and cut-off denim shorts was sitting in the first taxi. He looked at Charles hopefully. "Do you need a taxi, sir?"

"As a matter of fact, I do." Sir, he thought. Jesus...

The boy jumped to his feet and stepped aside so that Charles could step into the already open, sliding side door. "Where are you headed?"

"East Chop."

The boy looked worried. "Um...okay." He ran around the van and stepped up into the driver's seat. He turned his key in the ignition. "Do you know how to get there?"

Charles smiled at the boy's reflection in the rear view mirror. "Yes. Don't worry. We'll get there. What's your name bud?"

"Bobby!"

Of course it is. "Nice to meet you Bobby. I'm Charles." Charles pointed behind them. "You're going to want to make a u-turn here and drive down Lake

Avenue to East Chop Drive and then make a right hand turn. Then you just keep driving until we reach my house."

"You got it Charles!" Bobby pressed a bare foot onto the pedal. A couple of gearshift adjustments and they were on their way.

The barefoot driving made Charles laugh inwardly. College kids driving taxis barefoot... only on Martha's Vineyard. Once they turned onto East Chop Drive, the traffic was minimal. The lighting was more and more sparse the further up the Chop they went and when they got to Laurie's house, the only light was the light at the corner across the street, one house down.

"Nice house Charles!" Bobby said.

"Thanks. It's not actually mine. It's my girlfriend's place."

"Nice girlfriend."

The word 'girlfriend' rolled around in Charles' head like a pinball with nothing to stop it. He might just like the sound of it. "Yes, she's all right."

"I hope I live on the Vineyard someday...in a house like this would be awesome! On the beach? That would be wicked cool." Bobby turned his attention to a sheet of paper that had his fee schedule on it. "I just have to check what you owe me. I don't know if East Chop counts as a local run from Oak Bluffs or not."

Charles reached into his wallet and pulled out a twenty-dollar bill. "Will this cover it?"

Bobby looked at it with alarm. "Oh man! It won't be that much! It will either be seven or nine bucks. I'm just not sure which. I just have to check..."

"Take it. You made me smile tonight and you have no idea what a feat that was. Seriously, have a good night." Charles motioned for him to take the bill. He did.

"Wow! Thanks man!" Bobby beamed. "You have a good night too!"

Charles slid the side door open, stepped out, and slid it closed again behind him. He watched as Bobby, still beaming, pulled out of the drive, almost ran over a bush, and headed back into town. The van turned the corner not a hundred metres away and was gone from sight. Charles stood there for a minute in the night air. The only sounds were hidden crickets and unseen softly rolling waves. Charles reached up and rubbed his face with his left hand. He yawned. It was quiet on East Chop.

*   *   *

Charles had been home an hour when Laurie got in. He was showered and changed and finished his first glass of wine. It had been a healthy one, emptying the open bottle that he had found in the fridge. There were still three more bottles in there. A fact that made Charles very happy indeed. When Laurie walked in the front door, he heard her toss her keys into the bowl in the front hall but then she went directly upstairs without saying anything. Charles sat and listened to her moving around upstairs and waited. He heard the shower run. It ran for a very long time.

"That was possibly the worst day of my life." Laurie said when she finally came down the stairs and

286

entered the kitchen. She had changed into the Lululemon baby blue and brown yoga outfit that was Charles' favourite. "If it wasn't the worst, it was a contender." She pulled her hair back into a ponytail.

"I'd have to agree with that." Charles unscrewed the lid from a fresh bottle of Kim Crawford Sauvignon Blanc and poured a liberal glass for each of them. He went to put the remainder of the bottle in the fridge, thought better of it and took the bottle out. He passed one glass to Laurie and they headed to the back deck, wine bottle in tow. "Let's sit outside."

"Sure." Laurie took her glass and followed him out to the back deck. "Did Keith call?"

"No." Charles sat down in one of the Adirondack chairs and took a mouthful of wine. "What did you say to Jack?"

Laurie grimaced. "Do we have to talk about that?" She took a big sip of wine and then sighed. "Okay. I told Jack the whole story... right from the beginning. He did not take it well. He really did love her. He did know about the affair but he had no idea that she was mixed up in any of this. He's been working so much that he has hardly even seen her. Those times he said she was sleeping? She wasn't even home. That's why he was so strung out. She should have been at home getting comfort from her husband over the death of her father but she was out getting comfort from the other man...the man who killed him as it turns out."

Charles nodded in acknowledgement of the irony.

"When we were done, I took him to the police station. Barton was there, having just arrested Frank Zito. I had Barton drive me here and then take Jack home in my car. He'll pick me up again tomorrow around noon. Barton will stay with Jack for a while if not the night. They're friends...sort of."

"What about Frank?" Charles asked.

"Let him stew. He can spend the night in the tank. We'll deal with him in the morning. The two crewmembers are in there too, separately of course. One of them will roll over by tomorrow. We'll get all the answers we need. That should be the end of it... man, would I ever like a murder weapon." She took a healthy swig from her glass. "Jeff and Gavin had better be all right or you're going to see police brutality that will make Law and Order look like Wyle E. Coyote and Roadrunner..."

Charles didn't comment on the police brutality. He knew she was just talking. She was upset. "They will be fine. I promise."

"You promise?" Laurie looked at him with the beginnings of a wine induced calm.

"I promise." Charles smiled at her. "Have I ever lied to you?"

"Not so far." Laurie grinned lasciviously. She rubbed her toes up his bare calf.

"See? You can trust me then." Charles liked the feel of her smooth skin on his leg.

"I don't know...you could be setting me up for a whopper of a lie."

"Doesn't sound like me but if you want a whopper-"

288

When the phone rang inside, Laurie jumped and ran for it. "That could be Keith!" Her wine glass fell from the arm of her chair and shattered.

"Laurie!" Charles lifted his bare feet as quickly as he could. Glass flew across the deck in every direction. They would definitely have to move this party inside. It would be impossible to clean up the glass at this time of night. Best leave it until the next morning. Most of it could be just swept under the deck but Charles wasn't willing to risk it now. He reached down and picked up the glass stem. There was none of the bowl left. It was in small pieces on the wet cedar deck. Charles stood and tried to find clear spots to step. "Jesus Christ..." He muttered under his breath. Gingerly he put down one toe after another. With each step he was prepared to spring his foot back at the smallest inkling of a shard of glass penetrating his skin. Unscathed, he made it to the back door. Charles reached for the handle and pulled it open. When he did, he cut his thumb on the stem in his hand. "Damn it!" Charles shook his head at his own stupidity and went in the house.

Charles walked up to the kitchen sink and turned on the cold-water faucet. The water flowed into the pot in the sink and Charles stuck his thumb under the running water. He listened for Laurie's voice. Nothing. "Well... was it Keith?"

"No... it wasn't" The man behind him said.

Charles whipped around to find a large man with his left hand around Laurie's neck and his right hand holding a gun to her temple. They stood in the front hallway with their backs to the front door, facing the kitchen. The man was Richard Brooker, Steve Christie's partner from the Chinese restaurant. Charles could hear Marcie Cunningham's voice in his head, *'Then you had him killed!'* She had screamed at Joe Zito. *'You or your goddamned partner or your brother!'* At the time, Charles had assumed that he hadn't heard her right. He thought she had said 'your partner, your brother'. He thought she had meant one person. It had never occurred to him that there were three of them. That explained the Chinese restaurant connection.

Charles looked at the anger in Laurie's eyes. She was scared but she was angry more than anything else. "Hi Richard." He said calmly.

"You remember me...I'm flattered." He spat.

"Why should my memory be any worse than yours?"

"Because I didn't ruin your million fucking dollar business and I didn't kill your fucking partner...yet." He pushed the gun into her head. Where it rubbed her head was becoming red and swollen.

"There's nowhere for you to go Richard. I know we're not exactly in downtown Oak Bluffs but that gunshot will be heard. We're halfway between the hospital and the cop shop. There's no way you'll get off East Chop."

"I don't have to. You've got Frank in jail and those two assholes from Joe's boat. One of them will give me up tomorrow morning. I'm fucked anyway." He looked down at Laurie's face. "This way...you and the cop aren't getting out either."

The doorbell rang, startling Richard. It was just enough. Charles grabbed the pot from the sink and threw the cold water at him. In reflex, Richard brought his arms up to shield his face. Laurie elbowed him as hard as she could in the kidney and he toppled forward. Laurie turned quickly and elbowed him again on the back of the neck. At the same time her knee came up and met him square in the nose. There was a crack. Richard yelped like a dog. When he came up his nose was purple, bleeding, and swelling. Laurie kneed him in the nuts and he fell to the floor. Two hundred and fifty pounds of potatoes landed heavy and hard. Laurie was on him quickly. She flipped him over and brought his right arm up behind him, jerking it hard and high. Richard screamed in an unnatural pitch. It looked like his arm was about to leave its socket if it hadn't already. Charles ran past them and up the stairs. He returned immediately with Laurie's handcuffs. He tossed them at her; she caught them in mid-air and cuffed him. Charles sat on the bottom stair. Laurie sat on the floor. They were both breathing pretty heavily.

Charles rubbed his face and then motioned with his head. "Who's at the door?" He asked.

"Oh...I don't know." Laurie stood up and turned the door handle.

"I brought pizza!" Cathy Hurtubise said. "I was bringing one for Keith; I thought I'd bring one for you guys too."

Laurie opened the door and stepped aside.

"I figured you guys would need something to sop up all the wine you'd be drinking and..." Cathy stepped in the door and looked at Richard Brooker lying, wet, and crumpled on the floor. She looked at Laurie and then at Charles and back at Richard. "Who's that?" She asked.

"That's Richard Brooker. He just tried to kill Laurie." Charles said.

"Oh." She looked down at him disapprovingly. "You don't get any pizza."

33

Charles and Laurie sat in The Black Dog Tavern. They were waiting for the ferry. The last time Charles had been on the Vineyard, Laurie had brought him to The Black Dog for breakfast before he had to catch his ferry in Oak Bluffs. The breakfast had been excellent but the mood had been sombre. This morning was no different except that this time Charles was leaving from Vineyard Haven. The Black dog Tavern sat on the beach and they had a window table. From their wooden seats, they would be able to see the ferry pulling in. Charles watched Laurie carefully. She stared out the window, focusing on the tall ships moored at the Black Dog dock, avoiding his eyes at all cost. She wasn't one for emotional scenes and when they were inevitable, she fought them tooth and nail.

"The weather's good." Laurie said. She reached for her coffee mug without looking for it and had a mouthful of coffee. Then, she set it back down beside her plate that had just recently been piled high with Eggs Benedict. "It will be good for travelling."

"Yes..." Charles said. "It sure makes it harder to leave though."

"Then don't go." Laurie's voice wavered so much, it came out in a whisper.

"Pardon?" Charles asked.

Laurie cleared her throat and tried to regain her composure. "I said, then don't go." Her eyes were glassy and watery.

She turned to him and stared at him in the eye for the first time that morning. Even when they had visited Jeff and Gavin in the hospital, she hadn't looked at him. She had been cheerful in their visits but it was overdone, fake, and almost robotic. Charles knew that she had been happy to see the two of the men awake and in stable condition. He had been too; however, there had been a fragile tone in her voice, superficiality in her speaking. Especially when Jeff had brought up Charles' departure. Laurie had excused herself to the bathroom. Jeff, Chris, and Charles had all given each other that look that ensured they all knew what was really going on and when she came back they had quickly changed the subject.

"Just don't go." She said again.

"I have to." Charles said. "You know that."

"No, I don't know that. You have to eat, breathe, and sleep. After that, everything is a choice." Laurie's eyes locked on his and would not let go. "Do you want to go?"

"No." He said without hesitation. "No, I don't want to go." He really didn't.

"Then don't. You can stay for up to six months less a day. Right? Before you get in trouble with your country or mine. Right? Six months?"

"Yes. That's right."

"Will your family bring you some of your stuff? If they came on a vacation?" She asked.

"I'm sure someone would. Someone would have to bring my cat too."

"Your cat? Jesus Christ! Fine, your cat." She smiled and took his hand. "Please...stay."

"All right. I'll stay." Charles laughed when he said it.

Laurie jumped up and leaned over the Black Dog's small table and threw her arms around him. She laughed out loud. The restaurant was crowded but she didn't care. Her body shook with emotion.

Charles held her tightly. He laughed with joy at the feel of her, at the smell of her. He laughed. He couldn't remember the last time he had been so happy. The sun came in the window, lighting them.

"That's fantastic!" Laurie said as they both settled back into their seats. "That also means that you can stay to see this case completely buried!"

Charles looked at her in astonishment. "Buried! Of course!" He leapt to his feet and pulled his wallet out of his pocket. He put two twenties on the table, more than enough to cover the bill, put a coffee cup on top of them, and then raced toward the door. "Come on!"

Laurie chased after him in bewilderment. "Do you mind telling me where we're going?"

"Edgartown!!" He said. He pulled open the passenger side of the police cruiser and slid into the now very familiar seat.

"Okay. Edgartown it is." Laurie turned her key in the ignition and backed out of their parking space. It was taken immediately by an SUV. This was parking Martha's Vineyard style.

*   *   *

Laurie pulled the police cruiser into the drive of the Christie house. It was still lifeless and empty. This time when Charles got out of the car and looked at it, he didn't see omens and demons. He saw hope. Maybe it was the morning light on the gables but the house seemed brighter. Laurie closed her car door when she stepped out of the cruiser and began fishing for the house key in her pocket.

"What we need is in the backyard." Charles said excitedly.

"Are you going to let me in on this little secret or not?" Laurie asked.

"If I'm wrong, I'm going to look like the biggest dork but if I'm right..." Charles ran around the house to the backyard. Laurie followed closely behind him.

"I've got news for you: You're already the biggest dork I know."

Charles stopped at the stone path. He got on the path and started walking. Just as before, on one stone he wobbled, the stone made a metallic clack, and Charles tripped. "Help me move this stone!" He dropped to his knees and dug his fingers under one side of the large slab. Laurie did the same on the other side. They pulled the stone across the lawn to expose a shallow hole underneath. In the hole was a machete. It was dark and crusted. "I believe that is your murder weapon. If you swab it, I bet you'll find Steve's blood. I also bet you'll find Richard's prints. Why else would he be so worried about being turned in? If there wasn't evidence of him being the murderer, it wouldn't be worth the risk."

Laurie stared at him in amazement. "Why wouldn't he just get rid of the evidence? Destroy the knife?"

"My guess is that one of the Zitos hid it for insurance. Joe's dead and Frank might just be willing to make a deal if he had this ace in the hole... get it? In the hole?"

"That was awful." Laurie rolled her eyes.

"I thought it was brilliant." Charles grinned.

"Your deductions are brilliant but your jokes are awful. You're not funny." Laurie said.

"Marry me Chief Knickles." Charles said.

"You're not funny."

"I'm not trying to be." Charles looked at her in the depth of her blue eyes. He took her hand in his. "Marry me, Laurie."

Everything was so still.

"I will."

Fin

51547219R00166

Made in the USA
Middletown, DE
03 July 2019